THE ONLY SON

ALSO BY STÉPHANE AUDEGUY

The Theory of Clouds

THE ONLY SON

Stéphane Audeguy

Translated from the French by John Cullen

Harcourt, Inc.

ORLANDO   AUSTIN   NEW YORK   SAN DIEGO   LONDON

© Éditions GALLIMARD, Paris, 2006
English translation copyright © 2008 by John Cullen

www.HarcourtBooks.com

This is a translation of *Fils Unique*.

The author thanks Le Centre National du Livre
for supporting the writing of this book.

Library of Congress Cataloging-in-Publication Data
Audeguy, Stéphane.
[Fils unique. English]
The only son/Stéphane Audeguy;
translated from the French by John Cullen.
p.   cm.
I. Cullen, John.   II. Title.
PQ2701.U34F5513   2008
843'.92—dc22   2007049572
ISBN 978-0-15-101329-6

Text set in Adobe Jenson
Designed by Jennifer Kelly

Printed in the United States of America
First U.S. edition
A C E G I K J H F D B

In the end, my brother grew so bad that he went away and disappeared entirely. Some time afterward, we heard that he had gone to Germany. He never wrote, not even once. He has never since been heard of, and this is how I became the only son.

—Jean-Jacques Rousseau,
The Confessions, Book One

THE ONLY SON

$\mathcal{Y}$*esterday*, the entire nation of France bore the remains of Jean-Jacques Rousseau into the crypt of the Panthéon, formerly known as the Church of Sainte-Geneviève. The crowd, like the glory of the great man it honored, was considerable. But in that immense throng, there was not one who knew that the illustrious Jean-Jacques had a brother; that this brother was in attendance at the ceremony; and that I was he.

The Republic knows how to recognize its thinkers, but only after they are dead. Thus it spares the living the effort of reading them. Had I declared myself at the entrance to the Panthéon, had I revealed my identity by some dazzling, incontrovertible proof, I should have been feted and revered. The crowd loves to see that great men are likewise afflicted with a little family; the sight impresses the humble and consoles the mediocre. But I said nothing. I write this account with no hope that it shall be read and no fear that it shall not. I have decided to address my words to you, Jean-Jacques. Later, I shall tell you why.

I was eighteen years of age when I saw you for the last time. Now, I am drawing near to ninety, and there are many things I must tell you. Speaking to the dead is an old man's privilege, at an age when privileges are few. Why should I hesitate to invoke your ghost, when everyone in the street feels entitled to do so, calling upon you as the Christ of the Revolution? For many years, people have been naming their children after you. Your sainted face can be found on painted plates. You are the object of the devotion of many a patriotic mother, the cause of miraculous conversions to the superior interests of the Nation, the inspiration for vocations in botany or music.

Of course, no one reads your work anymore. What purpose would be served by doing so? The Revolution has turned your dreams into reality. Men who interpret the words of spirits which communicate by tapping upon tables make the dead say what the living wish to hear; nations do the same in their celebrations. This truth probably explains why the Convention determined to exhume your body, to snatch you out of the sweet earth of the Isle of Poplars, where you had lain in peaceful decomposition since the year of grace seventeen hundred and seventy-eight, and to haul your remains in a slow progress from Ermenonville to Paris, there to install them in new lodgings at great expense.

That such an inveterate debauchee as I, a man never touched in any way by the imbecile fear of the gods, should sit in the front ranks of the spectators assisting at the deification of a virtuous Rousseau invented by the butchers of the Terror— this was a situation not without irony, but irony died with the former world. I was accorded a place of honor in the tribune of representatives, not, to be sure, as the brother of the illustrious Jean-Jacques, but as a veteran of the Bastille. And there I sat, Jean-Jacques, watching your funeral cortege approach along the iron railings of Luxembourg Palace, down the middle of a festooned street. Atop your hearse stood a statue in your image, crowned by Liberty and surprisingly ugly. Our little platform, laden with flags and notables, faced the street opened by Soufflot in seventeen hundred and sixty. An inexplicable odor of death hung over the whole proceeding; in the end, I ascertained that the stench emanated from the press of poor, dirty bodies thronging to see you, Jean-Jacques. It seemed as if the common people had died, but remained ignorant of the fact, like the ghosts in some old tales; no one had the heart to tell them the truth, and they had already begun to stink most fearfully.

Two days previously I had been present at your exhumation in the park of the Château d'Ermenonville, the property of your loyal friend, the Marquis de Girardin. To those of us who witnessed the event, your corpse looked nearly intact. Having been placed in a raised tomb, it had remained there, inaccessible to vermin, for more than sixteen years. It was, however, dry as a stick, and it broke in a thousand places when the laborers tried to lay it upon a sheet. Your monumental urn contains naught but a handful of bones and desiccated skin and brittle hair.

Perhaps you did well to die before this revolution which claims you as its prophet, engulfing you sometimes in an ocean of saccharine compliments, and sometimes in the sea of blood spilled on the guillotines. I doubt my ability to give you an adequate representation of the cataclysms it has been our lot to endure. Consider, for example, that the month of October, the present month, no longer exists. We have twelve new names for the months of the year, and we owe them to one Fabre d'Églantine, whom I knew well in days gone by: a bad poet if ever there was, a swindler in his spare time, and a traitor to his country. The treacly inanity of his revolutionary calendar, with its newly minted months—"Misty" and "Snowy," "Hot" and "Vintage"— did nothing to hinder that dung beetle of Parnassus from giving proof of the most wolfish cruelty: In September of last year, when the Parisian mob, mad with fear and hatred, burst into the jails of the city and slaughtered thousands of prisoners, Fabre d'Églantine greeted the barbarism with unequivocal approval. Such are the times we live in. Early last April the Committee of Public Safety decided, most opportunely, to dispatch the odious rhymester to the guillotine, but we have kept, alas, his calendar. Thus it seems that time itself has come off its hinges, and although I am certainly not one of those who regret the passing of the old world, I despair when I see what the new one has become.

I am resolved to write the story of my life in plain terms and to describe my experiences as I lived them, without alteration or deletion. I know the terrible motto you chose for yourself, Jean-Jacques: *vitam impendere vero*, "to sacrifice my life to the truth." To that end, you lived in a solitude I could never have endured. I loved too much the company of women, and the society of men: two worlds wherein one must lie to others if he does not wish to lie to himself. But I believe I have not been unworthy of you. I have sacrificed the truth to my life.

My name is François Rousseau. You, whom the Nation chose to honor yesterday by depositing between Descartes and Voltaire in the crypt of the Panthéon, were seven years my junior. You were eleven when I left our native land, never to return, Jean-Jacques. Can I claim to know you better than those who buried you yesterday? I think I can. 'Tis true that we were brothers only through the coincidences of blood, which are hardly worth more than the few drops of seed which cause them; nevertheless—I say it openly—my mere existence wins me the right to address you. Here is how the idea of composing the present memoir came to me. A friend lent me the first volume of your *Confessions*, which had just appeared. I did not like the title, because it stank of the sacristy and stale incense. For all that, I read the work straight through, though not without great

4

irritation. On the vast stage of your pride, all the persons who figured in your life, from the humblest to the most illustrious, appear in decidedly minor roles. You see fit to mention your brother François only three or four times. For a man who claimed to tell the whole truth, you had an extremely odd notion of it, so much so that I believe it will be a pleasant endeavor to give those pompous confessions of yours the *thrashing* they deserve. Moreover: I have thus far in my life had better things to do than to write, and here I am come to the end of my days. I shall write now, or never.

PART ONE

Childhoods

You speak so falsely of the time of your birth that I am obliged to lead the reader back to the period of my own. I first saw the light of day at dawn on the fifteenth of March in the year seventeen hundred and five, in a fine, cold house in the upper city of Geneva, at number 40 on the Grand-Rue. In memory of our proud French Huguenot forebears, the Christian name chosen for me was François. At the time, Geneva was a republic, but so greatly has the meaning of this word changed that I am compelled to specify that it was a republic in the ancient Spartan or Athenian sense. By this I mean that a handful of aristocrats, a tenth of the city's population, governed it absolutely, with power over matters of religion, money, and law. The rest of Geneva's inhabitants formed a great mass of indistinguishable people who had access neither to the good name of citizen nor to the rights that it conferred. None of this prevented the bourgeoisie of the city from striking noble poses and putting on airs of ancient grandeur. Our father, Isaac Rousseau, belonged by birth to the class of Genevan citizens whose degree of citizenship surpassed that of other Genevans; our mother Suzanne, née Bernard, was also a product of this privileged group. Our parents both rejoiced in their lineage, in a manner peculiar to zealots of a reformed religion: They believed themselves to be utterly humble, and the thought made them quiver with pride.

I shall give here but a scant report of my early childhood. The perusal of your *Confessions* has at least taught me this: One should distrust his memories of his own tenderest years. For families are like people; they lie with every breath. As soon as the children are able to listen, the elders tell the tales which they, the storytellers, find pleasing. To this rule, the Rousseaus were no exception. I have in my memory a thousand anecdotes that reveal what kind of nursling, what kind of child, I was. Should I listen to my heart, I would believe those tales my own; but reason and memory softly murmur, assuring me that all such accounts are based on old stories regularly retold by my grandmother, my mother, and my father. In the end, by dint of repetition, they themselves believed their fables true, much as I suppose priests do: Having so often repeated the fable of creation, they are persuaded that they know the origin of the world. I shall leave unrecorded here my clearest memories, the ones that show traces of the sentimental style so dear to the Rousseau family; indeed, I shall begin with what happened before I was conscious of anything at all, and which seems sufficiently picturesque to deserve my relating it.

I was born, the first of Suzanne Rousseau's sons, in the month of March in the year seventeen hundred and five. Some few days after the blessed event, my father, Isaac Rousseau, left us without a word. In one and the same movement, he abandoned my mother, Geneva, and Europe. So mighty was his impulse to leave that it propelled him all the way to the suburbs of Constantinople. Why so impetuous a departure? The familial legend was silent on this point, and in after years, our parents showed scarcely any tendency to engage in domestic quarrels. Did Isaac Rousseau himself know the reasons behind his abrupt exile? He never seemed much disposed to self-examination and sometimes almost surprised himself by being so emotional, so brusque in taking certain decisions. Can one ever know the first causes of a man's private actions? Be that as it may, to this day I love that strange violence in my progenitor's character, which seems to offer some explanation of my own temperament. In my time, I have myself been prone to sudden bolting and swerving, like a skittish horse. I shall speak of this tendency later, when the occasion presents itself. A penchant for adventure—a rarity, generally speaking, in Genevan blood—seems to have coursed through the veins of several Rousseaus; one of our uncles died, a ruined man, in the province of Louisiana, and neither you nor I have belied that adventurous bent.

But let me return to my birth and my father. At the end of the month of April, seventeen hundred and five, Isaac Rousseau took up residence in Pera, a charming faubourg of Constantinople, far from his wife and son. There was no lack of work for a competent watchmaker, and our father was a meticulous, scrupulous artisan who established himself immediately and easily. Why had he chosen Constantinople among all other great cities? At the time, it abounded in whores of every nationality. I should not be surprised if he visited them most assiduously, for I must have inherited from someone the inclination to debauchery, which has determined my life and which, as nearly as I can judge, my mother did not possess in any measure.

My father left soon after I was born; what would become of me? I scarcely dare imagine, my poor Jean-Jacques, what your trembling, melancholic imagination would have made of that situation, had by chance you and not I been the firstborn of the children of Isaac and Suzanne Rousseau. How many heartrending melodies you would have drawn from that magnificent and mournful violin of yours, and what torrents of tears your readers would have shed throughout the whole of Europe! In my case, however, the truth is that I did not miss Isaac Rousseau at all. Of course, had I been five, or ten, I should have wept for the loss of an adored and feared father. But I was a nursling at my mother's breast; I missed nothing. I was ignorant of the sweet necessity of paternal authority, and even of the existence of that strange appendage to the couple I formed with my mother: my father. My imagination was limited to the narrow circle of my feeble senses. I loved the person who nursed me, rocked me, swaddled me. How had Isaac and Suzanne Rousseau met, paired, divided? I shall never know. All that remained of her capricious husband was a bawling baby; she would not engage a wet nurse and hardly left my side during the first three years of my life.

Without confessing it, and perhaps even without daring to admit it to herself, Suzanne—who reclaimed her maiden name—discovered that being no longer burdened with a husband suited her quite well, as did to an even greater degree the fact that, as a married woman, she was exempted from finding herself another one. Suzanne's mother had come to live at her daughter's side in our tall dwelling, which was built of gray stone. Though not rich, this curious Bernard household was in comfortable circumstances because of the income from some small but high-yielding patches of land. We had an elderly housekeeper, two chambermaids, and a cook. And so I grew up, surrounded by women, in one of those gynaecea to which the inequality of the sexes confines widows and abandoned wives.

For several years, I was the prince of this little realm. Each of the women around me practiced virtue without ostentation; none of them associated with men. They did not think of this as something missing from their lives. Chastity is a habit swiftly acquired, provided one gives it no thought, but it is not without consequences. To be quite honest, vapors rose from these ladies' cunnies to their heads and troubled their judgment; they treated me like a prodigy of Nature and greeted my smallest progress as a miracle effected by the hand of Providence. Under this regime of imbecile idolatry, I was very much at my ease, though more, alas, like a young boar in his wallow than like a future citizen of Geneva. It happened, therefore, that I learned to walk later than other children without anyone's taking notice of the fact. Other backwardnesses of mine met with even odder treatment: When at seven years of age I still soiled my breeches, the circumstance was found picturesque and droll. On the other hand, as soon as I was capable of recognizing some of the most common words, whose form I merely retained and which I only pretended to read, the household resounded with praise: Never had such a prodigy been seen; to find another example of such precocity, one would have to go back to the illustrious Ancients. If I laughed, I was the most charming creature in Geneva; if I raged, my imperious character foretold an exceptional destiny. In short, I lived like a favorite lover, more caressed, more combed, more rubbed, and more perfumed than a lapdog, exhibiting also, I believe, a lapdog's stupidity and servility. As I was not corrupt from birth, I was often sensible of how outrageous this conduct was, and secretly troubled by its extravagance; but soon I stretched out upon the soft eiderdown quilt of self-love. My inane Genevan paradise enthralled me like opium. How could I have resisted it? But like every illusory paradise, this one allowed a glimpse of an unhappy end to come.

My ladies thought they were providing me with an education by going into ecstasies over everything and nothing; in that cold and insipid happiness, however, I remained in the larval state. It is a good thing, no doubt, to follow one's inclination; but the path must lead upward.

Here it seems fitting that I should expatiate somewhat upon she who reigned over the first years of my childhood. One simple consideration can never be too often reiterated: A child is poorly qualified to describe his parents, for he encounters them at an age when he has no more judgment than an animal. In this, we are all children of mothers and fathers unknown. Doubtless, this is a fact that shocks the sensibility of children as they grow older, and so they construct effigies of those beings and come to believe, in the end, that they knew their parents well. I therefore offer an old man's conjectures as to what he observed as a child, what was told to him after he reached the age of reason, and what he was able to glean surreptitiously from the conversations of his elders. Let the reader distinguish the truth in all this, if he can; I shall not endeavor too much to betray my model; and should I fail, I shall at least have traced a portrait of myself. To begin, let us consider Suzanne's convalescence and how she recuperated from her confinement and the loss of her husband: When it became clear that Isaac Rousseau would not return, it was believed that my mother would never recover from so heavy a blow. For fifteen days on end, greatly weakened by my birth, she wept her heart out. No doubt, those tears contained as much humiliation as anger. She knew she would have to suffer the stares of her fellow Genevans, particularly those of the women. By her marriage, Suzanne had incurred the envy of some of them, as Isaac, given his profession and some future inheritance, was assured of a certain degree of prosperity. She had to ward off the danger of ostracism, which in a small republic such as Geneva was insupportable. During the fifteen days that followed Isaac's flight, Suzanne often received the pastor of her parish, a zealous neophyte who dedicated himself body and soul to his flock, and who came to exhort her to Christian stoicism. The pastor spoke little, but he spoke well. Suzanne heard him not; she wept. It is with tears as it is with the other fluids of the human body: If they are discharged excessively, they dry up. The pastor was chaste but handsome. Soon Suzanne began to listen to him more closely and to weep much less. She was coquettish, and prudish, and beautiful as a flower. In the evening, at her toilet, she probably deplored her red eyes and saw two little wrinkles she had never seen before. Decidedly, so many tears were quite unsuitable for a young Christian woman. She therefore determined to overcome the trial Providence had sent her. Before long, the pastor seemed even more handsome, and perhaps he showed himself less chaste. I knew him in later years. He blushed whenever he came upon me unexpectedly in one of the streets of the city, and I assume that there were times when Suzanne could not but keep me by her side while the pastor sacrificed at her altar. Fornication is as effective as any lullaby.

The Bernard family owned some land and was in no manner impoverished by Isaac's departure, and before much time had passed, men began to lay siege to the house. Well content with these attentions, Suzanne yielded to none of her suitors, nor did she discourage any. She was pleased to be virtuous and pleased to have at all times the power to cease being so, should one fine day the fancy take her—a double and delicate pleasure, in which the self-esteem of coquettes finds easy accommodation. All these assiduous gentlemen thought it a clever practice to caress the son in order to please the mother whom they wished to swive. At three years old, I was the doll on display in Suzanne's salon; she passed her days in rigging me out, knowing that together we made a charming sight. I grew up in an atmosphere pervaded by the scent of rut, yet without the ability to recognize it; it remained the perfume of a part of my life. By way of passing the time, some of my mother's gallants began pricking up their ears for clever remarks from me. Inevitably, I became a reliable supplier thereof; at the age of four, I produced them with the regularity of a clock, and I learned, without understanding, to make equivocal plays on words, much to the delight of my mother and her stable of eager stallions. In order to prevent gossip from reaching unreasonable levels, she invited her neighbors to her salon, and their presence allowed me to complete my training: I quickly learned how to proffer charming compliments, make adorable faces, tie ribbons as gifts for visitors of the gentle sex, and hurl myself upon my *maman* with that delicious freshness proper only to the most carefully schooled monkeys. Children find a pleasure in deceit ten times greater than any other; I am certain that I knew more than my share of that delight. I appeared every day on the stage at number 40, Grand-Rue, and otherwise rarely ventured outside its walls; the neighborhood brats flung stones and spat at the pomaded little fop who stared them up and down.

During my fifth year, I lost my grandmother, who died in the spring, and, at the beginning of winter, our old housekeeper. Those sad events occasioned a new role for the young François Rousseau upon his mother's stage. An air of restrained grief, a well-turned allusion to eternal life edified the entire parish. Once I brought myself to tears as I evoked the poor deceased. I thought myself sublime; I was cruel and cold. I had but the vaguest notion of death, but I went into mourning with voluptuous distress. In the end, the pastor, seeing through my affectations, took me aside and upbraided me: It was not fitting for a true Christian to grieve overlong after an ancestor, to say nothing of a simple domestic, had entered the Kingdom of Heaven; genuine grief was not so ostentatious as mine. In short, for the first time in my existence, I had come across a person who was not taken in by my feigning. I heard this priest with a good grace, and he departed content with me, that is, with himself. But from that day, I regarded Christianity as vaguely suspect, since it desired me to put away the little mourning costume that suited me so well, and also the handsome shoes with the black buckles. Let the reader pause to consider what a wretched child I was: I had just lost two of the persons who had raised me with adoration, and I wept heartily for the end of my mourning clothes. Alas, far from effecting my mother's return to a just sense of proportion, the passing of those two women gave the signal for redoubled extravagance. From this point on, the life of the entire household revolved around me, my games, my whims. Suzanne began to seize every opportunity to speak in the foolish affected way our century considered a sign of good form when addressing young children, and the servants, both old and new, imitated her. At last, practically an idiot, I reached the age when one is supposed to be capable of reason. Physically, I was a winsome little piglet, blond, as smooth as cream, and chubby as a cherub; morally, I was as ignorant as a calf, well satisfied with the world and with myself. The coquettish behavior of our servingwomen would have damned a saint, and I had not the temperament of a recluse. They produced effects upon my sensuality; one day, I became aware of a stiffening erection. The ladies laughed immoderately. Bare-arsed and eager to display my rigid member to my mother, I hurried from the kitchen and ran triumphantly to the room where she was resting. Have I invented what I am about to recount here? I cannot say. My mother, reclining languidly on her bed, could not pretend to be unaware that her son responded to her affection in a manner decidedly more virile than was fitting for a child. She bade me sit down and, half amused, half embarrassed, asked me various questions which I understood not at all. I therefore remained silent, which my mother believed to be a sign of precocious delicacy on my part. Suzanne thought I was feigning ignorance, and in her desire to show me that she was by no means duped by this stratagem, she plucked up her courage, described the fitting way for me to dispose of my virility, and demonstrated her meaning with vigorous movements of her hand. I scarcely had time to apprehend the pleasure which overcame me before she wiped me off with her batiste handkerchief and, blushing a little, ordered me to leave her room, which I did without a word. Never did my dear mother repeat this experience, and the subject was never mentioned between us. On the other hand, I presume that the household received certain instructions in this matter, instructions whose exact formulation I should have liked to know, for from that day, the least of my erections was greeted with preferential treatment. I still savor the delightful memory of the clean cloth the cook used to wipe me off, and of my mother's chambermaid's mouth; it always seemed so soft to me, despite her beautiful teeth, which to my wonderment I never felt at all.

I failed to see the least evil in any of these domestic games, and I have no doubt they contained none. I knew what fornication was because I had observed dogs in the streets of Geneva, and little peasant boys, less prudish than the city dwellers, had advanced my knowledge with thorough and detailed descriptions, which I received in exchange for pieces of white bread. But I should have been astounded, horrified, despondent to learn that the little attentions those ladies lavished on me morning and night were related to the original sin that was the frequent topic of our pastor's discourse. As for my mother, she formed the habit of coming to my room each evening to tuck me in, a task she performed with a sweaty eagerness which greatly excited me, for she bent over me in such a way that her bosom was almost entirely exposed. I nestled my head against her breast, inhaling, with the voluptuousness of a lover, the scent of flesh and almond milk, which would always remain my first conscious sensation. I was doubtless too young for such sensual feelings; often I recoiled of my own accord from that abyss of pleasure, which made me uneasy. But I should perhaps have flung myself into it like the mad, weak, and foolish little sultan of a sterile harem had not Isaac Rousseau returned to Geneva one morning, without anyone's having thought it necessary to mention his impending arrival to his only son.

Suzanne had written to Isaac in Constantinople. The chroniclers of the Rousseau family saga declared at this point that she had reconquered her husband through the subtlety of her pen. Neighborhood gossips added that one fine day Isaac Rousseau had suffered some rather delicately situated burns and had preferred to have them treated in the noble Republic of his forebears, which counted among its citizens the best physicians in Europe. Be that as it may, Isaac proved himself an attentive husband after his return. Many men have the sentimental pox; for them, a recurrence of conjugal affection takes the place of remorse. The month was September and the year seventeen hundred and eleven when he returned to his country, where he at once impregnated his legitimate spouse; and on the twenty-eighth day of June, seventeen hundred and twelve, a second son was born to them. They named you Jean-Jacques, and in later years I could never hear your admirers, in their affectionate fervor, refer to you by your given names without recalling your birth: One morning I was led to a cradle, in which a tiny, wrinkled thing wrapped in spotless swaddling clothes lay sleeping. I was informed that this worm was my brother. Uneasily, I leaned toward the creature that had robbed me of my mother's tender attentions, and it seemed to return my gaze. I could have hated you, Jean-Jacques; if I consider the consequences your unexpected birth had for my life, I think that perhaps I ought to have hated you. But in fact I loved you at once; it was one of those sudden attachments one can neither explain nor get over. This did not at all diminish my jealousy. The first fifteen days of your existence were for me a period of despair, as I was no longer the cynosure of every eye.

Nine months earlier, a giant with a face as dark as a Negro's had lifted me off my feet, held me in the light from a window, and replaced me on the floor with a laugh of delight; so I had a father, after all. That joy was short-lived. When Isaac Rousseau examined me with greater care, after an absence of six years, he flew into a rage. He had left behind a ruddy infant, wrapped up like a Hindu idol, bawling and sturdy. He returned to find a little pink and white doll, a very model of affected manners. You doubtless remember better than anyone else, Jean-Jacques, that for the men of those days, education consisted in turning a boy into a man, the sooner the better. Isaac could see no good in the man such a boy as I would become. Europe had not yet read your *Émile*, and our father was a simple man, a man of his century. He found me ridiculous. He ordered my pretty curls sheared, which duty our cook performed, all the while gnawing her nether lip in vexation. My father next commanded that a suit be made for me out of rough gray cloth, simply cut, and he formally forbade all future adornments of ribbons. I wept a great deal; I even stamped my feet; and when this sham proved unsuccessful, I rolled upon the floor. My antics had a great effect on Isaac. Without hesitation, our father unbuckled one of his shoes and struck me several sharp blows on the head with the flat of the sole, which had been carved out of solid oak. I bled so much that for an instant, in my surprise, I left off moaning. My mother and her servants uttered loud cries; but seeing that the master of the house still clutched his lifted shoe and seemed resolved on administering the same treatment to them, those ladies at once ceased their wails. I was in despair—or so I believed. Today I consider myself most fortunate to have regained, though somewhat late, the father whom no one expected to see again, and whom I did not even know I had lost. Fifteen days later my outward appearance was that of any other Genevan boy. The rascals in our street gawked in amazement at this metamorphosis; for a while in the beginning, they scoffed and scolded a little, but soon they accepted me as one of them. And so I left behind the confusion of my early years and entered into the society of my kind; my life was beginning.

Apprehension had hovered over your birth. While still unborn, you were considered the tangible sign of our parents' reunion; through a sort of sentimental superstition, everyone thought of you—although no one said so—as a portent of what the future held for the house of Rousseau. Your first moments augured ill; you were born at the end of the month of June and appeared unlikely to see the end of July. When you were baptized, in haste, on the fourth of July, the ceremony seemed more intended to secure as soon as possible the salvation of a soul which there was no hope of keeping among us than to welcome a new Christian into the community. Death struck indeed, but it spared the child: Suzanne Rousseau, née Bernard, died unexpectedly on the seventh day of July, seventeen hundred and twelve, at a moment when she was thought to be recovering from her childbed, which had exhausted her. I have promised myself to tell my story as it happened, and I will keep that promise; let no one judge too harshly the child that I was. Twelve months earlier I had had a mother whom I cherished without knowing anything of the vast world beyond her, and had possessed neither father nor brother; I lost the first at the very moment when I was given the two others! I was seven years old, and I have already disclosed how behindhand I was in grasping the realities of existence. The blind workings of fate inspired in me neither philosophical reflection nor rebellion. I discovered the streets of Geneva; they were my first school; I was pleased to meet persons unconnected to me by blood or servitude. I believe this to have been my first taste of equality. I say it plainly: I was but little incommoded by my mother's death. Perhaps it was difficult for me to take seriously the disappearance of that theatrical creature; during the obsequies, I thought for a moment that she was going to rise up before her funeral procession and complain of the discomfort of her coffin. My coldness amazed many, and I thus acquired a reputation as a monster of ingratitude, which has never abandoned me since. As for the little bawler whom everyone pitied, who was presented to me as an example, and who wept chiefly for his lost milk, I was sorry for him, the poor thing. In my confused fancy, Jean-Jacques, I imagined that you were to become for our father what I had been for our mother, and I was very near the mark.

In your *Confessions*, you call me a rake, you say that I was a libertine before I was old enough for libertinism, and your words are true: I embraced that vocation with enthusiasm, because it extracted me from the family circle. Free men do not belong to their families; if they have one, it is the one founded by themselves. That ordinary men are content with taking on the color of their surroundings, as certain insects are said to do, is only right; their survival depends on it. Solitary men have other guises, which do little to protect them. I repeat: In this we were brothers, Jean-Jacques, and in a sense more profound than that of the accidental consanguinity of two random beings.

With the death of Suzanne Rousseau, our existence changed. In the eyes of my father, I was the incarnate emblem of his departure for Constantinople—that is, of a past that he apparently did not like to remember. Nothing about me pleased him, and especially not my interminable expeditions into the streets of the city, from which I returned muddy, exhausted, and unable to give a decent account of the course of my day, having passed it in brawls and petty thieveries. At the same time, our father was disconcerted to find himself so soon a widower. After having been so long content to be free of his wife, he had absolutely fallen in love again with that capricious and beautiful woman, only to have fate cruelly snatch her from him. The widowed Isaac brought to bear on you, Jean-Jacques, the entire weight of his affection. You were puny and sickly and constantly in need of attention; I was robust and loved the street, with its games and its shouts. In other circumstances, I might have loved my father, as he might have loved me. Fate decided things differently. Isaac had a confused sense of my having escaped him. It often happened that he gave me a beating for no other reason than his surmise that since I had returned home so late and covered with dust, I must have been planning some filthy prank. That you and I, Jean-Jacques, should play together like brothers was out of the question, lest my loutish brutality exercise some influence on you; besides, I frightened you from the moment you were old enough to spend time in my company. Our father liked to weep in your presence, declaring to all how much you resembled your mother. Such effusions occurred daily, for Isaac kept you at his side in his watchmaker's shop. You early showed a form of precocity—that of the sick and spoiled child—with which I was quite familiar; people went into raptures over your childish words, just as they once had done over mine. You and Isaac read interminable novels together, in which chimerical knights spoke of love to highborn shepherdesses.

I should have conceived a ferocious jealousy of you had I not known the street, and I might have returned to my ribbons and my foolish infatuation with my person had a resident of the Grand-Rue not taken a liking to me. A Frenchman living in exile in Geneva, he had no household and no children. I never discovered what he saw in the peculiar little fellow who paced the paving stones of Geneva with a novice's conviction; in any case, however, he took into his head the notion of giving the child an education. This unhoped-for ally, the freest and most generous mind I ever encountered in the country of my birth, was named Maximin de Saint-Fonds.

The Comte de Saint-Fonds was at that time no more than forty years old. He sprang from an old family whose seat was in the environs of Aix-en-Provence. His father, the Marquis, had brought him up to take pride in his name and to be humbly conscious of the duties it imposed. The Saint-Fonds name had been valiantly represented in all the Crusades, and the family had produced martyrs and war leaders of the reformed faith during the disturbances of the sixteenth century. Though Protestants, the Saint-Fonds family was not forced to leave France at the time of the revocation of the Edict of Nantes, for before the beginning of the persecutions, and to general astonishment, the Marquis, grown quite pious in his old age, had converted to the Catholic faith. So well acknowledged was the old gentleman's probity that no one dared to think he had acted in fear of reprisals. At sixteen years of age, young Maximin, the Comte de Saint-Fonds, had seemed worthy of his name, and was a source of great pride for his father. He rode and hunted with admirable skill. He mastered the subtlest details of courtesy without sanctimony or pedantry. All that was lacking to make him aristocratically complete was a sojourn at the court of the King of France; in this matter he gave proof of his independence of mind, proceeding so well that he escaped what he considered, in his heart of hearts, a ridiculous duty. Maximin de Saint-Fonds loved his century; he esteemed everyone's merits, whether bourgeois or worker or peasant, priest or man of quality; and he could not understand the fascination of the news from Versailles, of a procession in Aix-en-Provence, of a masked ball. To him, the young aristocrats of Provence appeared as they were: civilized and vain. Those callow dandies sensed in young Saint-Fonds the fiber of true nobility, that which does not stem from accidents of blood and land. It infuriated them, so they hated him and took revenge by speaking ill of him.

As an old feudal lord, Maximin's father affected disdain for the administration of his properties. For such tasks there had always been chamberlains and overseers and stewards. One received them twice a year, out of kindness, and that was all. On the other hand, the Marquis was most rigorous on the subject of the considerations due his rank: Each year his sharecroppers, his tenant farmers, and the notables of his villages were obliged to participate in a long ceremony of homage, during which the old gentleman, stern and lean, wearing a crown, and seated on a blue and gold dais, condescended to accept from his people complicated bows and bags full of gold. Convinced that his son would soon do honor to his name, the Marquis de Saint-Fonds stepped calmly into the Eighteenth Century, which would see the last representatives of an order once thought eternal led to their deaths. At first, all was well between the Marquis and the Comte. Maximin grew up as the son of a noble lord; at fourteen, in observance of custom, he rogered some peasant girls. It was not long before he discovered that he preferred to roger peasant boys. One evening during the grape harvest, his foster brother, in honor of his fifteenth birthday, initiated him into these pleasures in the back of a barn. Saint-Fonds emerged from the initiation enraptured, except that for several days he felt some discomfort when sitting, as his foster brother employed a rustic roughness in all his activities. In the eyes of the old Marquis, this ancient vice, excusable among the young, recalled to him his own boyhood and simply seemed to herald a strong character. By the time he was sixteen, Maximin perceived that he had already gone through all his paces in the arena where, it was supposed, he would spend his life; and that the rest of his existence was going to consist in executing, with all the skill of the well-taught rider, those same figures. The prospect horrified him, and he resolved instead to live in a way which would benefit his fellow man as well as himself. He opened his project to his brother, a year younger than he, and that powdered monkey, for whom the highest good was the hunting of woodcocks, stared at him in amazement. Maximin developed a passion for the vast estates of the Saint-Fonds family, for their farms and their fields, their pastures and their forests. He soon became aware that the overseers and stewards appointed by his father were working in close collusion and robbing the Marquis like highwaymen. After years of petty larcenies, of timid but multifarious plundering, this small band had grown emboldened, and for the past two years they had subjected the Saint-Fonds woodlands to periodic felling. The timber thus obtained was sold at a derisory price to accomplices, who set out to resell it at five times that sum in Marseille. By means of divers accounting ruses, casks of wine were regularly lost, but these casks miraculously found discreet purchasers in Spain or Savoy. In the abundance of his riches, which he believed himself to disdain, like all those who to be rich have required but to be born, the Marquis de Saint-Fonds remarked nothing. His son weighed whether to inform his father of all his discoveries, but he doubted the revelations would bring about any change. The Marquis was capable of having the ringleaders hanged and then replacing them with men of the same caliber; he would never consent to look into the actual administration of his patrimony; furthermore, it was only the humblest peasants and the day laborers who really suffered from the state of things. In the fire of his youth, Maximin thought he could reform men and habits, and thus give his aristocratic condition the sublime significance he so desperately wished to find in it. He wrote to a bookseller in Leiden in the Netherlands, requesting the most modern books on a wide variety of agricultural subjects. Soon the pruning of almond trees, the fashioning of barrels, and the art of crop rotation held no more secrets for him. Nor did he neglect to acquaint himself with all current practices as well as with the profound wisdom passed down through the ages in the crude form of proverbial sayings. For the benefit of the men who were thieving from him and who had looked upon him at first with anxiety (as the reader may imagine), he assumed a somewhat inane, moralizing character, endowed with short sight and vague ideas. Relieved to find him so stupid, the subjects of his investigations allowed the heir of Monsieur le Marquis to go everywhere, listen to everything, observe a great deal, and ask as many questions as he wished. Little by little, Maximin initiated some improvements: He increased the yield of the most unproductive lands; he rationalized the use of dung from the paternal stables. In secret, he accumulated evidence against the thieves and sought the means to forestall such plundering in the future. As the measures he introduced augmented the paternal revenues, he postponed from year to year the moment when he would have to inform the Marquis, all the while hoping that the old man would make the unhappy discovery of his farmers' thievery himself. But during the year seventeen hundred and five, the whole of Provence was struck by a series of calamities which were to have immeasurable consequences.

The spring of that year was terrible, with late frosts and violent hailstorms. The summer was still worse: Water—and therefore fodder—was everywhere in short supply; an extreme drought burned all the rye and wheat. The poorest folk, the day workers, could find no more hire for their labor. By the end of September, pitiless Nature had driven hundreds of beggars out upon the roads of Provence, where they straggled along in the most extreme destitution. The people had to renounce bread, the price of which had taken flight. In Gardanne, two bakers were attacked, robbed, slain. The authorities dispatched an army corps, which hanged about fifty starvelings in the neighboring woods. Further incidents occurred. Some priests organized processions, but their God turned a deaf ear. Many wretches survived in the sun-scorched scrubland by gnawing on roots and sucking the moisture from the sickly mosses. In the woods the carcasses of several infants were found meticulously cleaned by vermin. Their mothers, knowing that they would not get through the winter, had killed them at birth, but lacked the strength to bury them. At the end of the summer, and at great expense, Maximin finally succeeded in obtaining the delivery of victuals, paid for out of his own purse, which he ordered to be distributed in the countryside; but his father, having learned of the matter, flew into a rage and commanded his son to cease all occupation with this nonsense, which was unworthy of a gentleman. Maximin refused to obey, and the Marquis did not speak to him again for several months; but when the winter was at its most rigorous, a scandalous affair captured the attention of respectable people and brought father and son closer together.

Emboldened by the Marquis' sovereign indifference to the plight of the beggars, who were dying en masse, and struck by seeing a large majority of the peasants reduced to the most abject misery, an odious little set of Saint-Fonds farmers, whose prodigious incomes were now threatened, conceived the fearfully ingenious project of extracting their future revenues from the only provision of which there was no lack: the population itself. To this end, the farmers learned that in Marseille an eight-year-old child, whether boy or girl, provided it was handsome and healthy, could be sold for its weight in gold. The famine had attracted to Provence shady characters and carrion feeders from all over Europe. Some of them had come to set up as pimps, but they were in need of accomplices with a perfect knowledge of the region. Within a few days, arrangements were made to install some ten little beds in a secluded farmhouse two leagues from Aix. The farmers themselves traveled on all the roads of the Saint-Fonds domains, visiting hamlets and isolated farms.

To each family, they offered the charity of taking away one of their children, along with the immediate succor of a piece of silver and, still more precious, some victuals. Debased by hunger, parents turned over their handsomest offspring; the mothers wept but complied, finding consolation in the thought that at least these would be saved from misery. The Saint-Fonds farmers were able to fatten their new stock at small expense. When the physical condition of one of the little wretches was deemed to have progressed sufficiently, he or she was bathed, thoroughly deloused, and given clean clothing, under the pretense that a benefactor had offered to take the child into service at his home in Marseille. The child would swallow this tale and make an enthusiastic dash for the closed carriage waiting in the courtyard. On the way to Marseille, the henchman charged with conveying the freight to its destination would stop in a sunken road and repeatedly violate the child, whether male or female, unless the purchaser had reserved, at a high price, this first use for himself. The next evening the carriage arrived at the gates of Marseille; delivery would take place in a disreputable inn, a sort of trading post frequented by thieves and seditionists, where anything and everything was bought and sold. On one such evening, a young boy and girl were consigned to a notorious libertine, the Duke de ——, who had stipulated that they should both be virgins. Unable to restrain himself at the sight of such fresh, tender flesh, he determined to enjoy it at once, in that very inn, and disregarding all considerations of discretion, ordered that a room should be made ready for him. It was the old gentleman's fancy simultaneously to throttle and bugger his victim; the child's desperate kicks and spasms of suffocation plunged the Duke into a cauldron of appalling delights, from which he emerged ashamed, but thoroughly gratified. He subjected the young girl to this treatment, after which she lay fainting and bleeding on the sheet where he had flung her. The Duke paused to inhale some salts, and then, advancing upon the dark cabinet where the boy, bound and gagged, awaited him, he unlocked the door. But his intended victim had freed himself from his bonds; he gave the wooden panel a violent shove, striking the libertine's face and knocking him down. Then the boy broke a shutter, leaped down into the rear courtyard of the inn, and soon found himself on the stony path that led to the main road.

By the time the old man had regained his senses, it was too late. As luck would have it, that night a squad of armed police was on its way to the inn, where reports had led them to believe there was traffic in counterfeit coin. The terrified young boy recounted his misadventures to the officer in charge of the troop. In an instant, the inn was surrounded. Two men of the watch, sword in hand, burst into the chamber of infamy indicated by the child; a servant intervened and was killed. The Duke, who had readjusted his clothing, confronted the intruders and, certain of his impunity, invoked his illustrious name. The officer was summoned. A man of experience, he knew what the Duke de —— was, both in Provence and at court. The officer therefore humbly begged him to be so good as to explain the reasons for his presence in that place, promising the Duke absolute secrecy. There were numerous witnesses to the affair, there were victims, and it was imperative that justice be done. The Duke perfectly understood the veiled threat and made a complete confession. Then he left the inn, furious and relieved. The following day, the Duke's purveyor was arrested at his farm in Gardanne. As this was a particularly dainty brute, the officer in charge of the arrest had only to threaten him with torture, whereupon he revealed the names of the farmers and all the details concerning their vile commerce. The affair was thrust into the bright light of day and exploded like a summer storm.

In Aix-en-Provence at that time, and especially in the Parliament of that city, there was a strong Catholic party whose members, scenting the potential backslider in every convert, had never stomached the Saint-Fonds conversion; moreover, this accursed abjuration had prevented them from getting their hands on the riches of the Saint-Fonds family, which were considerable. With the Farmers' Affair (as it was already called), those ferocious Catholics believed themselves in possession of the means to dishonor the name of Saint-Fonds. To flay a freshly converted Protestant and trafficker in children was a prospect exceedingly tempting to their zealous imaginations, and in unusual concord, the Jesuits and the Jansenists of the city agreed to collaborate in an effort to destroy the reputation of the Marquis de Saint-Fonds. They well knew the impossibility of openly attacking the man, but they also knew that their purpose would be served should the Saint-Fonds name be uttered in such a trial, should the judge take care to recall to whose property the wretches capable of such heinous deeds were attached, should one throw in, without seeming to touch, perfidious allusions to the new ideas hawked about by the Comte de Saint-Fonds, and should some abusive lampoons be drawn up and posted by night, assailing those great noblemen who tolerated, authorized, perhaps even organized, such shameful trafficking on their estates. The pious notables of Aix-en-Provence knew all of this. They could well judge the weight of such craven baseness, because it was the everyday currency of their careers. Artfully concerted, such sounds sufficed to create that sewerlike gargling known as a rumor, which made the Marquis de Saint-Fonds, in the eyes of the people, and while the famine persisted, an ogre from another age, a monster which it would be pleasant to hate, as a consolation for dying.

Happily, the Marquis was not friendless, even in Aix-en-Provence. Promptly made aware of the cabal against him, conscious that the scandal was public and the arrest of his tenant farmers imminent, and stung in his pride of rank, the Marquis reacted with that inflexible dignity which was second nature to him. An antique *droit de justice* authorized him to exercise the offices of police and judiciary throughout his domains. Saint-Fonds himself set up an inquiry into the whole affair, outstripping the Parliamentary judges, who were entirely given over to the party of the devout. In one of the great halls of the château, and only two days after the repulsive incident at the inn, the hearing of the crimes' instigators began. The trial lasted three days, at the end of which the farmers were broken on the wheel and burned. Their bodies, reduced to ashes, were solemnly scattered to the four corners of the Saint-Fonds lands. Through a remarkable act of clemency on the part of the Marquis, the families of the condemned received authorization to change their names. But the judges of the Parliament, furious to see themselves thwarted by the old man, protested his act of outdated justice, claiming—not without reason—that the discovery of the crime had taken place out of Saint-Fonds' jurisdiction, and that the right to rule in the affair was theirs. To these dogs, enraged at the escape of their prey, the Marquis de Saint-Fonds flung a few tasty bones: Orders were given that the criminals' worldly goods—their houses and their furniture, their lands and the profits from their villainous commerce, amounting to thirty sacks of gold coins—were to be entrusted to the most pious and most wise President of the Parliament of

Aix-en-Provence, on condition of his distributing them among the most deserving members of that august assembly. The which was done, and the matter closed.

Having warded off the dangers of opprobrium and dishonor, the old Marquis de Saint-Fonds, who had not faltered during the whole of the trial, became ill on the day following the executions and withdrew to a bed in his private apartments. His temperament had received a fatal blow, for though he had saved his name, he had also known the humiliation of publicity, and most of all, the concatenation of tragic events had enabled him to see with his own eyes, even among his peers, the universal triumph of the vulgarity he abhorred, because it put nothing above the attraction of money. In the beginning of the following year, the Marquis de Saint-Fonds died suddenly, like a blasted oak. With great dignity, Maximin led his family in mourning, but he absolutely refused to assume his father's title. The Marquis had perished from being a man of the past; Maximin sensed that he could suffer a similar fate for being a man of the future. The changing times had engendered legions of upstarts, and Maximin looked around him and saw the eldest sons of the greatest families paying court to flibbertigibbets whose grandfathers had not even owned shoes, but whose fathers, grown rich in the commerce of grain or the manufacture of casks and moved by some absurd pride, wished to endow them with a noble name. The Saint-Fonds family was rich, but in the manner of former times, that is, in land, in movable and immovable property; the new Marquis would be unable to escape an alliance with some new monarch of banking or spices. Maximin recoiled from such arrangements; moreover, he loved persons of his own sex too much to desire a life constantly exposed to the public view. In addition, his efforts to increase the production of his ancestral lands collided against the ignorance of the peasants, who could not comprehend the making of any changes in the usages of this world, not even in the manner of pruning fruit trees or pasturing sheep. Finally, the spectacle of that pack comprised of the notable citizens of Aix in full chase after his father had moved him profoundly by reviving a memory of his youth which, as he often told me in later days, had determined the formation of his sensibility and his philosophy.

When Maximin was thirteen, his father took him to Avignon. As they reached the city a trial was coming to an end; a young cobbler from Villeneuve had been judged and condemned to death. The unfortunate young man's crime was that one night, in his village tavern, he had exchanged with his neighbor at table some seditious talk, which an informer had hastened to relate to the police. A copy of an obscene lampoon against some of the local notables had also been found in his shop. A new judge had recently been appointed in that jurisdiction, and he believed it his duty to give a show of severity in order to intimidate the people and please the powerful. He was merciless; he sentenced the young man to the stake. The cobbler, an industrious worker, was not poor, but the trial, which lasted three weeks, had ruined him; thus he had not the means to pay the executioner to suffocate him at the beginning of his torment. The laws of the city of Avignon did not yet include the use of the sulfur shirt, which possessed the signal virtue of asphyxiating the victim at the first touch of the flames. And so, for the first time in ten years, the city prepared to burn a man alive, on a fine afternoon in spring. The Marquis de Saint-Fonds wished to seize this opportunity to complete his son's education and instill in him a thoroughgoing horror of vice, a sentiment he did not often enough discern in the taciturn lad. He himself led his young son to the foot of the pyre: twenty armfuls of firewood piled up around a stout post six feet high. A small man, naked to the waist, was led to this stake. Under his father's watchful eye, Maximin dared not turn aside, and, calmly horrified, he gazed upon the whole spectacle without seeing it. The executioner's assistants stood behind the stake and hoisted the doomed artisan onto a small platform. A priest came up beside the Marquis and his son to exhort the condemned man while the assistants bound him tightly to the stake. The cobbler did not vouchsafe the priest a word of reply, and the latter withdrew. Then the cobbler began loudly to proclaim his innocence, said that he did not deserve to die for a few words spoken at table, and seemed launched upon an ample discourse; but the executioner knew his business. In an instant, he kindled some faggots, which had been smeared with sulfur and then artfully placed here and there in the woodpile. The roaring of the flames quickly began to cover the cobbler's voice; the smoke sent him into harrowing fits of coughing. Suddenly, the cords binding him to the post burst apart; the surprised wretch staggered forward, managing two steps. Then he plunged into the flames.

When it is methodical, barbarity is forgiven. To render it odious, a blunder sometimes suffices. The crowd, which the instant before had relished the horror of the all-too-rare spectacle, was shocked by such frightful cruelty. After the cobbler's body rolled down almost to the spectators' feet, the executioner sought to repair his error by pushing the victim into the blazing pyre with the end of his pike. Then the fellow gave forth a strange howl. This was too much for the good people: Within two minutes, the angry murmur of the crowd turned to shouts, stones began to fly in all directions, and soon the executioner's head was set on his pike and carried around the ramparts. As for the executioner's body, only scraps of it were later to be found. The Marquis de Saint-Fonds, wielding his cane, made a path through the throng and led his son to safety. When, after an hour, the crowd had not dispersed, the commander of the watch gave orders to fire two cannons charged with grapeshot at the execution square. Afterward, thirty lifeless bodies lay on the paving stones. That night, the cobbler's remains were discreetly carried to the river and thrown in. By the end of the following month, Avignon had a new judge and a new public executioner, who was formally authorized to make use of the sulfur shirt, should the need arise. The Marquis returned to his lands with his son and heir, pleased with the stripling for having borne the entire scene with the fortitude proper to a Saint-Fonds. He never suspected what horror had overcome the boy, nor did he see that the fickleness of men, the barbarity of their justice, and the infinite possibilities of human suffering had formed a permanent knot in Maximin's heart. After the return to the paternal château, the boy tried to understand. He read widely in the works of all the historians and philosophers, but no reasoning, no wise words ever diminished the force of his first indignation. He saw that the history of States resounded almost ceaselessly with the din of battle, and that public punishments meted out by a system of equivocal justice nurtured the lowest instincts of that abject menagerie known as human society. He gained knowledge of incredible torments, which did honor to the inventiveness of their devisers from every part of the world: in the empire of China, where they practiced the art of cutting a culprit to pieces while he remained alive, thus killing him as slowly as possible; in Turkey, where unfaithful wives were suitably chastised by being placed naked in a sack with several cats, and the sack then flung into the sea. Europe was not at all behindhand in such matters. For years, the cobbler of Avignon haunted Maximin's nightmares. There are some men who will always scent, wafting from dull and highly civilized moralizers in philosophy and religion, the reek of the savage beast, crouched and ready to spring. At thirteen years of age and without even understanding what he was about, Maximin de Saint-Fonds entered the secret confraternity of those who love men too much not to hate humanity. His Christian faith was affected by this, but he remained a Deist: The ubiquitous spectacle of the diversity of life caused his generous soul to imagine a benevolent Creator, to whom he refused to give a particular name. Such was the man who, at thirty, should have become the new Marquis de Saint-Fonds, but who judged, not without reason, that this was impossible.

Maximin proposed to his younger brother that he should become Marquis in his stead. The young man accepted enthusiastically and went at once to the family chapel to thank Providence on his knees. In the tedious family council which ensued, it was agreed that Maximin would keep his title of Comte, but on the express condition that he retire abroad, never more to appear in Provence. The other members of the family were surely not displeased to be rid of their eccentric relative; they had got wind of his persistent inclinations and were uneasy about his habits; but they feared even more the libertinism of his thought. For Maximin de Saint-Fonds, through all those years, had not ordered from his bookseller in Leiden only weighty treatises on botany or the physiocrats' best monographs. This enlightened nobleman's library was arranged in two sections. On the shelves of the first, available for perusal to any visitor, could be found, in scholarly disorder, English manuals of gardening, all the sages of Antiquity, and all the works published by Monsieur de Voltaire. The shelves of the second section held every obscene volume ever produced in Europe, every work which miscreants and blasphemers have bequeathed us from the past. In Maximin, the debauchery of the body had engendered that of the mind, and he had thrown himself rapturously into those books, filled with new ideas, which avoided censure by donning the mask of gallantry. Announcing to the family council his determination to remove to Geneva, Maximin de Saint-Fonds made preparations for his departure.

Now, the choice of Geneva has perhaps amazed the reader, and it requires a word of explanation. One may well ask, in fact, what the devil would impel a tranquil Deist, an ardent sodomite, an amateur physiocrat, and an enlightened admirer of obscene literature to settle in Calvin's gray and virtuous Republic? In the first instance, the Comte required a city of some size, where he could savor the pleasure of being forgotten by the world. He thought Geneva a cunning choice, as it was, for a man of Maximin's tastes, the least welcoming State in Europe. He had concluded, since it was unthinkable that a creature such as himself would choose Geneva for his domicile, that there he would be better concealed, and safer than in Paris, for example, where the so-called Greek vice was on display everywhere, especially among fashionable aristocrats, who were therefore at the mercy of the honorable Lieutenant-General of the Police. This official was possessed of enough privy information to make all the lads in the capital sing in chorus and did not hesitate to use it when the need arose. It seemed to Maximin better to take up residence in the city of virtue, in the heart of righteous Europe. When his austere disguise grew too heavy, he thought, he would advance some clever pretext and set out on a journey to Venice, Madrid, or Paris, where he could always find means to satisfy his carnal appetites. But first, Maximin de Saint-Fonds must

seduce Geneva. Had the city known what man it was who aspired to its hospitality, it would have repulsed him in horror.
Saint-Fonds conceived the simplest of stratagems: He wrote to
the Republic, declaring that the Catholics had given him no
peace since his return to the true, reformed religion and that he
desired to practice the faith of his ancestors closer to its living
source. He did not fail to evoke the shepherd and his lost sheep,
the prodigal son, and his own personal fortune. Geneva immediately let it be known that Monsieur de Saint-Fonds was
granted permission to purchase a house in the upper city. In the
beginning of the year seventeen hundred and six, he arrived in
Geneva and settled into a house at number 20 in the Grand-
Rue; he also purchased several tracts of farmland, as well as two
smaller properties he intended to oversee more closely. One of
them, located at the gates of Geneva, contained pastureland and
was suitable for rearing livestock. The other, at Péron, on the
slopes of a mountain in the French Jura, was to serve for his
agricultural experiments and justify all his departures on the
road to Paris. Finally, on the subject of his behavior, Maximin
de Saint-Fonds had resolved to adhere to Descartes' precept:
When sojourning in a foreign country—and to such a man,
every country had long since fallen into that category—one
ought to adopt the customs and usages of its inhabitants.
Throughout the time of his residence in Geneva, this Frenchman earned the admiration of the natives by attending services
twice daily and practicing a constant but discreet charity; so that
when I met him, Maximin de Saint-Fonds was, as far as the
Genevans were concerned, an honorable citizen, nor would the
suspicion of any turpitude have occurred to them when he took
me under his wing in plain sight of the whole town. This is all
that I have been able to reconstruct of the life of my benefactor. As to his benefactions themselves, I shall have more to say;

that subject contains enough matter to occupy me at length! But first, I begin with our meeting.

In the spring of the year seventeen hundred and fifteen, Saint-Fonds, who seldom left his house, and even more rarely walked anywhere, took notice of me among the urchins wearing out their clogs upon the Grand-Rue. The young in each of their little societies follow the abominable example of adults and take great pleasure in tormenting one of their kind. In our neighborhood at that time, the role of the scapegoat was played by one Christophe. No one could say exactly what had earned him this disgraceful fate: his piping voice, perhaps, or something hunted in his eyes, which were those of a misnurtured, mistreated child. Christophe was the son of a cloth merchant who, partly out of idleness and partly out of the rage common to husbands when they must raise a bastard, beat him like a carpet. The poor child passed his days in the streets, where he sought with horrible obstinacy the company of his peers and found this devotion remunerated with a continuous rain of blows and insults, which he bore with the feeble stoicism of a child who is not loved. That day, he was the butt of a jest even more repugnant than usual. Some idle brats spat on the filthy street and compared their work; they convinced Christophe that he could win their friendship had he but the courage to lick up a few of those gobs of spittle. I observed the scene from a few paces away, shaking with rage at such vulgarity. The trembling Christophe was already on his knees, bending over the dungy mud, when I could hold myself back no longer and, without thought, ran to his aid. Surprise worked to my advantage; with several well-placed kicks, I laid two scoundrels in the dirt. Christophe stupidly decamped, and I was left to face his tormentors alone. A violent blow in the back knocked me down, and the little band set about giving me a proper thrashing. In an effort to escape, I began to crawl on my hands and knees, when in an instant the group scattered to the winds, like a flight of swallows. I got to my feet, but in the sudden movement the blood rushed to my brain, and I lost consciousness.

Saint-Fonds—since it was he who, by dealing out heavy blows with his cane, had dispersed my valiant adversaries—had me carried inside his house, under whose windows the battle had just taken place. We entered a strange little salon, filled with objects the nature of which I could not at all understand. I was laid upon a sofa and a towel placed on my head. My rescuer complimented me on my chivalrous valor and asked me, with a hint of irony, what the victim was to me. I confessed that I had acted less out of affection for Christophe, who disgusted me as he did the others, than out of indignation at the baseness of his torturers. Saint-Fonds was doubtless pleased by the frankness of my reply. Drawing up a chair, he sat beside the sofa where I lay and asked me a thousand questions about my family and my occupations. He spoke to me with the courtesy one ordinarily reserves for his peers; I was sensible on that score, child that I was, not knowing that Saint-Fonds—as I would quite soon discover—spoke to everyone in that unchangingly polite tone, without regard to rank or fortune. He bade me rise and showed me, in the large glass cases which filled most of the room, curiosities from his treasure trove of old and rare objects and specimens from his collection of natural history. I scarcely liked books, but I had a passion for the things of Nature. I asked him many questions about his herbarium, to which he responded with a good grace. An enormous vessel wherein floated a two-headed lamb greatly astonished me. As dusk was falling, Saint-Fonds had me served a small meal and then accompanied me to the door, inviting me to come and visit him again. I returned the very next day, and all the following days.

Saint-Fonds often confided to me that he had not thought of me with concupiscence during the earliest period of our acquaintance. I am willing to believe it. I was the first person he befriended in Geneva. He believed that he had found in me the companion he sometimes missed; this mirage was doubtless the cause of his eventually disregarding the iron law of his debauches, for he put his life in danger with what might look, from the outside, like the corruption of the child of a Genevan citizen. For that matter, I hardly know anymore how he came to take liberties with me. I seem to remember that it all happened quite simply. In such matters, Saint-Fonds was neither a brute nor a fool, and his sensuality, which demanded little from him, would not have led him to force his attentions upon me had I displayed any horror of them. I was ten years old, and the ardor of my temperament was beginning to show itself. I had forgotten the expedient taught me by my deceased mother; Maximin obligingly refreshed my memory, and I considered curiously the milky, sticky effusion, which I had never seen before. He explained its nature to me and showed me how to produce the same effect on him. At first, I believe, I saw in this nothing but a natural extension of our tête-à-têtes amid his collections of curiosities. At nearly a century's distance, I consider the innocent child I was to have been right. We ought not attach to such actions moral values which they do not contain: false values, born of the imaginings of depraved priests, and which are none the better for being shared by the majority. Those games of my youth did not engage me for life; but I have never been able to refuse pleasure, whatever its source, and if I have preferred the company of women, it is simply because I have followed my sentimental inclination. I recall that once Saint-Fonds was taken with the fancy of offering me his fundament. I considered that wrinkled rump with little appetite; I have always been, with regard to arses, somewhat particular. By tradition, the Saint-Fonds males had low posteriors, with flat, hairy buttocks: nothing to inflame me with desire. The excellent Comte sensed this and did not insist. There was little conformity between his sexual temper and my own; he had the nobility to recognize our difference, and we remained as father and son. On occasion, he solaced himself with polished waxen pricks of his own fabrication; I willingly assisted him, and it was a wonder to observe how easily such bulky objects disappeared into that noble bottom, proof that Providence, if it did not explicitly desire these harmless games, at the very least permitted them. Many years later I learned that practices of this sort were called "antiphysical"—that is, unnatural—love. Saint-Fonds made me swear never to mention them, but he never thought fit to tell me why. To him and to my mother, I believe, I owe my lifelong enjoyment of the pleasures of the bedroom, unmixed with any moody humors, and my experience of raptures so intense, their only danger was that I sometimes desired to die of them.

And so I formed the habit of knocking at the door of number 20 in the Grand-Rue every afternoon. Saint-Fonds led an orderly life, in which I had my place. He broke his fast early, and from six to eleven in the morning corresponded with all of Europe—with bourgeois, enlightened noblemen, scholars, artisans. They exchanged recipes for eliminating plant lice from rosebushes, advice on the best method of draining clayey soil or of fattening excessively acidic land at small expense. After lunch, the Comte withdrew to read in his library; his most beautiful Bible was ostentatiously displayed there, resting on a magnificent reading stand. Maximin would double-lock the door, turn his back on his handsome reading stand, settle himself in an armchair, and reread, for the twentieth time, Pierre Bayle's *Dictionnaire*, a treatise by Fontenelle, or one of a thousand other works, until six o'clock in the evening. It was by interrupting his reading five afternoons a week, from two until four o'clock, that Saint-Fonds undertook to give me lessons. He perceived that books intimidated me. I had pretended to scorn them, out of fear of being unworthy of them. We began with lessons upon things. I learned the names of stones and their properties, and how plants are named and classed. In our second year, I conceived a passion for animals; I wanted to understand the mystery of monsters, for the two-headed lamb remained the object of my fascination. Saint-Fonds casually showed me an intact copy of the first edition of the great Ambroise Paré's treatise *Des monstres et prodiges*, observing as he did so that he doubted whether I was capable of deciphering the author's old-fashioned language. From the height of my eleven years, proud child that I was, I claimed knowledge of our French tongue, and Saint-Fonds' ruse succeeded admirably: I desired to read. He pretended not to notice my mistakes as I read the illustrious surgeon's prose aloud and made a show of understanding it. A half hour passed in this way before I cried for mercy and confessed my ignorance. It was then decided that Saint-Fonds would read the text to me; that I would ask him to explain unfamiliar words; and that for his part, my good master would add comments whenever he thought them necessary. When I entered the cabinet in the beginning of the following week, a surprise awaited me: Saint-Fonds had, with his own hands, built me a little oaken bookcase and placed it beside his writing desk. It was the first object which had ever belonged to me. We agreed that whenever I began to read a book, it would be kept there, and that there it would remain after I had read it to the end. For a long time, Paré's tome occupied the case alone. I still remember the joy that seized my heart one dark winter afternoon, when, thanks to a thick volume of Plutarch, we reached the end of my first shelf.

After our lessons, the Comte would ring for his old servant Théodore, who had followed him into exile from Provence, and we partook of a hearty collation, conversing all the while. At seven o'clock, I returned to my paternal roof. Families are odious little dramas, Jean-Jacques. Parents, the sovereigns of those chimerical realms, have a frightful penchant to assign us our parts in the play. I was the idle, nasty rogue; you took over my former role. I loved you, but I looked on in anger as the mask of the exemplary child, which you never removed, took root in your flesh. You returned my affection, I believe. You ran to me whenever I entered the door, but partly because the performance took place under our father's tender gaze. This irritated me, and sometimes I rejected you, thus eliciting from him cries of protest against such ingratitude. And so we drew apart from each other, with little ado. The consequence was that I was all the more assiduous in my studies.

My apprenticeship with Saint-Fonds lasted three years. Our method was always to proceed from experience, and the Comte, who took a childlike delight in his role as private tutor, excelled at giving everything an air of charming nonchalance. One day, our father was afflicted with a terrible toothache. I was extremely struck to see so tough and stoical a man writhing in pain for hours on end, and I related this to Saint-Fonds. He seized the occasion to convey to me some knowledge of that part of the human machine. He began by giving me first hot water to drink, and then cold. My young teeth were not insensible to this treatment, and we consulted a medical treatise, whose plates showed, delicately drawn, our dental nerves. Saint-Fonds next asked me some questions concerning my father's alimentary preferences. As long as I had known him, Isaac Rousseau had been mad for sugar, a fondness his sojourn in Constantinople had only increased. This did not seem to surprise Saint-Fonds, who said that the nations which eat sweetmeats excessively have the foulest teeth, and those which know no sweetmeats the soundest. The most daring experts in the matter recommended that one should clean one's teeth. To this end, some time after this lesson, I received a little ivory box containing some indispensable utensils, a gift from Maximin, and I formed the habit of using them every day, to my lasting benefit. From oral care we passed to different dietary regimens, considering which organs they stimulate and which they run the risk of weakening. Soon dietetics were no longer a secret to me; to that science I owe my prolonged state of good health, as well as the fact that, since I turned sixty, I have always looked twenty years younger than my true age. And so each season brought me a share of new, useful, solid knowledge. I lived better, I tried to think justly, and I felt more and more subtly. What more could I have wanted? However, I observed that all this improvement did not come without an increase of melancholy: In proportion to my mind's development, I grew more and more detached from the superstitions, vulgar beliefs, and false idols which men invent out of fear of the only world, namely this one here below. As for you, O my only brother, you acted the puppet in your little Genevan theater. You two—you and Isaac—frequently played touching scenes: When he clutched you to his bosom, telling you how greatly you resembled your poor, deceased mother, you wept with him; in his workshop, you read aloud to him from asinine old novels. The best books spoiled you; you affected some antique poses found in a volume of Plutarch. In the end, a sense of melancholy overcame me, and I understood that I was alone.

Summer was approaching. As he did every year, Saint-Fonds had to betake himself to the farm he possessed in France, just outside the town of Péron, a day's ride from Geneva. On this occasion, he presented himself at my father's workshop and requested the favor of my company. Isaac Rousseau, delighted to be rid of me, gave his blessing. We left toward the end of the month of June, seventeen hundred and nineteen. La Charmille was a modest farm. The overseer who dwelt there sufficed to carry out most tasks, seconded by day workers when occasion required them. There was also at La Charmille a young Denise, the girl in charge of tending the cows, a fresh, rosy peasant not yet sixteen years old, who considered the Comte a saint, because he had taken her in without trying to violate her. Denise had grown up not far from there, at Ferney, and had scarcely known her father; some time since, her mother had lost her peasant's clearheadedness and grown infatuated with a swindler, a native of Lille, who was trying to withdraw from his financial entanglements before the justice of men dispatched him to the next world. The fugitive had retreated all the way to Ferney, thinking that nearby Switzerland would always offer him an asylum from the police of his own country, and in Ferney he had been fascinated by the relative affluence of some cunning breeders of livestock, who twice a year sold meat on the hoof to the citizens of Geneva at exorbitant prices. The handsome Lillois therefore set about wooing the village's only widow, his elder by twenty years, and his suit was so successful that he married her at the end of winter in seventeen hundred and fifteen. With the coming of spring, the dashing husband, observing that Denise was nubile, believed himself authorized to enjoy her fresh favors. When Denise resisted and called for help, the fellow had no other recourse than to tear his own shirt and accuse the unhappy girl of having tried to force upon him an abominable act of incest. Denise's mother knew her daughter's probity, but she was infatuated with her Lillois. She remained deaf to the appeals of her heart, and heeding only her cunt and feigning to believe her husband, she gave her daughter a small sum of money and a formal order to abandon Ferney. Weeping, Denise obeyed.

In September a market of newborn livestock was held in Chambéry, and it was there, in the muddy rear courtyard of a tavern, that Denise had met the Comte de Saint-Fonds, luckily for her, as she was on the verge of falling into the clutches of a churl who would have finished what her mother's husband had tried to begin. Saint-Fonds elicited some conversation from the young girl, who was a servant in the tavern. He engaged with her and, when the market ended, brought her back with him to his property in Péron. The austere overseer of La Charmille liked Denise; this excellent man believed in the eternal perdition of the human race and consequently gave proof of remarkable tolerance and uncommon courtesy in his dealings with every representative of the damned breed. To him Saint-Fonds consigned Denise, who knew a good deal about cows. In less than a year, she had flourished and grown more beautiful while holding absolute sway over her master's cattle, which numbered some ten head. The boys from the neighboring farms courted her assiduously, believing her the Genevan's mistress and dreaming about the dowry he might well bestow upon her. Denise was a girl of feeling, and she gave herself to none of them. Such was the beautiful, lovable, tender creature whom I saw coming toward me across the courtyard at La Charmille on the twenty-first day of June, seventeen hundred and nineteen. I was dazzled by her. I had on my side the freshness of youth and that discerning air which city dwellers affect when they visit the country, and to my great good fortune, Denise liked me as I liked her. The Genevan sluts by whom I could have been initiated into the mysteries of women disgusted me, for they lacked delicacy. I was a virgin in these matters, and if I was familiar with the most refined representations of lechery from having made my way through the second section of my mentor's library, I was, in regard to amorous sentiments and practical experience of womankind, absolutely ignorant. The awkwardness of my address, my fashion of gawking at her openmouthed, in short all the blunders which would have turned away another, disposed Denise in my favor. We had arrived at dusk. Night came quickly. We must give thought to retiring. Denise showed me the way. We were lodged in the barn, in two neighboring rooms; these were, to tell the truth, two mattresses in the hayloft, above the stable. We had to climb up to our beds by moonlight. Will the reader believe me? When Denise complained of the cold and asked if I would consent to bring our pallets together so that we might keep each other warm, I thought her prone to chilliness and was silently amazed because we had the benefit of the musky heat that was rising from the stable. We were in our shirts. I brought my bedding next to hers, lay down, and turned my back to her. She pressed herself against me, and I felt her breath tickling the nape of my neck. Finally, I turned over. We embraced each other as though we had always done so. The rest may be guessed. It was by the light of a beautiful full moon that the difference of the sexes, to which I had hitherto given but little thought, first became apparent to me, and I found it admirable.

The following morning Saint-Fonds was obliged to climb up the little ladder to extract me from the leaden slumber in which my tender mistress had left me. As was her wont, she had risen before dawn, and in her modesty had not dared awaken me. Saint-Fonds tenderly contemplated the two pallets lying side by side. I saw that he had secretly hoped for this conjoining of his two beloved protégés. In an access of gratitude, I threw myself at his feet, weeping and kissing his hand. He began to laugh in order to keep from bursting into tears in his turn and bade me rise, telling me that I was to learn at Péron the rudiments of bovine breeding as well. He revealed that Denise had been enjoined to make a decent young cowherd of me during the time of my sojourn. I went down to the stable to find my tutoress. Saint-Fonds went walking for the rest of that day, and we did not see him again until dinner, over which he presided, asking me many questions about the progress of my instruction; but I detected about him an air of sadness. Did he regret our past intimacy? I have often thought so. A sort of paternal fiber had grown in him, and he conformed to it.

Denise did indeed teach me the rudiments of her calling: the proper care of beasts in the stable, how to lead them to pasture, how to brush and examine them for ticks, and the art of milking them without risking a blow from a hoof, as well as that of preparing cheese and allowing it to mature. The days slipped past like the wind. Denise and I had the evenings at our disposal, while Saint-Fonds retired to his room to verify his accounts or contemplate the purchase of some new agricultural implement. We climbed exhausted to our nest above the stable. Denise threw her skirts and petticoats over her head and stood before me, naked and trembling, in the bluish moonlight, while I gazed upon her with delight. Sometimes she said, laughing, that she took after her animals; her forms had a similar opulence. She sat atop me, I drew her close, we rolled upon each other. I never tired of caressing her powerful flanks, her white, well-muscled thighs. She laughed at my enthusiasm, then let herself be excited by my caresses, and finished by joyously burying my member between her thighs. From night to night, I grew ever more skillful at the business of the lover, which I have always considered the sweetest of all servitudes. One region of the female anatomy hitherto unknown to me was the object of my particular admiration, and I handled it with fervent caution. Denise gave me to understand that it was not forbidden to bring my face nearer to the part in question, and one night I found myself nose to nose with an adorable, fleshy bud, covered with finest skin, and which at once inspired in me a reverence that was to endure as long as my life. I heeded both my mistress's discreet instructions and the inspirations of my fancy, imparting as much speed as I could to the movements of my tongue and my fingers. A sigh more deeply drawn than the others informed me that luck was smiling on the neophyte, compensating for his inexperience. When I rose, smeared with her effusions, I was resolved to renew the exercise immediately, as I believed that I had performed it with some success. I learned from my companion that the frail organ must be allowed to rest from time to time, and that, as with our pricks, it required intermittences whose subtle seasons were best respected. Then Denise fell asleep in my arms, and I dared not move; I reflected at length upon the wonders of the human machine.

The day following that night was a Sunday. I hastened to find the Comte, who was taking a dish of chocolate in his room. I reported my discovery to him. As the reader may suppose, Saint-Fonds had little information to impart about the tiny appendage; all he knew to tell me was that it had been baptized with a Greek name that meant "little key," because it was there that the key to women's pleasure apparently lay; he promised, however, to order a dispatch from Geneva that would satisfy my curiosity. This he did, and fifteen days later I could leaf to my heart's content through the finest atlases of the human body which the universities in Bologna, Montpellier, and elsewhere had produced, as well as the best treatises on the physical structure of woman. I had to bow to the evidence: The clitoris had but scarcely drawn the attention of medical science. The most learned men spoke not of it, yet I came to prefer the most learned to the mediocre, for these surpassed one another in idiocy upon the subject. Some of them approved the cultures which followed the wisest course, that is, those who excised the diabolical excrescence, which was responsible for the uterine rages of the most ungovernable hussies; others claimed that it was a sort of penis, which, impending over the uterus, recalled the superiority of the male; still others maintained that the very indecency of the gaping female parts sufficed to explain why woman had yielded to the Evil One, and that it was not the act of a good Christian to excite any female flesh not necessary to childbirth. These and similar inanities heated my brain to such a point that I immediately resolved to refute all such sorry metaphysicians. I did not reveal my project to Saint-Fonds, whom I wished to surprise with my reasoning. After turning the mystery of the clitoris over and over in my mind, after having discarded all the absurd justifications for its existence and all the dull moral condemnations of the poor organ, I finally had an illumination. The clitoris appeared to me as an irrefutable proof of the nonexistence of God. This interesting idea came to me one evening, when the moonlight was shedding some of its light upon my adorable, monumental mistress: The sublime grace of her body, the tempestuous discharge which had left her prostrate, her delighted laughter, my own raptures, her tender neck, in whose hollow I buried my head—all that seemed perfectly summed up in that little button of pink flesh, as essential and useless as life itself. That so minute a part of the female body enclosed so much pleasure was, strictly speaking, the true miracle of Nature. To believe in a god, when the world offered us Denise and her sisters, was a presumption of those whom life had endowed with a bilious temperament, of the unfortunate whose lot was poverty here on earth, and of the mighty, who had long understood that superstition could be of use to them. Such, in substance, was the pretty philosophical system which I, at the venerable age of fourteen years, secretly committed to paper.

At the end of some weeks, enchanted with myself and my system, I gave Saint-Fonds a copy of my first philosophical work. He read it at once, and I did not remember ever having seen him laugh so much. I took umbrage; he laughed still more. Beside myself, I summoned him to answer for his hilarity: Had any author ever, to his knowledge, so magisterially conjoined an apology for the clitoris with a defense of atheism? He replied that I had truly taken a new path, whereon no one had ever preceded me. I could not endure raillery and should perhaps have raised my hand upon the excellent man had he, recovering the smiling seriousness which quitted him but rarely, not perceived that I was far from jesting, and had he not taken it upon himself patiently to make me understand wherein my system, however appealing, nevertheless fell somewhat short of perfection. In the end, he found a way to congratulate me, saying that although I had not a philosophical turn of mind, my treatise clearly showed originality, which was, according to him, the feature of my work worthy to be retained. I remained vexed and demanded in an injured tone that he give me a proper refutation of my philosophizing. He needed no persuasion, and in no time at all, he fulfilled my demand, amusing himself in passing by demonstrating that the clitoris, which I had made the cornerstone of the edifice of my thought, argued rather for the existence of a divine architect. For if the Creator in his infinite wisdom had conceived the womb as the seat of woman's punishment, through which she was condemned to the pangs of childbirth, and if he had conceived the prick as the indisputable sign of male authority over female passivity, it was then necessary to consider the clitoris as a consolation accorded to humans saved by Our Lord Jesus Christ, and as a means of tasting, before the Day of Judgment, moments of truly celestial bliss. Thoroughly crestfallen, I left my master. I was mean-spirited enough to avoid talking to him almost completely during the following week; then I forgot the whole thing and never again set myself up as a philosopher. However, the day came when I had to leave La Charmille, that laborious, fruitful life, and the delights of shared love! One may rightly assume that my farewells to Denise were punctuated by tears and sighs. The Comte promised me that we would come back to Péron for the feast of Saint Médard in June. I returned to Geneva joylessly, under an already autumnal September sky, with nothing ahead of me but a long exercise of patience. Had I known what misfortunes awaited us in the city, I would have refused to set foot there.

When we saw each other again, we wept for joy, Jean-Jacques. As for our father, he was quite disappointed; he had hoped that I would never come down from the Jura Mountains, and that he was rid of me forever. Out of pique, he summoned me that very evening and commanded me to choose a trade within the hour. The protection afforded by Saint-Fonds had habituated me badly upon this point; for a long time, I had not given any thought to my rank in the society where I lived isolated from my peers, and now, suddenly, the hand of that society clapped me violently on the shoulder. I replied haughtily that I had never considered the matter and to my thinking there was no reason for him to consult me, given that it was incumbent on the citizens of Geneva to choose a trade for their sons, and that those same sons had nothing to say on the subject. This too-proud response did not please Isaac Rousseau. He raised his hand to strike me, and of course you clung to his clothes to restrain him. I was an ingrate, an unnatural son. Greuze would not have disowned such a picture as we formed. I ran out of my father's house without a word and disappeared into the night.

The very next day I returned to the Grand-Rue. Saint-Fonds listened to me with neither approbation nor disapprobation, which discomposed me somewhat. In the end, I grew tired of my own lamentations. Then Saint-Fonds remarked that I was surely not a man who would refuse to enter a trade without first carefully deliberating on which one I should be likely to accept. The Comte proposed that we examine together the kinds of employment open to me. He mentioned first, not without mischief, the vocation of the priesthood, making reference to faculties of theology, benefices, a regular life, and promised to buy me some office. I cried out in protest. Then, no doubt, I wished to be a domestic? I replied that I would rather die than serve. Commerce, perhaps? Renewed outcries from me. At this point, the Comte fell silent. I reflected, and it occurred to me that I had not for so much as an instant considered the purport of my father's charge. I raised my eyes to Saint-Fonds; we understood each other without a word. He pointed out that watchmaking was a pleasant and profitable occupation, and that I could, as I pleased, carry it on in any country in Europe, or even in the New World, should I wish to go there. In short, I returned that very day to the Rousseau family's little stage, resolved to play my part and obey the paternal injunction. Not without annoyance, for in my sorrowful imagination I saw the sweet caresses of my Denise moving farther away from me, perhaps forever. I returned to my father's house, I threw myself at his feet, I implored his forgiveness; and once again, my poor Jean-Jacques, you burst into a storm of tears, which in turn made Isaac weep, too. I agreed to enter into an apprenticeship. The laws of Geneva, which regulated all things, required its artisans to engage their apprentices at the beginning of each year, and my father informed me that it would be impossible for him to find, in the remaining months of that one, an artisan who would consent to take me under his wing. I had gained a year's reprieve. I hastened to request leave to absent myself from Geneva during that time; our father, thoroughly relieved by my sudden conversion, granted my wish without quibble. He asked only for my word of honor that I would return to Geneva, ready for obedience, no later than the last day of the month of September, so that he might present me to my new master. I gave him my word. Then, despite the lateness of the hour, I went again to Saint-Fonds' house. He was reading in his bed, waiting to congratulate me on my success. He decreed that I should depart for Péron within the hour and commanded that his best mule be saddled for me.

Denise, who was not expecting me, swooned with joy. The overseer released her from her day's duties, and I assisted her, trembling, to our bed of love, where I set about proving to her that I was no figment. Our love frolics were interspersed with tears, for Denise had received from her mother news that was to change the course of her life. The man from Lille, her mother's husband, had died of a nasty fall taken while leaving a tavern (some called it an even less reputable place) in Lyon. This time, it appeared, Denise's mother had reconciled herself to widowhood, but not to solitude. Having remembered that she had a daughter, she had inquired after her all over the region; a horse dealer from Chambéry, whom she encountered in Coppet and who knew Saint-Fonds, had put her on the right path. Now Denise contemplated returning to the land of her birth, where the prosperity of her family's farm would allow her to marry well. The excellent girl wept when she told me this. I entreated her not to let our imminent separation weigh on her and told her that I, too, would soon have to alter my life and enter a trade. And we spent the most wonderful months of my existence together. Denise, as imbued as ever with gratitude to Saint-Fonds, did not wish it to be said that she abused his kindness at the end of her employment, with the result that never, in the memory of the Jura, was a herd of cows attended with more love, more jealous zeal, than those of Monsieur le Comte. For my part, I passed my days browsing without the least discernment among the laden shelves of Saint-Fonds' library. I merely wanted to be able to announce to him, upon my return, what Herculean labors I had performed. Thus our sole occupations were work and love. Some delicate spirits will find me uncouth, but I say that this humble life was the best I ever had. Later, in Paris, I knew luxury; I have always taken pleasure in it and almost never refused it; but those days in the barn sufficed me then, and would suffice me today, should some benevolent genie propose to snatch them out of the void of the past. As for my dear Denise, I never saw her again; may she have known happiness in her marriage in Ferney!

That year of mine, like the others, had to end. And so it did. Denise and I bade each other farewell forever, and I forbear describing the scene. I left on the twenty-eighth day of September, resolved to keep my word. On the afternoon of the thirtieth I was within sight of the gates of Geneva when, raising my eyes to the Alps, I saw a violent storm turn in our direction, cover the town with thick clouds, and inundate the main road. In a few instants, this tempest was upon us: Saint-Fonds' poor mule, which had just spent three months grazing in the meadows of La Charmille, that is, in something like the earthly paradise of mules, reacted very badly to the sudden change of weather, threw me into a ditch, and disappeared into the neighboring wood. I lost perhaps an hour in beating the underwood for the creature before I remembered that the guards of the watch in Geneva were charged with closing the city gates at nightfall and keeping them closed throughout the night. I began to run, drenched and buffeted by the storm. I reached the southern gate of the city. The guards saw me as I came on, but to my misfortune one of them recognized me. I was one of those little scoundrels who, for years on end, had played some ferocious pranks on him and his comrades. They were delighted to close the gate in my face and then taunt me at great length. I responded by insulting them copiously. Luckily, like all the shiftless idlers of the Republic of Geneva, I knew a forbidden passage: I crept into the ditch, followed it west along the walls, reached a low, timeworn gate, and slipped between two loosened bars. From there, I sneaked into an abandoned guard post; I emerged upon a terrace, climbed over a wall, and jumped down into the street.

I had underestimated my adversaries' subtlety. They were there, infuriated by my recent insults and overjoyed to chastise me. My struggles availed me nothing; they gave me a thrashing, bound me hand and foot, and dragged me to the watchhouse, where there was a dungeon used, perhaps thrice a year, to confine transient drunkards, and which stank of stale urine and regurgitated wine. I implored the guards in vain; they remained unyielding, and I spent the night in that place. Early the next morning, in exchange for the contents of my purse, the most perfidious villain of the troop agreed to notify my father, who had to suffer the humiliation of traversing the city by the side of a sergeant of the watch. As we walked home, I dared not speak. Isaac Rousseau declared himself weary of my outrageous conduct; I had failed to keep my word. Although he had no doubt that I could produce some excellent explanation for my failure, this time he refused to listen to my reasons. I was a renegade without honor; he cursed the day I was born; he invoked my deceased mother and all the saints in Paradise. His tragic tone made me laugh in spite of myself. Unfortunately, Isaac discovered my mirth, and we changed our destination at once: He wished to consult his former brother-in-law, our uncle on our mother's side. I quaked at the thought of the family council that seemed to be in store for me. Our uncle Bernard, at scarcely forty-five years of age, was a worn-out old fellow who was good for very little, and therefore he believed himself justified in deciding everything. But this former soldier did so with such authority, with the self-assurance proper to imbeciles, that the Rousseau family had formed the habit of seeking his advice in moments of crisis. He received us gravely and entered into the paternal indignation with great conviction. My uncle had the ear of the director of our fair city's house of correction, an establishment which was the admiration of Protestant Europe, and from which the Catholics themselves, it was said, spoke of drawing inspiration. The director was accustomed to aiding in the repair of disordered families; moreover, telling himself that there was no smoke without fire, he took my father's anger at face value. And so I found myself, for a peccadillo and without the faintest hint of a trial, condemned to one year in the house of correction on the grounds of dissipation, a vague term which punished the person without soiling the name of a family known to be honorable. I was brought there that very evening.

In the Rue de la Miséricorde, a basalt façade, almost blind, monastic: Geneva's house of correction, which we called the Hospital; a narrow courtyard flanked by individual cells (meant to avoid the emulation in vice produced by the dormitories in boarding schools), but without doors, so that the supervisors might exercise their absolute authority at any moment; instead of windows, different sorts of loopholes, so that the constant sight of the heavens might inspire sublime thoughts and ideas of repentance. Fifty boarders shared repulsive nourishment, a great change for me from the dairy foods of my beloved Jura. Approximately ten tutors, chosen for their scrupulous probity, lived in the Hospital with us; they dispensed elementary scraps of knowledge, which, in order not to attract attention, I pretended to discover under their instruction for the first time, as my companions in misfortune did. These tutors were admirable men of active piety, sincerely convinced that redemption was possible for everyone on earth and that their consecration to this infinite task and to the incessant exercise of patience it required was pleasing to their God. Within those walls, I witnessed the practice of the superior form of charity, namely that which is given without the least concern for recompense—and which probably proceeds, saving the grace of those enthusiasts of humility, from uncommonly great pride. Nine times out of ten, their heroic efforts were wasted, but they were generous enough to forget all but the tenth case. Subject to the tutors' orders were about thirty supervisors, for the most part ignorant and unwashed, who stood in horrid contrast to our devout preceptors. In dangerous contrast, too, because the latter were too naive to imagine the depravity of the former, who threatened us with the wickedest cruelties if we should dare to think about seeking protection from our masters. Those brutes had found their Paradise in the Hospital. Their infamies were various: Some limited their pleasures to tormenting the youngest among us with absurd bullying and punishments; others committed rape. During my very first night, the head supervisor, the worthy leader of this band, came to my cell, awakened me, and sat on my bed. He smelled of stale sweat. He inspected my face first, bringing his lantern close to my nose. I was naked under the nightshirt the Hospital had provided; he examined me meticulously to make sure that I had been washed and shorn and cleansed of all vermin. His voice was soft and his manner unctuous. He counseled me that I should sleep with my hands outside my bedclothes, so that I would be prevented from causing irreparable damage to my modesty; thus did he express himself. As I quickly perceived, the style employed by this man and his ruffians was a mixture of our masters' admonitions, surreptitiously overheard in the refectory; of the mercenary prose employed in the sacred pamphlets which peddlers hawked and which one found, for economy's sake, torn into smaller pieces in the latrines; and of their own obscene imaginings. After that first exhortation to goodness, the honorable head supervisor asked me a thousand questions. While he spoke, I deliberated: Should I deliver a kick to his groin? Should I try to rid myself of him in some subtler fashion? He wished to know who I was and, especially, what miserable misdeeds had brought me to that place. Not wishing to disappoint him, I alluded, in a hesitating voice, to crimes of lust. He urged me at once to describe them in the greatest detail, so that he might know the extent of the evil and that we might together, by taking the long and tortuous road of humiliation, make our way to the glorious citadel of grace. As he spoke these words in his short-breathed murmur, he ran his hand over one of my thighs. In answer, I invented debauches which would have made the most hardened libertine tremble. Feeling along his breeches, I discovered a majestic but still partly limp engine; I redoubled my caresses and my obscenities. Soon a sigh deeper than the others apprised me that the honorable head supervisor's pleasure had, for this evening, run its course. He took out a handkerchief and wiped his prick with a somewhat crestfallen air. Once his member returned to the flaccid state, the poor devil did not conceal from me his bewilderment at finding that a creature so young could wallow in such pestilential filth. He seemed to fear that my disordered mind had begotten the chimeras he had seen. He returned to his bed, which was set up in a sort of vestibule on the same floor as the older boys' cells, including my own, but I never again received a nocturnal visit from him. After our encounter, I later learned, he resumed his attentions to his little favorite, practically a child, a fat, white idiot whom he buggered nightly, greatly savoring the boy's tears. My bold defense had been successful.

The inmates of the Hospital formed a very disparate group, whose ages ranged from twelve to twenty-four years. For the first six days, I was not authorized to speak to them, because it was customary at the Hospital to put new arrivals in isolation, in order to lead them more swiftly to complete repentance. At first, in the naïveté produced by solitude, I fancied that my fellow prisoners were indomitable free spirits, and I rejoiced that I would soon meet them. My illusions were quickly shattered. The stupidity of most of my fellows was abyssal; no one, having once conversed with them, could be surprised to find them where they were (prisons are populated by scatterbrains and fools; the cunning never set foot there). I had envisioned original personages, but the majority of those creatures had been driven to crime by poverty, with no more exercise of will than twigs carried along by a torrent. A small number of them had been honest boys, whom the death of a father, a catastrophic harvest, or a family quarrel had thrown upon the roads, far from their village. A tiny minority, the least intelligent, exhibited genuine, active, absolute dispositions to vice. It was in the Hospital in Geneva that I lost all my admiration for the brigands who had fascinated me in my early years. In the end, I felt pity for them all, for the dregs of humanity present a spectacle of infinite sadness. But every existence contains empty moments; those twelve months, calm and dreary, slipped by. I was permitted to send letters, but I did not avail myself of the privilege, certain that anything I might write to Saint-Fonds would be read. Toward the end of my stay in the Hospital, I amused myself by composing a letter in which, aping the florid style of the head supervisor, I promised to conduct myself more properly in the future. Copies of this letter were sent to my uncle and my father. In September, seventeen hundred and twenty-one, I left the Hospital, neither more nor less dissolute than I had been when I entered it. Eager to be reunited with my trusted counselor, I hurried to the Grand-Rue, and fell down in a faint at his door when I found it draped in black. Maximin de Saint-Fonds was dead. Théodore found me on the steps of the house when he returned from ordering his master's coffin.

I was sixteen years old, and I was astonished that men died. I imagined that my teacher would have mocked my naïveté, and I tried to be reasonable. But then I thought of my mother, dead nine years before; and for the first time, I cried, both for her and for him. I questioned Théodore, who hovered like a grief-stricken shade, about the Comte's death, which had left me almost an orphan. Among the Saint-Fonds family, cancers were a solid tradition. The Comte's disease had fed, as it were, upon his well-preserved youthfulness and vigor, and had struck him down within a few months. He died two days before I came out of the Hospital. Fortunately, he had had sufficient time to make his confession and to attend to all the dispositions required by his scrupulous character and his rank. He was borne, by his command, into his library. He charged Théodore with taking down and casting into the fire each of the volumes on the shelves of the second section. The task occupied Théodore for several days, and never did he give any appearance of knowing what was inside those books. When the pain consuming his stomach became intolerable, Saint-Fonds began to avail himself of the opium grains he had reserved for just such an eventuality, for he never affected the false stoicism of refusing to take up arms against suffering; he would not run the risk of dying like an animal when he had lived as a man. He hastened to put his affairs in order, closing the sale of his dwelling and judiciously organizing the dispersion of his collections of curiosities and learned works to the best libraries in Europe. He also arranged for the payment of a generous pension to Théodore. In the end, he swallowed a chocolate enriched with ten grains of opium and lay down calmly, never to rise again, certain that the benevolent Author of all things here below would see into his heart and not damn him for having avoided the useless torment of his disease.

Théodore was unable to finish his account, as I could not bear to hear any more of it. He offered to show me the body, which was lying upstairs. I refused, wishing to remember Saint-Fonds only as he was when alive. Not long after, the Comte's remains were transported to the family tomb in Provence. The Saint-Fonds family saw fit to bury him embalmed in a triple coffin under an extravagance of white marble, winged angels, and elaborate garlands. Why would they not let him decay in the earth which he loved better than any of them, to nourish it and merge with it entirely? After having accompanied him to the end, Théodore retired to the village where he was born, at the foot of the Saint-Fonds château, where I doubt if he long survived his master. Nothing then remained of Maximin de Saint-Fonds' passage through the Republic of Geneva, except for the good he had done to his fellow men and the seeds of life and truth he had sown in the heart of a ten-year-old rascal named François Rousseau. The said miscreant sought a way to honor Saint-Fonds' memory; emancipated from churches and gods, he was obliged to invent a form for his mourning. And I well believe, my dear Jean-Jacques, that you will understand what I did. One brisk, cool morning, under a dazzling sun, I departed from Geneva. Going northward, along the west shore of the lake, I walked up to a height whereon Saint-Fonds loved to meditate. The spot overlooked the gray roofs of the city; from there one could clearly observe changes of weather; and when the sun shone brightly, it was possible to make out the feverish movements of men on the roads and the decks of ships. Your rake of a brother remained there for a long time, bareheaded, savoring the kisses of the sun and the buffets of the wind; he gave thanks to the beloved departed, and before Nature, which is indifferent to the disasters of men, he undertook to live his life as intensely, as singularly, as the Comte had lived his own, *to live his life* and not the ridiculous roles perfidiously offered him by the theater of the world. Then the solitary young man again went down to the city, and three days later, his father took him to Louis Augustin, artisan watchmaker by trade, in whose workshop he was to enter upon his apprenticeship.

Between my sojourn in the house of correction and my apprenticeship occurred a comic episode about which I am obliged to say a word, because it holds a place of honor in the admirable labyrinth of your *Confessions*. Our father quarreled with a man who, I believe, was an officer; Isaac thrust his sword into the fellow's arm and had to leave the city. You were put to board with a pastor named Lambercier, who lived a few leagues from Geneva, in the little village of Bossey. Isaac was very concerned about you, and, as I was at leisure, I promised him I would visit you in Bossey now and again. You were in your tenth year. Both of us passionately loved argumentation, and in this domain you gave proof of an astonishing precocity. The subject of one of our most fervent debates was heroism. I spoke of your infatuation with the great figures you had found in Plutarch. You maintained that there were some men, extraordinary from birth, whom nothing could prevent from accomplishing great deeds. You confounded Plutarch's heroes with those bad novels you two devoured, you and your father, all the more religiously because they had once belonged to our poor Suzanne; tales of nothing but secret births, princes disguised as beggars, combats sublime in their magnanimity, and miraculous coincidences. I replied that there was no such thing as Destiny: that in my opinion, a farm laborer could make a good king, provided that enough trouble was taken to educate him in kingly matters. We were certainly both right and both wrong, as is necessarily the case in debates of that kind. When our lively imaginations dictated images to us, we took them for thoughts, and so it became impossible for us to accept or bear the least contradiction; and that impossibility led us to believe ourselves absolutely irrefutable. In the heat of our conversation, we went to extremes: I told you frankly that your heroes would not have been able to bear an apprentice's life and that it was less difficult for the leading figure of Rome or Troy to strike grandiose poses than it was for the lowliest servant of a house in a seedy quarter of Geneva, where he was badly lodged and badly fed, simply to be a man. Had you been able to do so, I believe you would have struck me, Jean-Jacques. Instead, with a smooth transition, you declared peremptorily that there was no injustice here on earth, that each person received what he deserved. I resolved to give you a lesson. But I was far from supposing what bizarre use you would later make of it!

I describe the affair as it happened. And to begin, I must say a word about the circumstances of my misdeed: As the reader may have guessed, I was still, for the Rousseaus as well as the Bernards, the Ne'er-do-well; as for you, Jean-Jacques, you enthusiastically performed your role of the Virtuous Child. In the past, I had been blamed for some few pieces of mischief, some petty thefts committed by you, and you had neglected to declare your guilt. Two days after our philosophical jousting match, I secretly returned to Bossey and began to spy on you, waiting for the propitious moment: I had a precise and fearsome idea of how I would exact my revenge. A maidservant in the house of your host, the pastor Lambercier, was in the daily habit of putting his daughter's combs to dry in a room where you often sat reading. I waited for a long time, hidden in the garden. At last, you came into that room, where no one but you and the servant ever entered. You took a chair near the window, hidden behind a screen, and began to read in a low voice, your back turned to the fireplace, where Mademoiselle Lambercier's combs were drying. The maidservant finally left the house. I slipped soundlessly behind you, plucked one of the combs off the mantel, broke it, and replaced the pieces. I left the house as I had entered it and hastened away from Bossey without being seen by anyone: I had to be beyond the reach of all suspicion by the time the broken comb was discovered. I ran to Geneva and through the city gates without attracting notice. Alas, some unforeseen circumstances, which I shall soon relate, prevented me from enjoying my farce and then revealing to you that it was one. In fact, I quickly forgot that puerile incident, and it would never again have risen to the surface of my memory had I not, sixty years later, discovered in Book One of your *Confessions*, to my great surprise, the last word on the little adventure. And I firmly believe myself to be the only reader whom your account of the incident has ever caused to burst into loud laughter. The servant found the broken comb; the crime could have been committed by no one but you. You energetically declared your innocence. But the Lamberciers did not offer the same inexhaustible indulgence your father would have shown in such a circumstance. Everything pointed to you. Your wickedness provoked wounded indignation. And if you were punished, it was less for having broken the comb than for your obstinacy in denying it.

Any child but you, any child without your extreme sensibility, without your talent, would have forgotten such an incident (what child has not suffered a similar injustice?). Most of us would have disregarded it or consoled ourselves with thinking of all the times when we remained unpunished. You reacted differently, Jean-Jacques. Wrapped in your toga, perched on the platform of your *Confessions*, you turn that Affair of the Broken Comb into the worst injustice ever committed in the memory of humanity, a second end to the terrestrial Paradise! In your place, I should have sought, I should have found the solution to this enigma, I should have questioned the neighbors, one of whom must doubtless have taken notice of me; you preferred your own truth. To many of the first readers of your *Confessions*, this incident, placed at the beginning of the book, gave proof of a streak of utter ridiculousness in its author. What? Make an entire drama from this one insignificant scene? Your former friends, the Encyclopédistes, mocked you, and, as I have said, I did no less the first time I read you. Well, then: We were all wrong. You were the first to think that such trivialities were worth recording, the first to write in that way, at the human level, the first to give voice to the unique protests of ordinary mortals. Fewer than ten years after the publication of the first volume of your *Confessions*, thousands of Jean-Jacqueses made in this country a revolution of a kind never before seen; many among them had read your works. Each of them fought against some ridiculous injustice which he had suffered; many others imitated them without knowing why. Together, they brought down an iniquitous society. Such was your singular genius, Jean-Jacques, and I have a hundred times regretted that you died before you could measure its scope: You believed yourself alone in the world, and in the end you nearly were; you thought yourself unique, and because you were, an army of your kind rose up to change the order of things. Would you have recognized this revolution as your work? I am certain you would not. But I was there, and I tell you plainly: They were right to invoke your name.

———

But let us return to the period after I left the Hospital. By that time, I was looked upon, in the family circle, as a thoroughgoing imbecile, a downright fool, who could not even see where his interest lay. I considered in depth the advantages I could derive from this bad reputation. I showed myself disinclined to chat; I discouraged all attempts at elevated conversation; I never uttered any opinion that fell outside the range of insignificant mediocrity. I had been the scandal of the family; now nobody gave me a second thought. I was alone and at peace. A master badly in need of an apprentice had been found for me. Isaac personally accompanied me to Louis Augustin's workshop. Contrary to my fears, the art of the watchmaker delighted me, even though I could not say the same for the company of the venerable Augustin, a sickly, irascible old man, an admirable pedagogue, and for the rest a master like any other, since, in order to pay me as little as possible, he decided that I would lodge with him in his house, in a filthy alley in the lower city.

From the moment I sat down at Master Augustin's table, I understood why aspiring apprentices were not jostling one another on his doorstep. His journeyman was there, a watchmaker named Léveillé, hardly "awake" as his name implies, but a near if not complete idiot, with marvelously agile fingers and excellent taste in the decoration of watches. The housekeeper, Monique, a chubby, mustachioed former sutleress, round and solid as an oaken barrel, relegated me at once to the kitchen, where she gave me a gruel which was, to my taste, rather thin. I found it odd that I should be exiled in this fashion, apprentice as I was, but it was my first evening, so I put on a good countenance and waited for old Augustin and his journeyman Léveillé to finish the supper the harpy served them. At last, she handed me a cold and meager plate, with meat so lean I feared it owed less to the poultry market than to some stray cat. Despite my hunger, I did not eat all that was set before me. I regretted this decision a great deal the next day, when I discovered that supper constituted what passed for a feast in that gloomy household. The housekeeper slept on a straw mattress in a small lean-to where I, too, was assigned a pallet on the floor. I retired first and blew out my candle, and in the darkness Monique came and lay down in her accustomed place. The thought of my Denise seeing me in that alcove made me smile more than once. I had not, for an instant, an idea of any amorous adventure. The venerable Monique regarded me as if I had been an abandoned puppy taken in by the master of the house; I learned that she had once been old Augustin's mistress. As a good second, Léveillé, who had his eye on succeeding to the old man's workbench, in the meanwhile succeeded him in Monique's bed, as I was soon able to ascertain. Every night, by the light of a candle, this lusty fellow of thirty years plied the ample sutleress, who bit a corner of her scarf so as not to disturb anyone; in the darkness, with her mastiff's face no longer visible, the rounded contours of her flesh, trembling under the buffets of her vigorous paramour, did not form a disagreeable spectacle. In the end, I grew overheated. The journeyman, his business done, went back to his room without a word. The scene was repeated each evening; my chamber companions never seemed to be inhibited by my presence. On the tenth night, and while I feigned sleep, it happened that the candle had been moved, and I saw the matron peering in my direction, trying to see me, but without success. Until pleasure made her roll up her eyes, they never ceased searching for mine. After Léveillé left, taking his candle, I waited in curious anticipation, wondering what would be my neighbor's reaction. Doubtless made nervous by her own boldness, she lay unmoving on her mattress, but her breathing clearly told me that she was not dozing. Since the brazen hussy gives herself to Léveillé, I thought, why not play the idiot? I made bold to approach her on all fours, and then I asked her what had caused the sounds they made, and when she hesitated in her response, I inquired whether she was in pain, and whether Monsieur Léveillé had hurt her. Surely she suspected a jest of some kind, but I remained so stubbornly in character that in the end she took me for what I appeared to be. She shifted herself in the darkness, and the exhalations of her warm, perspiring flesh rose to my nostrils. Drawing me close to her, she said that I must not speak so loudly or I would awaken the master (this lie heralded my victory, for old Augustin, separated from us by a thick wall, slept like a log and snored like a sawmill, and nothing ever awakened him). I felt the curves of her hip and her thigh against my skin, but I remained as motionless as I could. She asked me if it was true that I knew nothing of the game she had played in my sight but a short while ago; I swore on the Holy Bible that I was telling the truth. At that point, she could contain herself no longer and, seizing my most protruding part with one hand, she grasped my buttocks with the other and threw me upon herself; then she demonstrated the maneuver with a few movements, and I fucked her with all my heart. When I rolled onto my side, covered with sweat, the excellent woman climbed atop me and presented to my mouth a fabulously thick bush. Its scents intoxicated me, and I hastened to devour that hot, musky fruit with a calculated clumsiness which greatly augmented her pleasure. She was not long in reaching a climax, and I joyously accompanied her. I began that evening to learn a truth of experience, namely that one must not judge a lover by her appearance or by the character she presents to society. The massive Monique was the sweetest and most enthusiastic of mistresses. I never tired of handling and contemplating her ripe, majestic charms. I have since enjoyed similar instances of good fortune, and I believe that the variety of cunts and bodies is no less great or less pleasing than that of faces. After all, a head has fewer charming folds than a cunt. Some sexes are stupid, dull, expressionless; others, by contrast, are pleasant and happy, like the faces of friends. In the end, I found that the nether face lies less than the other; and that is perhaps why the former is hidden, and the latter displayed for all to see. My line of reasoning applies equally well, I believe, to pricks. Monique's cunt had lived and made no secret of it; it seemed to regret nothing; serving it was never dull. Before long, she began to slip into my bed every morning. I never took off my simpleton's mask for her, for the idea of my stupidity excited her, as did Léveillé's, spurring her to a degree of recklessness she would not have reached with a sensible lover. One of those fine mornings, as we were recovering our spirits, Monique made me a strange confession there in the half darkness of the little room. If she bit a piece of cloth during her love bouts, she said, it was not to keep from crying out, for she was capable of restraining herself unaided. But when the cloth was in her mouth, she imagined that she had been gagged and that the highwaymen who were her abductors came in one after another and had their way with her, all the while declaring that her life would be forfeit if she uttered so much as a sigh. When she was obliged to share the lean-to with me, she said, her bizarre fancy had acquired a semblance of reality, which had driven her to discharges of pleasure such as she had never known. Those voluptuous imaginings, then, had emboldened her to seduce me. I pretended to understand nothing at all of this confession; had she believed I would understand it, she would never have made it. But the fancies of Dame Monique with the rag between her teeth, my own whims, which I shall have a later occasion to discuss, and the Comte de Saint-

Fonds' waxen implements have sometimes given me much food for thought. For although, at the beginning of my amorous career, I thought it curious that fate continually flung me into the arms of eccentrics, experience slowly taught me that when it comes to the commerce of the flesh, my fellow humans are quite fond of odd little rituals, some of which originate uniquely in the body, while others are entirely products of their imagination. I learned that these innocent singularities were comparable to parts of works so tiny that the uninitiated always think they can be done without, whereas in fact a watch will not run without them. The human machine has its own works, and moralists who wrongly condemn the brutishness of our desires know not how infinitely subtle are the motivations of human actions. This is what I thought about sometimes, during the long hours I spent patiently learning my trade.

I had served six months of my apprenticeship when I received from Saint-Fonds' lawyer in Geneva a small package, wrapped in waxed cloth and sealed; the man of law informed me in his florid style that Monsieur le Comte had been pleased to bequeath me the volume in octavo herewith included; he likewise gave me to understand that in his testament, Monsieur de Saint-Fonds expressed his expectation that the said book would edify me as it had edified him all his life long and even more, should it please God. When I read those last words, I suspected some prank on Saint-Fonds' part and waited until I was alone before I opened the volume. The red morocco cover bore an admirable title—*The Flowers of Sanctity*—and the first page announced to the reader that he would find gathered there the most inspiriting maxims of Christianity, chosen with loving care by the most eminent moralists of our Church. I read a few phrases at random and saw at once that they were not Christian in inspiration, and that Saint-Fonds must have prepared the work himself. Then I found the real title page, which indicated that the volume in my hands was a book called *On the Nature of Things*, translated into French by Maximin-Irénée-Tancrède, Comte de Saint-Fonds, from the Latin poem of Titus Lucretius, Roman citizen.

One of Saint-Fonds' regrets had been his failure to inspire in me a passion for Latin and Greek. I do not know very well what hindered me from taking to those languages. I was born a barbarian, and so I have remained. I learned enough of the classical tongues to know that I did not know them at all; and all that I have read, I have read in French. Sometimes, in jest, Saint-Fonds vexed me on this point, saying that he despaired of ever making me a scholar. I replied in the same fashion, declaring that my projects for the future did not include wasting away while poring over dusty parchments, and further, that the barbarians were, in their way, civilized. He teased me by pointing out that although I wished to be a pagan, I chose to deprive myself of an acquaintance with my pagan ancestors. In addition to such badinage, Saint-Fonds often spoke to me of Lucretius and deplored the lack of a worthy translation of the Roman poet's work. Therefore, in the privacy of his study, he dedicated himself to this task. I looked at the date on which this most particular work was printed and saw that my unexpected sojourn in the Hospital of Geneva must have prevented the Comte from giving me his present himself. As the reader has no doubt guessed, as soon as I had a moment of solitude, I began to read the book, and it was thus that I met Lucretius. I say that I "met" him: *On the Nature of Things* begins with an invocation to Venus, and at once I found myself inflamed, transported. Love at first sight exists in matters of the mind as well as in those of the heart. I devoured the work and carefully hid my new treasure.

Soon I knew it by heart, and I emerged from reading it cleansed of the last remnants of that Deism my teacher had tried to inculcate in me; for it seemed evident that the god whom Lucretius sometimes evokes is so subtle, so remote, that he can be got rid of without the world's ceasing to turn, and this is what I did, definitively, being persuaded that Lucretius himself, in his heart of hearts, did not think otherwise, and that he had presented things as he did only out of prudence. For the rest, everything in his poem enchanted me. To write about the nature of things seemed to me the only honorable task, the highest and the most direct, and it was then that to know the world became my single ambition. This book made me regret my ignorance of Latin. So much did I love the work that twenty years later, in Paris, I bought it in its original version, which I soon got by heart. In the blackest hours of my existence, I recited lines from Lucretius's poem as though it were a talisman. It seemed that the man spoke to me like a brother, whispering in my ear; this, I believe, is the miracle of poetry. Lucretius sings that everything which exists can be explained: mountains and lightning, rivers and winds; that it is possible to get to the bottom of all things: how dreams are formed, what sensations are, how to live, how to die with dignity; and that it is incumbent upon man to perform the immense and elating task of finding the individual causes of everything in this unique world where we exist. And for all that, he says, there is no need whatsoever to imagine gods living in ugly, uninhabitable palaces somewhere out of this world. I was delighted that one should say so simply that there was no heaven above the clouds.

And so Saint-Fonds had not abandoned me completely. Sometimes I recalled our metaphysical debates, but, fortified by my volume of Lucretius, I was thenceforth resolved to manage without the hypothesis of a divine watchmaker. Man appeared to me as a sort of automaton, but an automaton which could never be wound up again. I carried on a solitary dialogue with Saint-Fonds: I admitted, if I must, that one might declare ignorance of man's first cause, but I maintained most energetically that mechanics would, in the end, provide us with the ultimate explanation of living things. As the reader sees, I was no better a metaphysician at eighteen than I was at fourteen. It was also around this time that I conceived an ephemeral passion for research into perpetual motion. The Don Quixotes of mathematics chase after the squaring of the circle; those of watchmaking go in quest of perpetual motion. I pursued this study to the point of obsession, but in an access of lucidity, I saw myself running like a madman behind an insubstantial chimera, and that was the end of my sterile researches.

I had some talent for the subtle art of watchmaking, but I kept a goodly part of my most rapid progress hidden and carefully committed some errors in the hope that my apprenticeship would be prolonged, for I disliked that subaltern state less than the future which my family, without even having to think about it, foresaw for me. Sometimes, in the laborious silence of the workshop, I lifted my eyes from the bench and considered Léveillé: He had once occupied my place; soon he would take Augustin's. And there it was, the narrow circle inside which Geneva bound me! At the end of a year and a half, my pretended clumsiness had an effect which went beyond my intentions. Without a word to me, Master Augustin went before the watchmakers' guild and declared, most officially, that I must be recommitted, a hypocritical term signifying that I was not mastering the trade and that I was going to be brought before an assembly of the guild and subjected, with all pomp and cir-

cumstance, to an interminable philippic, after which I must beg
to be given the opportunity to repair my most grievous fault. I
heard all this from Monique's mouth, one morning in the month
of April, seventeen hundred and twenty-three. I went down to
the shop, where Léveillé had been working, as was his habit,
since dawn. So preoccupied was I by the fate impending over
my future that I failed to take notice of the mocking smiles with
which Léveillé favored me. In the end, growing bolder, he made
an exceedingly vulgar remark, the upshot of which was that
I should soon have to do without the breakfasts I was being
served in bed. Before the words had completely left his mouth,
he bit his lip, but the thunderclap had already burst: I understood that he had poisoned Augustin's mind; otherwise, the old
man, with his passion for watchmaking, would not have renounced his efforts to inculcate his knowledge in me. Outraged
by such baseness, I slapped my churlish rival in the face. He returned the blow, and I thrust him away from me so vigorously
that the unfortunate wretch fell over backward, his head struck
a chest, and he moved no more.

Was he dead? No matter; I believed he was. This time, I
risked losing my life as well as my liberty, and my age would no
longer protect me. I left Léveillé where he lay and ran to my
room, where I snatched up my purse before rushing out into
the street. I took the road to France, thinking to attract less notice on the most frequented highway. Before reaching the bor-
der, I turned in to a byroad, for I had no passport to show. I had
not bidden adieu to anyone. Did I truly regret that? I had become a foreigner in my own country. I had had a brother; I believed I had lost him forever, for at the time you seemed to be
the lifeless marionette that was our father's notion of a perfect
child. I was alone in the world, but the world held out its arms

to me. For each of their theorems, mathematicians seek the shortest demonstration, which they call the "elegant proof." I was happy to imitate those learned men.

I walked the whole day on the road to France. Would the Republic of Geneva lower itself to pursue so miserable a fugitive? I doubted it, but in fact I could never afterward discover whether or not Léveillé had died from his fall; to have— perhaps—dispatched that poor fool into death is the only deep regret of my long life. In any case, I left the main road. Traveling on hunters' and shepherds' paths, meeting no one, and sleeping in rocky shelters still empty before the coming of summer, I came to Nantua. From there I joined a group of day laborers, and after some long days of trudging we reached Mâcon, where I left them and struck out toward Dijon, for along the way I had resolved to seek my fortune in Paris. As I went, I gradually built myself, so to speak, castles in Spain, inhabited by lovable women. My solitary march was beginning to oppress me when I caught sight of a well-dressed old man, who sat under a great oak and seemed to be asleep. As I approached him, he turned his head in my direction. By his smoke-darkened spectacles, by his manner of leaning forward, I perceived that he was blind. He thanked Providence for my arrival, rose to his feet, and asked me to lend him my arm, which I did gladly. He inquired as to my destination, and out of an abundance of caution, I replied that I was on my way to Langres. He was also bound for that very place. I invented a plausible tale: I was going to Langres to learn cutlery. The blind man rejoiced in my youth, which he had determined from my gait, and counted on walking along in good spirits with my support. We got under way. He advanced at such a lively pace that it cost me most of my breath to keep abreast of him. He asked me a thousand questions; I lied as little as possible. Eventually, I confessed to him that I planned to continue on from Langres to Paris, where a master watchmaker had promised me employment (I uttered this puerile lie with the idea that it would bring me luck). My traveling companion asked me whether the Parisian watchmaker might not, by chance, be Monsieur B——. Although I had never in my life heard his name, I said that it was indeed he. This happy coincidence made us the best friends in the world.

My blind man said that his name was Bois-Robert. For a long time before retiring to Paris, he had commanded a regiment of soldiers from the Brie region. His affliction had not diminished his good humor. As agreeably as you please, he told me how he had lost the use of both his eyes during the Sun King's last campaign. He had not been hurt, alas, while performing some heroic feat, in which case his wound would have earned him a pension for life; he had simply been in the line of cannon fire in the regiment he commanded. He showed me, all along one side of his balding crown, the horrible trail of seeds left by the grapeshot. Night fell, as did a fine, penetrating rain. We took shelter in a small wood, and Bois-Robert, as a man of experience, taught me how to construct a makeshift encampment. Following his directions, I arranged a sort of lattice of branches we could lie on without touching the wet ground and a roof of foliage backed by our two coats. I peppered him with questions about Paris, a city he knew well. He warned me vehemently against the swindlers and robbers of every kind with which the capital teemed. At length, he sagely put an end to our conversation, for the night was far advanced, and the road was long. To give me patience, he promised to continue my instruction when I awoke; and I drifted off to sleep, content with myself, my lot, and my companion, whom fate had placed in my path.

A violent ray of sunlight awakened me late the next morning. My temples throbbed with terrible pain. I touched my forehead, sat up, and turned to Bois-Robert. He had disappeared, and curiously enough, my purse had done the same. In a fury, I dragged myself to a nearby stream. I washed my wound and felt a deep cut; the blind man had used a heavy hand. On one point, Bois-Robert had not lied to me: One must keep an eye out for Parisian thieves. (I learned his lesson so well that I reached the city without falling into another trap.) However, this misadventure greatly delayed me; without my savings, I found myself once again obliged to work. Luckily, it was now June, and the season had been precocious: I fed on mulberries and dandelion sprouts, chewing safflower seeds from time to time to still my hunger. Summer kills the poor even more effectively than winter. At the gates of Dijon, I had the good fortune of encountering a monk, who, when he learned that I was versed in mechanical arts, brought me to his community, where I was put to repairing innumerable small objects. Summer passed in this way, and it was September when I entered Dijon, bearing a certificate the good monks had insisted upon giving me.

My employment in Dijon was no different from any other I had known. Always confined within the bounds of an easy mediocrity, I felt neither the false joys of a brilliant career nor the pangs of hunger. In the archbishop's palace, the porter showed me to a workshop which turned out little clocks to be hung above chimneys, a product much in demand in Europe at that time. I slept with the other workers under the roof, lying on top of long tables; we dined on a thick and savory soup, which I ate with ample slices of black bread. My comrades obligingly warned me that the master, a man suspicious by nature, had the habit of subjecting each new worker to two proofs. It was not long before he put me to them. One day he carelessly left a few louis upon a table and went out to perform an errand in the neighborhood; I had no difficulty avoiding that trap. Then, one afternoon, his wife had me accompany her to town in order to carry packages for her, and as we returned to the house in the carriage, she rubbed herself against me several times, ostensibly jolted by the uneven cobblestone road. I remained incorruptible, politely rejecting her advances; such restraint was no merit to me, for she was as dry as a stick. A year passed before my companions in the workshop began to appear to me as what they were: fantastically boring louts. I bought a subscription to the first circulating library I found. This enterprise was conducted by the widow Tribu, a creature so frail and so gentle that she seemed to have escaped from one of the collections of fairy tales on her shelves. Madame Tribu, a woman past forty-five, was the only memorable acquaintance I made in Dijon. Conversation was her sole passion; I suspect that she had opened her little reading room in order to satisfy her desire, for she was the daughter and heiress of a rich wine merchant and had no need of her library's income. She appeared so prudish and so chaste that the idea of trying to make a conquest of her never occurred to me; I love solid pleasures too much to be one of those hunters whom the chase of difficult game fills with delight. Moreover, I have never thought it just to compare the sweet commerce of women with hunting, and not with war, either; I leave the fortresses to the warriors. One day, however, out of bravado, I requested an exceedingly obscene novel, and without the least flinching, the little widow disappeared into the room in the rear and emerged with a considerably worn copy of the work in question, which she handed me without a word.

———

My surprise must have shown on my face, for she laughed heartily, greatly amused to think how suddenly my opinion of her had shifted. She had observed me with attention, she said, since I had begun to frequent her library some six months before. She had assessed me according to a method she considered sure, as indeed it was; the books a man reads tell who he is. She had taken comfort in the reserve which I had shown heretofore, and which had confirmed the trust I inspired in her. When I made my obscene request, she had found me, for the first time, a little dull. From that day forward, the widow Tribu abandoned herself to the practically maternal affection she felt for me, and we became the best friends in the world. You will doubtless be surprised, Jean-Jacques, to see me discover friendship with a woman. The fact was that the widow Tribu, as she soon revealed to me, had some particular tastes which had little if anything to do with men. I confided to her my project of making my fortune in Paris. She was in complete agreement with this plan; in her opinion, a young, healthy man, resolute, clever with his hands, and lacking neither education nor nimbleness of mind, could not but succeed in Paris. The widow Tribu offered to recommend me to an important woman in the capital, a woman with a name of good augury: Madame Paris.

This Madame Paris had been, in the past, her best and even her most loving friend. Both Camille Paris and Rose Tribu— I could never call the latter by her given name in her presence— had, in their first youth, confounded the impulses of their virgin flesh with the appeal of the sacred. Each of them had felt a religious vocation which no one in her circle had bothered to examine; and no more did the Mother Superior of the convent of L———, in Normandy, for she anticipated handsome gifts from their parents, rich merchants of Rouen who, knowing that men required ampler dowries, were happy to pay far less in order that their daughters might marry God. Rose and Camille had been immediately drawn to each other. The year was sixteen hundred and ninety-four, and they shared a secret admiration for the mystical writings of Madame Guyon. These young girls of fourteen and fifteen were allowed to share a cell, and proceeding from mystical effusion to mystical effusion, one fine summer night it came to pass that Camille Paris, while fervently kissing her friend's pubes, was deflowered by Rose Tribu's delicate hand. They were in an analogous position at three o'clock in the morning a few weeks later, when the Mother Superior, having abused the melons of which she was so fond, surprised them on her way to the privy. The girls would probably have been forgiven these distinctly unspiritual exercises had a search of their cell not yielded a Quietist pamphlet extolling the mystical self-abnegation advocated by Madame Guyon. The Mother Superior of the convent of L—— was ambitious; she saw an opportunity to attract the attention of the court by furnishing to the adversaries of Madame Guyon and the gentle bishop Fénelon the proof that Quietism was a ferment of heresy. Her stratagem succeeded, but the two young culprits had to be sent home, where they were promptly separated and married, with dispensation, to two old gentlemen who could not afford to be particular; or whom hints of tribadism excited. Rose's lot fell to a certain Tribu, a prosperous fellow who did not touch her more than thirty times in his life and who left her a widow after barely six years. Camille was less fortunate. Her husband, a brute who loved naught but hunting and profit, was involved in obscure embezzlements with some sordid traffickers from Bordeaux. Patiently, Camille gained his trust, and by the end of seven long years, she had collected sufficient evidence of his wrongdoing to send the thief to the galleys. During one of the grand banquets which Monsieur and Madame Paris gave each year to open the boar-hunting season, Camille revealed her position to her husband, thus avoiding the possibility of being murdered in the first rush of his fury. He was obliged to put on an amicable show for his guests, the flower of Rouen society, and after they had all returned to their homes, Camille obtained what she had demanded: Paris allowed her to go, pretending to be overwhelmed by the scandal, but in fact relieved that she had not asked him for any money at all. Camille went directly to the capital, for Rose had chosen to take up residence in Paris in order to escape the abominable calumnies beginning to circulate concerning the circumstances surrounding her husband's death. To own a perfume shop had been the dream of Camille's youth; with old Tribu's money, Rose opened one for her under the arcades of the Palais-Royal. And so the two enjoyed three years of quivering passion. The shop began to give satisfaction, and the elegant women of the city paid it the honor of their custom. In the end, Camille Paris hardly left the Palais-Royal, while Rose moped in her apartment. She believed herself deceived; for some time, Camille had spoken of nothing but her new shop assistant, a young woman to whom she entrusted the establishment while she made the rounds of her purveyors throughout the capital. One day Rose followed Camille, who passed briefly under the arcades and then rushed to the gate of the Tuileries garden. A man was waiting for her there, and the two of them, apparently on the best of terms, mounted his carriage.

That very evening, during a long discussion with her mistress, Camille wept a great deal. With the passage of time, she had lost her taste for the weaker sex. At first, she had thought her sexual appetite was growing dull. But then an uncommonly enterprising male customer had seduced her, and she had been forced to admit the sad truth: Although she cherished the most tender and affectionate sentiments for Rose, she no longer felt that flaming passion which she had taken for love, and which had been but the fire of her youth; a fire for which, as she now knew, men were the best fuel. Rose had known enough misfortunes in her young life to refrain from turning this news into a violent tragedy. The two women separated sorrowfully, but remained friends. Not long afterward, Rose decided to withdraw to a town cleaner and more tranquil than the capital, whose incessant agitation was burdensome to her temperament, with its inclination to reverie. She continued to correspond with Camille, although as the years passed, their letters became shorter and arrived at much longer intervals.

Seven years went by. Life flows like a river, its course shaped by accidents of terrain; here it moves in slow, lazy eddies, there it rushes headlong into a chaos of noise and foam. In the early days of the month of May, seventeen hundred and thirty, on a bright spring morning, I left Dijon. I embraced the widow Tribu, who had written a letter to Madame Paris, in which she acquainted her of my imminent arrival. The road was dry and pleasant. With the sun warming my back, a little breathless because of my heretofore sedentary life, I savored the simple happiness of existence, conscious of the incertitude of my future, enriched by my past, and at last master and sole proprietor of my destiny. I was twenty-five. I was a man. I had resolved to travel on foot and to sleep under the stars. (It is always possible to evade gangs of armed bandits on the main roads of France, while her innkeepers despoil their guests as plant lice do rosebushes.) I shall say nothing of my journey or of the people I fell in with along the way, except to declare that I had no leisure for growing bored and that in those distant days everything appeared picturesque to me. When I think on them today, I wonder how I could have failed to see what I learned to recognize a good while later. For the beautiful country of France, around the year seventeen hundred and thirty, was in a very bad way. Most of the men I met were no freer than the inmates of the Hospital in Geneva. The day laborers and the tenant farmers were chained to the land they worked, subject to the double scourge of tax collectors and bad weather, whose caprices could destroy a long-awaited harvest and ruin a year's toil. The humble village craftsmen were caught in a tight net of regulations imposed by the State and public holidays imposed by the Church. The people of France lived bent under the weight of insatiable parasites: the priests and the farmers-general, the nobles and the officers, the high bourgeoisie and the petty nobility, and, to crown everything, the armies of ill-disciplined soldiers who from time to time trampled their fields and stole their provisions. Those who regret the old days confuse them with their naive youth. Has our Revolution changed all that? The answer, I see, is clearly no. The noble émigrés and all our enemies—that is to say, all Europe—have the upper hand; wars, reforms, and speculations have dealt France some terrible blows. Why deny it? But the Revolution has merely begun. We have shaken and broken some chains; other men will come and repair them; while still others will forge new ones. There is no need to be surprised by this. In any case, some will continue the struggle. We others have had our time. I am the ghost of a world which no longer exists, and of the one which preceded it. It is for this reason, Jean-Jacques, that I address these pages to a dead man, uniquely akin to me, in order to tell the story of how I have lived. As to the future, everything is possible; my past tells me so, for at the moment when I entered Paris, the old world whose center was Versailles seemed to turn so well that no one thought its rhythm could be altered in any way. History is a strange theater: The actors play without learning their roles in advance; one never knows which of them will appear in the next act; the denouement is never sure. Whether it is tragedy or farce I leave to the philosophers to determine; I know only that the play is worth the playing, and I return to my story.

PART TWO

Paris

I had no preconceived ideas when, as the summer of seventeen hundred and thirty was drawing to a close, I reached the outskirts of Paris; I hoped merely that the city would not in any way resemble Geneva. On this point, I was not disappointed. I wished to enter the capital dressed in my best clothes. Half a league from Paris, I found a stream where I could bathe and a thicket where I could change. Replacing my ordinary traveling clothes, a shirt and coat, I put on my finest suit, which was also the only one I possessed. I believed my suit to be in the best taste and of the latest fashion; it was the latest fashion in Dijon, where a tailor had cut it for me, and this was the same as the fashion in the capital, but five years behind. Following the advice of a coach driver, I had decided to enter the city from the south, as this was the most convenient way to reach the Saint-Germain quarter, where Madame Paris resided. At the moment when I passed the toll barrier known as the *barrière d'Enfer,* I brushed my garments. I wore shoes and stockings, shirt and breeches, and I was the most self-satisfied of men-about-town. I carried a passport with the stamp of the Artisans' Guild of Dijon, but the officer of the guard scarcely looked at this document, and in an instant I was in Paris. Night was beginning to fall. A light wind arose, and the city's powerful breath struck me full in the face. Before long, I would learn that the stench of Paris was proverbial; but I had always delighted in heady smells, and those pungent, mephitic exhalations inebriated me. I was hardly through the *barrière d'Enfer* when I stopped to savor the voluptuous aromas. Alas, my evening breeze had not arrived alone; it was joined at once by a downpour of rain. I advanced into Paris, passing magnificent gardens on my way. The rain doubled its force. In an instant, the street became a bottomless quagmire, which a rushing stream promptly divided in two, ferrying along an increasing quantity of filth and rubbish. In an effort to reach shelter, I tried to cross that torrent of mud, but I had guessed its depth badly. I sank in it to my knees and fell. At least, I thought, I no longer have to fret about taking shelter. I walked on, accompanied by a few pedestrians who were still on the street, doubtless foreigners like myself. To my right, some men dressed in Savoyard costume had taken refuge under a porch. They carried strange wooden arches whose use I could not fathom; as I later learned, they were little bridges, which persons of quality in Paris rented when they were surprised by sudden showers and wished to cross the streams rushing among the paving stones. To my left, some women sheltering under a tree openly mocked me. The reader may imagine what chagrin I felt at the idea of being the laughingstock of the first elegant females I passed! As to elegance, those ladies were the most impudent and worst-rigged trollops in the city, but I did not yet know how to recognize them. I stubbornly trudged on, going down the rue d'Enfer, while fiacres driven at full speed spattered me with mud.

A guard carefully wrapped in his ample coat declared that, luckily for me, the Saint-Germain quarter was not far. I followed his directions. The rain ceased, but the sun was unable to pierce the clouds, and night fell completely. I guided my steps toward the lights of a narrow street, crowded with pedestrians and lined with lofty façades; complex odors I could not distinguish floated in the air, which echoed with sounds familiar to me: those of tools striking metal and wood. Above all that, the modulated cries of the craftsmen and the harangues of the vendors produced so lively a scene that I reached the end of the street unaware that it was a bridge and that I had just crossed the Seine. I kept walking in the heavy evening air. I sensed something like the coolness of an underwood and, seeking its origin, perceived a garden, which I tried to enter in order to rest a little. A rather cocksure, high-horsed Swiss blocked my way with his lance. I asked him the reason for this interdiction. The smug young man puffed himself up inside his uniform and solemnly recited his rules: Entrance to the Palais-Royal was forbidden to soldiers, persons in livery, maidservants, persons wearing caps or jackets, schoolboys, scamps, vagrants, dogs, and workers. With an effort, I overlooked his insolence and asked the way to Rue de Bagneux. He laughed heartily and informed me that my goal was in the opposite direction. I was on the point of favoring this Swiss with a few sharp kicks when a Franciscan friar who was passing by took pity on a muddy, weary stranger and amiably offered to lead me whither I wished to go, for my destination lay on his way.

My guide explained to me that the numbers of the dwellings in Paris were not all visibly inscribed above their doors and that by a singular aberration, they ran from one end of the street to the other; so that number 19, Rue de Bagneux, the goal of my quest, faced number 2. When I named Madame Paris, my Franciscan looked at me curiously and took his leave. But there I was at last, standing before the house where the lady dwelt. Was it regarded as seemly in this city to ring at someone's door after eight o'clock in the evening and unannounced to boot? My pride recoiled from showing myself transformed into a statue of mud. But I knew no other place to sleep, and I reflected that my ridiculous state would doubtless work in my favor; and so I rang. A massive porter with a good-natured look opened the door, and without a word I handed him the widow Tribu's letter, which I had saved from the deluge. The porter obligingly invited me to step into the shelter of the porch. Upon one point, I was not mistaken; my clothes aroused general amusement, and several maidservants came and admired me while laughing up their sleeves. I tried to take their laughter in good part, and everyone seemed grateful. Down from the mistress's apartments came the order to return me to human form. The porter, Michel, undertook this task. He was a former sergeant, a gruff Gascon, covered with scars and crippled with rheumatism, and he appeared to be no great enemy of wine. He showed me into the courtyard: On the sides, two large stables, and before us, a simple white façade joyously pierced by vast windows; beyond the rooms, I could see the white footpaths of a garden. I had never seen anything more beautiful, but I dared not say this to my guide. Michel led me to an empty stall between two carriage horses, had me undress, and consigned my suit to a maidservant, who bore it away. He scoured me with dry straw, like a foal, and bade me put on a shirt from which a tailor could have cut two to my size. A quarter of an hour later, the housekeeper gave me back my suit, still steaming but almost dry, and miraculously clean. I was told that it was too late for me to present myself to Madame Paris, but that she had read my letter with interest and offered me her hospitality for the night. The reader may be sure I accepted with effusion! As I was preparing to make my bed on the straw of the stable, a maid as pretty as she was sullen came to usher me up the main staircase of the building to the second floor and then through a maze of corridors, up two sets of rather narrow stairs, and into a vast, charming room, hung with a pink fabric on which shepherds were wooing naiads. The maid withdrew; I undressed quickly in the darkness. A high bed stretched out its arms to me. An instant later I was snoring to my heart's content.

Michel, the porter, had taken a great liking to me. At five o'clock in the morning I woke to find him standing beside my bed, inviting me to share some chocolate with him in the kitchen. Our breakfast included large slices of white bread and some dry, crumbly ewe's-milk cheese, accompanied by a dark, musky wine. I did ample justice to all. Two maids, the cook, and Michel watched me intently as I ate. They wished to know what had brought me here, and whether I had some skill. When I spoke the word "watchmaking," Michel gave me reason to hope that Madame Paris would find employment for me and declared himself most pleased at the prospect; according to him, Madame Paris's household did not have enough men. I wished to know if they were unwelcome here. There was an outburst of general laughter, after which my companions informed me that 19 Rue de Bagneux was known throughout Europe as one of the most admirable bordellos in the capital.

And so it appeared that Camille Paris had not persisted in the sale of perfumes. This revelation served to double my curiosity in her regard. When all the others went about their chores, I remained with the cook, who gladly accepted my help, and questioned her about her employer. Madame was a beloved mistress; she paid well but dealt pitilessly with mediocrities. She was known in Paris as a woman of intellect, who had never burdened herself with a husband. Despite her advanced age, it was still she who gave the most fashionable young men of the capital their start in gallantry. One became the lover of Madame Paris just as, in days of yore, one was dubbed a knight by an experienced cavalier. She was often seen to have a favorite for the duration of a season, but he was never the same from one year to the next. Rumor—at this point in the conversation, I had to struggle to keep my countenance—attributed to her rather too warm a fondness for the fair sex; the rumor was inexplicable because she had never been known to act in such a way as might confirm it. With her favorite of the season, Madame Paris observed an unvarying protocol, taking him to her country house when the weather was fine and to the Opéra in the fall. Madame had dismissed the last of these temporary husbands in the very middle of the summer. He was the Vicomte de D——, an amiable, bewigged, complacent fellow intimately acquainted with the most trivial usages, the smallest infatuations of the latest fashion in Paris. The Vicomte had made less of his position than his predecessors; with great relish, the cook recounted to me the whole story of this affair.

The Vicomte had been with Madame Paris for seven months when his father, the Comte de D——, summoned him and the Comtesse. He had gambled away the entire family fortune, and even rather more than that. It had all vanished at the faro tables in the home of one of his friends, where the Comte had hoped to renovate a fortune already damaged by risky speculations in Negroes and cocoa beans. He was left with a choice: pistol or prison. The thought of prison horrified him. The pistol was no more to his liking, but it had its advantages. One avoided dishonor. One allowed his family a possibility of declaring bankruptcy and the hope of erasing his debts. In short, the Comte had made his decision, and he had thought it his duty to inform his wife and son. Madame de D—— threw herself at his knees. The Vicomte tried to ring for salts, but he lost consciousness. The Comtesse declared her preference for a dishonored but living husband. The Comte thanked her, saying that for the sake of a woman so generous, to sacrifice himself would be an easy undertaking; at the word "sacrifice," the Comtesse swooned in her turn. When she came to her senses, she was lying on her bed, and her fool of a son was at her side. She uttered a terrible cry: The Comte? The Vicomte calmly replied that he deemed it wrong to prevent so courageous a man from restoring solvency to the name of D——. The Comtesse thrust aside this unnatural offspring and rushed to her husband's chamber. An open drawer; on his writing desk, two sealed letters; and no Comte. An explosion was heard in the courtyard. Madame de D—— gave way to despair.

The Comte de D—— was found in a small room on the ground floor. He had fired his shot while standing before a mirror, to ensure that there was no risk of missing his mark. The Vicomte himself hurried to relate the whole story to his mistress, expecting to find comfort and consolation; for his joy at having at last become Comte was tempered by the hard blow of ruin, which would constrain him to sell lands and raise loans, all things which seemed to him quite tedious. The Vicomte was greatly surprised to receive from his mistress, in lieu of consolation, a magisterial buffet, followed by a vigorous remonstrance which could be heard in the kitchens. Outraged at having given herself to such a vile brat, Madame Paris dismissed him on the spot. The new Comte de D—— went away, and not long thereafter, to swell his coffers, he married the daughter of a merchant, a trader in coarse cloth who had grown rich in the Indies. At the same time, Camille Paris made his conduct public, which forced the despicable fellow to retire to his property in the Limousin.

My narratress had reached this point in her tale when she was interrupted by a chambermaid. Madame Paris wished to see me in her Spanish salon. The maid accompanied me. Overcome by shyness, I entered, greeted my hostess, and stood very straight. Sitting on a sofa, Madame Paris considered me attentively. What is called beauty has always seemed to me to be a cold and soulless chimera; and I have often admired a woman's face, even as its lineaments left my heart untouched. Madame Paris's body was small, but well proportioned; she was not beautiful, but infinitely attractive: the accomplished Parisienne, in a city where a thousand women of quality aspired to that title. Of course, she offered the pleasant features, the bearing of restrained vivacity, and the ease of conversation which are the passports required to gain entry into fashionable salons. But her charm sprang from deeper and subtler causes: the fragrance of a sensual woman; the intensity of her look, which always unsettled me; and, finally, a measured, captivating eloquence, of which she soon favored me with a demonstration. She interrogated me at length regarding Rose Tribu and asked me many questions about my life. As I was filled with the liveliest admiration for this woman, I replied frankly and simply to all her inquiries. She wished to know if I contemplated entering into her service, and I hastened to answer in the affirmative. Then she began to speak in a tranquil tone which formed a piquant contrast with the audacity of her words:

"You must know, Monsieur, that this house is what fools call a wicked place; and, I daresay, one of the best in Paris. We enjoy an admirable reputation, both among our visitors, who come here from all over Europe, and among our residents, who esteem themselves fortunate to work here. I keep a bordello, and I find no shame in that. Nor glory, either. Through Rose, you know enough about my past to do me harm; but I know Rose well enough to be sure that her trust in you was not misplaced when she disclosed to you certain secrets, which I pray you, if you desire my protection and have no wish to incur my anger, never to mention in Paris. Allow me to recount to you what became of me after she left, in order that you may understand what I shall expect from you.

"The perfume shop in the Palais-Royal prospered for two more years; then the capricious deities of fashion who had showered us with their favors decided to turn away from us. I closed the shop before I was utterly ruined and went to Brussels, where for two long years I lived a life of amorous intrigues. I wanted Paris to forget me, and two years in Paris are two centuries. An old English lord brought me back to France and installed me in this town house where I receive you today. He desired very much to marry me and was so ingratiating, so persuasive and charming, that I was very near to giving my consent, despite all the vows my terrible marriage had inspired me to make. Believing that I, as a commoner, feared for my independence, he summoned his lawyer, and in no time at all I became the sole proprietress of this house and all it contained. I did not have the opportunity to give him as much proof of my gratitude as I could have wished; six weeks later, he died of an apoplexy. I was left in a residence fit for a prince, but I possessed not even a hundred louis in ready money. To find a new benefactor, to submit to the protection of a nuisance whose sole merit would have consisted in his wearing breeches, was beyond my capacity. I resolved once again to grasp the reins of my fate with a firm hand. I assembled my people: I promised generous wages to all those who were willing to remain in my service, but they had to consent to receive but small recompense at first. To those who wished to retire, I offered a small pension; but I asked them, too, for a year's grace. One must believe, Monsieur, that I was beloved by my household, for only one member left us, a girl of twenty who for a long time had dreamed of returning to Compiègne and setting up as a seamstress. I then joined forces with a banker, mortgaged my sole possession, and began both to conceive and to realize a new kind of bordello.

"I wanted my establishment to be absolutely unique, and so it has become. During my sojourn in Brussels, I learned this: The vast majority of girls who live as courtesans are unhappy creatures, reduced to slavery and disgusted by their condition. Very few of them have chosen to live on their charms, and fewer still have been fortunate enough to avoid falling under the power of a bawd or a pimp. It was from among such exceptions that I sought to enlist my girls, determined that there would never be more than twelve in my employ, and all between the ages of sixteen and twenty. To each of them, I gave the education of a young woman of quality, not neglecting anything in that regard. Here in my house, these damsels received lessons in music, singing, and dancing; they were keenly encouraged to read; they were taken to the theater. Naturally, all that instruction had a cost, which was my wager on the future; I told myself that such a city as Paris must contain a sufficient number of extremely rich men willing to pay a high price for the charms of creatures as well taught as those from among whom they were wont to choose their mistresses, but who presented none of the coquetries and affectations, the greediness of gain, the insatiable hunger for attentions, the sullen airs flaunted to attract notice, which in this country mark the fundamental temperament of kept women. My bet was well placed; clients flocked to my door.

Faced with an excess of demand, I took the most sensible course: I raised our prices, which were already quite high, and refused either to engage more girls or to increase their work rate.

"As regards lechery, conversation, and proper salon manners, I myself undertook to instruct all those who needed instruction: I enjoined them never to accept anything they deemed degrading, whatever it might be, but I also counseled them not to be offended by eccentricities in the function of the amorous machine. Our clientele was soon the wealthiest and most refined in Paris. I also saw to the well-being of my domestics: eight chambermaids; a cook and her two assistants, one for meats and the other for pastries; and the porter, Michel, whom you have met and who is the soul of the house. This, Monsieur, is the story of how this establishment has reached the heights it enjoys today. I trust that it will maintain its lofty position. Now, you may well wonder how you could be useful to me here. Michel is becoming an old man. This is partly due to a misfortune; a year ago, he lost a beloved son, his only descendant. Since then, he is subject to distractions, to melancholies, from which his service suffers. I cannot imagine dismissing him, nor do I wish to compromise the smooth operation of my house. You could assist Michel as a man of all work; here it is always necessary to repair windows, oil doors, and perform other small tasks, as well as to undertake all kinds of errands inside Paris, as Michel will indicate to you. As for your watchmaking talents, you will see that we shall have no lack of employment for them. And as for our girls, you will make their acquaintance tomorrow. On this subject, one word, to which you must pay close heed: You are forbidden to lie with them, unless they request you to do so for the necessities of service. Do you want this work? Do not reply at once. First, if you will be so kind as to allow me to show you my establishment."

Then, without awaiting my consent and without seeming in the least winded by her long discourse, Madame Paris rose. Leaving her Spanish salon, she strode along a long corridor, with me following behind. The apartments dedicated to pleasure occupied the entire second floor on both sides of the courtyard. The day was a Monday, when the residents in Madame Paris's employ enjoyed their day of rest. The twelve chambers were empty, and we inspected them one by one. Madame Paris favored me with all the necessary explanations. Eight of the rooms, furnished and decorated in keeping with the simple tastes of the time, served for amatory encounters of the ordinary kind. The doors of these rooms were open; a closed door signified that the chamber was in service. The four other apartments could, for a supplemental fee, respond to more demanding, or more ceremonious, passions and were known as the "machine rooms." Most fortunately, the human fancy followed rules of recurrence, and the dominant passions of most of these gentlemen fell, without their knowing it, into one or another of a few broad categories. Each of the special rooms was fitted out like a little theater; an ingenious system of screens and false ceilings allowed the space within to be arranged in a thousand different fashions. There was the religious chamber: a bed of woven straps, two prie-dieux, a confessional, and, in two tall cupboards, everything that one could wish in the way of candles and ecclesiastical costumes, including the most common religious habits. On the same principle, the oriental chamber, completely hung with scarlet draperies and veils; the rustic room, with a floor of beaten earth and oiled paper over the windows; and the dungeon room, which was the one most likely to be frequented by the powerful, and where they would most often occupy not the elevated station of the judge or the executioner but the lowly place of the condemned. Such were the trumperies men purchased, day after day, in obedience to their most unbridled desires. In addition, each client could bring to his chosen room whatever accessories he might need, and the most meticulous of such gentlemen kept all the accoutrements of their bizarre lust stored in the house on Rue de Bagneux. I inquired as to the price of an ordinary session; Madame Paris named the immense sum of one hundred livres. As to the special sessions, each girl had the right to fix her own price, which, if she consented to some painful or repellent ritual, could reach incredible heights.

After we left the apartments, Madame led me into her garden and informed me that the time had come for me to reply to her offer. I was in the land of Venus, where desires reigned in all the variety of their powers; I thought of my master Lucretius, and I felt at home in that place, in the ferment of that life, triumphing over death. I kissed Madame Paris's hand, and thus I entered into her service. The following day Michel presented me to the residents of the house, who were having a music lesson. We interrupted it for an instant, and I was gazed upon by a dozen pairs of amiable eyes, whose owners I greeted as best I could. Each of them said her name, which I forgot as I observed her person; we went out; the lesson recommenced. I found the damsels charming, but not completely to my taste. Too urbane, too ironic mentally, too common physically; in a word, too French. I was glad of it, since it was unlikely that I would take the risk of trying to seduce them. Michel questioned me: Could I guess which of those young ladies was the one most in demand? I supposed that it was the striking brunette who had been the first to introduce herself. Michel complimented me on my taste, but smiled at my naïveté; the girl most ardently contended for was the one named Antoinette, a blond whose features, like her figure, had left not the slightest trace in my memory. I desired to know why she was such a favorite. Michel replied by pointing to the established fact, as he called it, that most men seek neither the beautiful nor the original, but the mediocre; as to finding out the reason why, he had given up the attempt. To be sure, he declared, the most beautiful whores in Paris became the most pampered mistresses; they were women whom men purchased in order to display them on their arms in the lobby of the Opéra, but whom, in fact, they cared little to fuck. And he cited the case of a certain Mademoiselle M——, a divinely beautiful creature whom fashionable young men had fought over for two years. A young English lord, in despair at the prospect of returning to London without a story to tell, paid a thousand livres for one of her nights, but in the course of it did not even try to possess her, making her promise never to reveal the omission to anyone. At dawn he left, well rested and well content, and soon he was back in his country, boasting about his mad expense, which was taken as the sign of a mad passion. Mademoiselle M—— avenged herself on him by making the truth known, and the young lord never set foot in Paris again.

A kind of small apartment, a boy's quarters, was set up for me in the attic. An order went out for two suits of clothes, simple but becoming, for Madame Paris, giving proof of a remarkable delicacy, did not impose the wearing of livery on those who served her. The light of day entered my room only through a bull's-eye, but I hardly had grounds for complaint, as I led a most industrious life. In the morning, in the absence of clients, I inspected the pleasure chambers and carried out small but necessary repairs, and, according to need, I assisted Michel in preparing the machine rooms; in the afternoon I remained on the alert, ready, whenever I was rung for, to carry in some refreshment or furnish some accessory. Sometimes a girl rang because a client, swayed by caprice or exalted by drink, was taking unwanted liberties with her; on such occasions, I presented myself with Michel, and we must have appeared serious enough, because only once did a fellow prove so obstinate that we were compelled to throw him into the street. In addition, I took care to assure that the water filters functioned properly; for thoroughly comprehensible reasons, the entire mansion was equipped with modern pumps, which carried clean, abundant water to every room, and which, once the investment was cleared, turned out to be less costly than constantly buying water from the carriers in the streets. In short, my role in the house on Rue de Bagneux was that of a jack-of-all-trades and master of none; the occupation corresponded mightily to my talent, which was, as I eventually understood, not to have any talent at all. Do not think, Jean-Jacques, that I am appealing to your pity. It is not unpleasant to be without talent. Men of genius are most often men obsessed; tied to the same picket, they always graze within the same circle, even when their picket is moved. As for me, I liked myself as I was.

The weeks passed, and I was granted no more private interviews with the mistress of the house, to my great chagrin. I caught a glimpse of her every afternoon, reading or sewing in the vast salon which opened onto the courtyard. The distance, the powerful impression made on me by this extraordinary woman, the overexcitement to which working amidst petticoats and creams subjected me, the surroundings of crumpled sheets and depravity—all of these led me to the conclusion that I must be in love with Madame Paris. The thought flashed upon me one fine morning, like a heavenly revelation; at my first opportunity, I climbed up to my attic, took pen, ink, and paper in hand, and wrote to Camille Paris an impassioned letter, which I thought original, and which, without reading it over, I slipped into her work basket at dawn the next morning. Then I languished the whole day in the throes of an uncertainty which I took for an indisputable sign of the most ardent passion. I did not have long to mope; a note from her summoned me that very evening. At the stated hour, I knocked on the door of my fair lady's apartments. She opened it herself, a beginning I thought augured very well. She bade me sit next to her on an ample bergère; I threw myself at her feet and kissed her hand in an indescribable transport. She made me stand up again. My waist was at the level of her eyes; she lowered my breeches with one hand, seized my already-engorged instrument, and began manipulating it with great vigor. I had expected some sweet dalliance, some words smothered in sighs, some exquisite defenses, perhaps even some reticence. It was not long before Madame Paris's heroic charge took its toll upon my surprised virility. When the moment had passed, she drew from her bosom a small handkerchief of fine batiste, wiped away the product of my juvenile fervor, and threw the scrap of cloth into the fire. Then she turned back to me—I had meanwhile sheathed my wrinkled, crestfallen weapon and sat down mechanically on the bergère—and spoke to me in approximately the following terms: "I have done you the honor, Monsieur, of receiving you today as I have done in the past: with frankness and friendship. Know that by speaking to you as I am about to do, I once again honor you with my trust. I do not know what can have convinced you that you love me, and I am particularly unable to conceive how you could have presumed such familiarity with me as to make me aware of your sentiment. I have read your letter. It does honor to your sensibility, but it speaks ill of your knowledge of the world, and still worse of your judgment. Were it not for the excuse of your age, were it not for the affection our good Michel feels for you, you would be in the street this very evening. When you addressed those declarations to me, did you give no thought to my position? Do you not know that in Paris the pox is easier to survive than ridicule? And this matter is far too ridiculous, both for you and for me. What would I do with such a lover as you? You would become pestilent before I had the time to find you amusing. What would you do with a mistress twice your age? You admire me, and you think yourself in love. It is the sign of a good temperament. For the past two months, I have observed you; you work a good deal, and you work well; but you have neglected to fuck, and all that fluid has mounted to your head. Men reason very poorly when their balls are full. Come, I have relieved you, and now you are purged. Put your hand on your heart; dare to tell me again that you love me; and if you persist without telling a lie, I swear I will be yours."

At this point in her discourse, Madame Paris became aware that I was foaming with anger. With an imperious gesture, she commanded me to remain silent and added these words: "Do not let your pride drive you to a mad response. Five days from now, at this same hour, if you present yourself to me, I shall know that you do not desire to quit my service. In the contrary case, I shall order that you be given a gratuity, as well as letters containing the warmest recommendations, and all will have been said. In this city you will find twenty masters who have not, as I have, the habit of speaking the truth!"

And the extraordinary woman pushed me toward the door. I went out, resolved never in my life to see her again. The following day, I performed my duties without any diminution of my anger. The day after that, I was still furious, and in my rage I gave myself over to self-pollution, mentally placing Madame

Paris in the most obscene positions my fertile imagination and my wide reading could suggest to me. By the end of the third day, my anger had become tempered, as all anger does, and I began to come to my senses. I dropped a word about my misadventure to Michel, who had the kindness not to laugh in my presence, and sufficient delicacy to refrain from giving me counsel. On the appointed day at the appointed hour, I stood before Madame Paris, who did not press her advantage, but rather made me feel, by means of a certain gentleness in her tone, that she did not hold my conduct against me. Ignorant though I was of Parisian manners in those days of my youth, I was nevertheless able to appreciate the extent of her generosity. Sincere gratitude gives rise to awkward but heartfelt words: I forthrightly declared that I had been a fool, and I reiterated the expression of my most genuine admiration. As she listened to me, she pulled from her sleeve a letter which I recognized; I cannot swear that I did not blush; she slipped it into the fire. And that was the end of the incident.

Our interview then veered in a much different direction. Michel had spoken in favorable terms of my manual abilities, and Madame Paris had decided that, should I consent to her proposal, I could render some new services to her enterprise. Certain clients of the house liked to have available for their amorous disports various accessories, tools in whose fabrication precious materials, such as ivory, as well as exceedingly delicate mechanisms, were often employed; but such utensils were not, in truth, among those which one could order without risk, or without embarrassment, from any respectable supplier. In order that I might form a more precise idea of the nature of my task, Madame Paris ordered that horses should be harnessed and her carriage made ready early the following morning; we drove to

Faubourg Saint-Jacques and into a vast rear courtyard. There, in a workshop, an Italian named Gondi produced articles of the type in question. I knew this old fellow a little, having more than once gone to him to take delivery of slender, carefully bound-up parcels, whose contents I was forbidden to investigate. Gondi had settled in the capital some thirty years before, having been expelled from Bologna for a sordid affair involving children; ten versions of this story were current in Paris. There passed in parade before his little counting table the flower of Parisian debauchery, but also discreet sodomites; scrupulous, prim old men; and seducers of every age, while ladies of good society stayed away from the place altogether, preferring to send some trusted servant in their stead.

Gondi received us in the courtyard, accompanied us through his shop, and made us climb a convoluted, stinking staircase up to his workroom on the third floor. It was a comfortable place, receiving the light of day only through high windows, which did not look out upon any other building, and it was equipped with a discreet exit to an often deserted street. Here Gondi kept a vast store of artificial pricks, meticulously aligned on racks which covered the biggest wall in the room, and displaying a remarkable variety of materials, sizes, and colors. There was also a long table bearing a great number of objects destined for obscene uses: finely worked chains and bracelets, artificial cunts, special armchairs, gloves, jewelry, and tools of all kinds. Gondi's handsome face, thin, spiritual, and penetrating of eye, was like a bishop's; his hands were especially admirable and noble, testifying to the fabulous skill they possessed. Otherwise, his appearance was common: short in the waist and crooked in the limbs. As for his moral character, he was a nasty piece of work. A shrewd tradesman quite aware that his long success, now somewhat diminished, was coming to an end, he had received from Madame Paris an offer to buy his cumbersome collections, his shop, and his workroom on the condition that he initiate into his art the person of her choice. She took her leave of us, and I remained with Gondi, who showed me, with a good grace, the most remarkable products of his labors. I shall not describe them in any detail here. Let the reader consider that the examination of the counterfeit *membra virilia* alone occupied us for several hours: Gondi had tried his hand at every size; at every material; at double as well as single models; at hollow extensions, which advantaged those who wore them; and at mechanical pieces—I, of course, examined these with great attention—to which a variety of ingenious springs gave a movement that was practically natural. Gondi had sufficient orders to occupy him for ten months; it was decided that during that period of time I would remain at his side, observing the secrets of his art before he retired from it.

A new and far from idle life took shape for me. I was twenty-five years of age; I was in good health. Early in the morning I carried out in Madame Paris's house the small repairs necessitated by the disorders of the previous night; then I hastened to Faubourg Saint-Jacques where I turned into Master Gondi's assistant. In a few months I mastered the principal skills of the craft, and I began to propose innovations. I was particularly proud of a certain spring of my own invention, capable of imparting to an armchair for men or women a movement which marvelously imitated the repeated shocks of a vigorous lover, and with a force which could be increased or diminished at will. I also conceived the idea of drawing up a catalogue of our products, and of giving them names. Objects made in the image of the prick were generally named "Prodigies," and of these we chiefly sold the models "Formidable" and "Insidious"; objects figuring cunts received the name of "Flasks," of which the "Elysian" and the "Maid" had good success; the chair which was my pride was christened the "Indefatigable." My afternoons were spent at the counting table in Gondi's shop. I learned to listen impassively while worthy gentlemen regaled us with long, muddled fables intended to make us believe that the dildos whose respectable measurements they recited to me in a trembling voice were destined for remote acquaintances whom they were helping out of pure benevolence or for some amusing experiment in physics. The end of the afternoon found me back in Paris, where I made certain deliveries. On occasion, I was asked for a demonstration of the goods, and I rarely refused such obligations of my trade.

The moment of Gondi's retirement came. I was obliged to choose a name for my role in the Parisian theater of secret pleasures. Madame Paris proposed "Laroche," a patronymic whose solidity she thought correspondent to my character; to this surname I added the Christian name of Bernard, in memory of our mother. Thus equipped, I made my entrance onto the stage of Parisian libertinism in the autumn of the year seventeen hundred and thirty-one and played my part there with great diligence throughout the following nine years. During that time, I came to know the most extraordinary individuals in the capital, all those of philosophical bent who were left unsatisfied by the insipid moralizing dear to the rising personalities in the philosophical party and whom rational thought had set on the path of sensual exploration. I learned much from my contact with them, for those men shared the harmless habit of conversation and a less innocent determination to convince their interlocutors. I diverted myself by contradicting them, embracing in opposition to Friday's client an argument with which another had belabored me on Tuesday. And when caught off guard, I had always the option of citing my Lucretius. Soon I, who never opened a book, acquired the reputation of a man of learning. I have ever been greatly struck by the naïveté of libertines; and something affected, something studied in their taste for libertinism has often kept me from thoroughly admiring them. So I never entered entirely into that coterie of the debauched; there, as elsewhere, I was alone.

All through those years, I received visits from representatives of the French police. Owing to a Swiss style of pronunciation I was never able to correct, the false passport which a powerful friend of Madame Paris had procured for me indicated that I was a citizen of Geneva, and therefore suspect as regarded both politics and religion. The first to present himself, soon after Gondi's retirement, was a small, affable man sent by Versailles. He desired to know the nature of my business, asked me for news of old Gondi, and expressed interest in my new models. Having fortunately been instructed by Michel, I did not venture the smallest dissimulation before this courteous and kindly representative of the forces of order, who had it in his power to make me rot in Vincennes prison or in the Bastille for the rest of my days. The man asked many questions concerning our most faithful and most eminent clients. He came to me, on this and other occasions, to collect some scraps of scandal, which would then enter into the composition of the obscene reports read every morning with great relish by the king and his favorite. Other police officers of all kinds visited me from time to time. To some I offered the opportunity to examine the box where I kept the income from the day's sales under lock and key; they inspected it carefully and returned it to me a little lighter. To others I made so bold as to propose a model of their choice, a tribute from the worker in the fields of pleasure to the master of the secrets. They generally agreed to accept the piece only because they wished to give it as a gift. Thanks to these prudent policies, I was never obliged to close my workshop.

Those years fled by in a rush. It seemed that the French had become more infatuated than ever with the progress of mechanics, and not just in the narrow domain in which I exercised my craft. In Paris, there was a vogue in automatons which was not far from turning into a passion; so much so, that from it the proprietor of a coffeehouse in the gardens of the Palais-Royal made a fortune at little expense: The beverages, common but high-priced, which were served in his establishment arrived upon his customers' tables without the visible intervention of any human waiter. As though by some operation of magic, they emerged from a hollow column which extended from under the table to the cellar below. This extremely simple device, from its being concealed, took on a fabulous prestige. The shrewd host, who had conceived the arrangement, profited not only from the drinks, but also from the chairs he had placed in front of the window outside; the curious hired them like boxes in the theater. The entire public loved this false prodigy and took great delight in finding it incomprehensible.

One morning I received a visitor, a large man whom I had never seen, with an air of gaiety and prosperity emanating from his whole person. At first, he did not reveal his name and questioned me with such imperious authority that I felt compelled to reply without hesitation. He desired to know whether I might accept a proposal for an utterly singular job of work, which diverged not only from good morals but also, and more dangerously, from the teachings of the most holy, Catholic, and apostolic Church. Such was his manner of speaking; I liked the frankness of his tone; and I admired his bold bearing. The person who had sent him was the issue of one of the greatest families of France and did not wish to appear in this affair; were we to come to an agreement, Monsieur B —— said, I should always and only deal with him. He was measuring me with his piercing eyes. When he gave his name as Monsieur B——, my face brightened; upon his asking whether I knew him, I replied that I had read his *Commentaries* on Lucretius. He posed me several questions on the subject of my philosopher. My replies must not have been too stupid, for he began to speak in an even freer and more open way and went into some details of his request. But before I relate them, it is proper that I should say here a few words about Monsieur B——, and about the occasion which had led him to my workroom in Faubourg Saint-Jacques.

Everything I knew about him disposed me in his favor. B —— had been a farmer-general in Provence, the home of Maximin de Saint-Fonds, and had made a fortune there, without ruining anyone, before retiring to Paris. It was said that certain religious authorities had finally, after long trying, got him dismissed from his functions as a farmer-general, for the man was violently, totally, and definitively atheist, and at no pains to conceal the fact. He gladly declared that he had been born thus, without a sense of the divine, and asserted that it was impossible to believe his atheism the product of personal rancor, for the good priests had provided him with the best education. His famous *Commentaries* on Lucretius had appeared in one of those editions which falsely claim the Congo as their provenance; naturally, he had not signed it; but the work contained a preface, written by his hand, in which he feigned indignation at the idea that a naive reader would draw from the book grounds for throwing down the true religion. According to common report, he received, in his mansion in Rue Saint-Honoré, all the scoffers and miscreants of the capital. Speaking little, listening much, and as attentive to the service as to the conversation, B—— attracted the best society, half of which came in order to be able to say they had done so, and the other half in order to satisfy their hunger for more substantial philosophical fare; and all of them left content. There was nothing of the debauchee about B——. He was known to have neither mistress nor minion. He seemed to feel no passion for the flesh, but cultivated the rarer and more refined one of facilitating the pleasures of his fellows; he was said to have given his best friend, for his fortieth birthday, forty nubile young girls chosen from among the most beautiful races of the entire world. In matters relating to the table, he was a man of boundless refinement and erudition. He was not averse to preparing food himself, and in general took such voluptuous pleasure therein that it was seen as the explanation for his complete chastity. He was truly an enormous man, though at first one tended not to notice his bulk because he was always bursting with energy.

He kept open house in Rue Saint-Honoré every Thursday and Saturday; moreover, on Mondays he received rather a small company made up of his closest friends, all of them scholarly and learned personages. This gathering was not, properly speaking, what was called a "day," and the few curious visitors who arrived uninvited were solemnly informed, while the entire house was lighted up with tall flambeaux and great bursts of laughter and loud talking came from behind the closed doors, that Monsieur was not at home. A few great noblemen, intimates of the master of the house, like him collectors of rare plants and animals, and proprietors of vast collections of curiosities; some prelates who were curious about all things and by no means too adamantly attached to the medicines they administered to their flocks; no bourgeois. Such was the composition, as B—— himself explained to me, of all his society, which notably included the illustrious Duke de C—— and wherein absolute liberty reigned, far from the stupidity of men and the ears of police spies.

Of the orgies which insulting lampoons sometimes denounced, there was not a trace in that odd fraternity. Certainly, all the guests were known to be impenitent libertines in their private lives. Each week, the Bishop of M—— left considerable sums at Madame Paris's house and other establishments of that sort, as the dainty tableaux he requested from the whores came with a heavy surcharge. The Duke de C—— had been the Caesar of the kingdom's last military campaigns, and was reported to be, like his model, every wife's husband no less than he was every husband's wife. Those two gentlemen, and a few others of the same caliber, assembled at B——'s house at around six in the evening. Servants carried in refreshments and withdrew at once; host and guests degusted cold entremets and slices of fowl served in chafing dishes, as well as oysters, which the master of the house loved to distraction, and of which he liked to say that their fragrance, to his thinking, surpassed that of the freshest cunts. The little company tasted everything and talked about everything, especially news of scientific progress, each member of the society contributing his share according to his inclinations. Everything which appeared singular and amusing in the world found an attentive and severe public there, including subjects falling within the infinitely diverse domain of human behavior; on that score, the elevated positions of these gentlemen furnished them with abundance of matter. Around the hour of midnight, the guests all withdrew, rested and content, and returned to their crowded social lives.

Toward the end of the year seventeen hundred and thirty-eight, a certain Vaucanson enjoyed a brief period of celebrity. He had patiently designed and constructed a mechanical duck. It was not, properly speaking, an automaton; the animal had more in common with a clock in a sitting room than with a creature in a farmyard. But, just as it was, Vaucanson's duck inflamed imaginations as rapidly as it enriched its proprietor, who charged a fee for his demonstrations. Those who had seen it said that it drank like a real animal and, what was even more extraordinary, that it digested as well; however, no one was capable of saying exactly how these delicate operations were carried out. Monsieur B—— and his little coterie desired to see the prodigy for themselves, for the court and the town, which lavished such praise upon the shy engineer's mechanical duck, had in the past shown themselves as naive as the populace at the Saint-Germain's fair, amazed by the snake-man and the bearded woman. Was not Monsieur de Vaucanson but a clever street entertainer? Monsieur B——, charged to invite the man and his duck, contracted for a demonstration at an exorbitant price, for he greatly desired to penetrate the secrets of the object's manufacture. Either the thing was genuinely astounding, or B—— suspected some fraud; in any case, he refused to be duped. Now, B—— was far from possessing the technical knowledge required to unmask an impostor of that order or to admire his mechanical genius. And thus he conceived the plan of introducing me into the little company, under a false identity, so that Monsieur de Vaucanson, who refused to assent to any examination of his machine by other men of his art, would not be wary of me. Everyone was to address me with the title of the Comte d'Artois; I would examine Vaucanson's machine with an air of indifference, and then I would make my report to B—— and the other gentlemen. As the reader may easily guess, I accepted his proposal.

The following Monday afternoon a squadron of purveyors arrived at the house in Rue de Bagneux where I awaited the instructions of my master for one evening. Meanwhile, I was combed, perfumed, dressed in the latest fashion, shod with new shoes. I, who loved nothing so much as to go about in loose clothing, with no wig and no suit, was turned that day into a fashionable gentleman; for although clothes do not easily make the monk, they do wonders for the coxcomb. My host's carriage transported me to his house. I entered a salon of great pomp, draped in blue, and I was presented to half of the most illustrious men in Paris. True greatness is without affectation; the gentlemen addressed themselves to me with remarkable friendliness. We moved to a dining room, where the guest of honor had passed the last two hours, bustling about his invention.

The duck was awaiting us; and Vaucanson stood bareheaded at its side, greeting his audience. Overcoming his natural timidity, he undertook to show us his invention. Pieces of metal were the duck's essential components. It was covered in a sort of copperplate mold, its engineer having eschewed a naive imitation of plumage. Monsieur de Vaucanson opened the mold for us, and we were able to examine at leisure the animal's complicated machinery. In the end, the learned man invited the Duke de C—— to feed the beast. The Duke placed a grain of wheat in its beak. The mold had been left open so that we could follow the operation: First, the food slowly descended the duck's gullet, drawn down by simple gravity; next, the wheat dropped into a kind of vase, which represented the stomach, and at the bottom of which lay a thickish liquid; and there the grain underwent a slow dissolution. The Bishop of M—— questioned Monsieur de Vaucanson upon the composition of this brew, but the engineer energetically refused to reveal the recipe to us. Soon the grain lost its original appearance; the liquid grew darker; the residue sank to the bottom of the stomach, where it was pushed by a clever arrangement of pistons toward a sphincter, which served to compress it. Finally, amid absolute silence, Monsieur de Vaucanson's duck released one of the little green droppings which for weeks had elicited cries of admiration from the whole city of Paris. The process was repeated once, this time with a bit of white bread. And that was all. Monsieur de Vaucanson was thanked and generously rewarded. He bowed quite low. His assistants came in to dismantle his machine, after putting up a screen to conceal their work from our view. I asked the engineer if he had attempted to give his creature autonomy of movement (for the duck he presented to us had no legs, being placed upon a pedestal containing the clockwork components necessary for the moving parts of the digestive system). Vaucanson replied that he did not aspire to compete with the Creator in all things. We thanked him again most courteously, and he took his leave. Then we returned to the blue salon, from which the remnants of our dinner had been removed.

After Vaucanson's departure, the dinner guests were pitiless in their judgments; the unfortunate man was torn to pieces, and so was his beast. The ferocity of these gentlemen of ungoverned imagination attested to their disappointment. The idea of a new Prometheus successfully imitating Nature had so fired them with enthusiasm and expectations that the droppings extruded from Monsieur de Vaucanson's fowl seemed meager in comparison. Vaucanson might well delude the weak brains of polite society or gratify an audience befogged by Christianity and secretly rejoicing at man's impotence to equal Nature; but with my host and his strong-minded companions, the engineer had small success. Monsieur B—— asked me to state my opinion. I held back a little from the general assault. I began by observing that none of the machinery involved in the automaton's functioning was new and suggested that our man's only discovery might be the digestive liquid, the composition of which I could but guess at. However, I said, one could hardly consider the operation a perfect digestion, since it could not make blood or provide the nourishment necessary to maintain the entire animal. In conclusion, I opined, the poor duck, without being a fraud punishable by hanging, was nonetheless far from the equal of its model, and hardly worth all the noise it had caused. The moderation of my speech made a good impression on my audience. I was asked numerous questions; then, when B—— rang for supper, I rose to take my leave, but the whole company cried out with one voice that I must stay.

That supper was a wonder. Everyone spoke wittily about nothing and everything. The evening advanced, and as the wine of Champagne went round again, someone observed that there was one function the duck had no hope of performing: that of generation. Producing shit was not so great an exploit as producing sperm, he said, all the while looking at Monsieur B——, whose chastity was the object of much jocularity among his friends. When the loud laughter which greeted this sally had died down, Monsieur B—— calmly declared that to meet such a challenge, he needed my help. He desired me to build not only a creature endowed with an accomplished digestion—here the Bishop of M—— suggested the name "Cloaca," which was unanimously adopted, and the first name "Adam" added as further mockery—but also a mechanical lover, to be christened "Hercules," capable of indefatigable swiving, so that he might prove to these gentlemen that the miracles of lechery they made so much of were not very extraordinary. The whole assembly turned toward me. I promised the cloacal Adam, I promised the lusty Hercules, and I received their cheers. A toast to my health ended that memorable evening. The next day Monsieur B——, who was perhaps the only one of the party who remembered his promise, set about keeping it. He came to Rue de Bagneux to see me and to win Madame Paris's approval. The excellent woman agreed to everything, since by that time I had in my workroom in Faubourg Saint-Jacques three assistants, sufficiently advanced to fill the majority of the orders I received.

I revealed to B—— my old hobbyhorse of perpetual motion. He warmly exhorted me to take up my work again and allowed me a comfortable sum for my materials and tools. We agreed that such an enterprise required a private workshop, quite vast and quite discreet. In the spring of the year seventeen hundred and forty, we found a suitable place at the gates of Paris. It lay on the slopes of the hill of Chaillot, within the property known as Chemin des Vignes, and it was the remains of the country house once owned by an eccentric old banker. It included stables, which he had desired should be magnificent and which still were: lined with panels of a strange wood, almost garnet in color, as tall as a man; adorned with an incredible luxury of metal fittings; and divided into immense stalls. B—— had a portion of this structure transformed into a library and a bedchamber. The saddle room became a workshop, from which, by means of two large windows newly opened in the wall, I enjoyed a view of Paris: the dance of the vehicles on the Cours la

Reine, the dark expanse of the Champ-de-Mars. Under the windows was a long oaken table, covered with all the tools necessary to the working of wood, leather, and metal. How many times did I leave my bed at dawn and stand at my table to watch the sunrise, while the clouds above the rooftops fled eastward! How many times did I see the starry evening sky slowly spread night over people and things! Ten years passed while I lived among those vineyards, on a verdant island where I knew so much joy. What would be the use of explaining to the uninitiated my decade of groping about, of meditation, of trials? Suffice it to say that with the passage of time, I came to find Lucretius's explanations of the subtle mechanisms of digestion, in the fourth book of his poem, oversimple. It was not that I called into question his devotion to the material explanation; on the contrary, I told myself that I should descend to degrees of description still subtler, still deeper, than those he had managed to reach—that I must, in short, refine materialism and not, like too many dunces in the medical profession, ascend spuriously into the absolute void of religious belief, up where the mind encounters no resistance, surrounded as it is by emptiness on all sides! The further I progressed in the knowledge of man, the more I admired the vital energy of his apparatus.

During much of that time, I had forgotten Geneva and all the Rousseaus on earth, but then a certain Jean-Jacques began to cause a sensation in the capital. At first, I hesitated to believe that this man was you; but then I learned that he was nicknamed "the Citizen of Geneva." I read a few of your articles, dedicated to music, in the Encyclopédie of Messieurs Diderot and d'Alembert; B—— was one of its first subscribers. Then I began to observe your star as it rose into the kingdom of France's changing sky: One of your essays won a competition in Dijon;

the account of it which I read in the *Mercure de France* was followed by responses, refutations, polemics. A work written by your hand was presented at Versailles and at the Opéra, and thereafter you became so famous that I congratulated myself on having changed my name. (I heard a few songs from your opera *The Village Soothsayer* and found them quite dull.) But a scandal tainted your reputation: It was said that you had refused to go to Versailles and join the flock of courtiers in that farmyard, and it was further said that Denis Diderot had reproached you for the refusal, on the grounds that you thus rejected a pension and bread for your children. I felt I had a brother again. While I considered having your address found out and going to pay you a visit, B—— announced his imminent departure in order to accompany one of his friends to Geneva, where he would place her in the care of Dr. Tronchin, the illustrious physician. (If I understood his implication aright, the woman was suffering from a cumbersome burden not made in the image of her husband.) I requested my protector to conduct some discreet inquiries while in Geneva concerning the Rousseau family and, more particularly, concerning the Citizen's brother, one François, whom I claimed to have known in times past. Without (I believe) being gulled by my half lie, B—— carried out his mission. Upon his return, I learned from him that my father was dead. I owe it to truth to admit that this news hardly stirred me. I felt a certain gratitude to my father for having set me on the road to man's estate; but I had never had sufficient time to know him. The voice of the blood too often speaks in obscure oracles, and whether or not he and I could have been close is a mystery I shall never resolve.

As to one François Rousseau, B—— brought me some sad news: He had seen a letter in Geneva written by François' brother, Jean-Jacques, in which the latter stated that the former was dead. Our father was dead, Jean-Jacques, and you wanted your inheritance. You had a brother without whom the thing was impossible, for it had to be shared with him. He had disappeared so long ago that you lied to the Republic of Geneva, saying that you knew with almost perfect certainty that François Rousseau was no longer in this world. Your subterfuge failed, but you were not wrong to write those words; to become a stranger, not to my true self, but to the little marionette which society desires us to be, that it may manipulate us at leisure— that was the law that ruled me. And when I cast a look back on this world, which I shall soon abandon, this is what I am proudest of: I have lived *my* life. How many men have gained the right to set down those words? That little meanness of yours regarding our common inheritance irritated me, and I gave up the idea of seeing you. But enough of us; I return to my researches.

In the beginning of summer in the year seventeen hundred and forty, I assigned one stall to our cloacal Adam and another to our amorous Hercules. Betraying an innocence which today makes me blush, we had concluded that the secrets of the digestive process were simpler than those of coupling. I had never previously given any thought to the miracles of digestion, but— doubtless emboldened by the success of my sexual devices and sustained by my Lucretius, my watchmaking skills, and my munificent patron's money—I was confident of penetrating the secrets of life in a few months, perhaps in a few years.

First of all, it was necessary to fix upon a working method for the accomplishment of the new and untried tasks I had set myself. I have always mistrusted inflexible men, stopped clocks which pride themselves, twice a day, in giving the right time; but the hour is always the same. Nevertheless, the design of my automatons required that I should proceed according to some reasonable plan, and I was determined to neglect nothing that might assist the success of the grandiose project. And so we— that is, Monsieur B—— and I—wrote letters to the learned men across Europe who had debated the questions which absorbed us. A few imbeciles referred us to the Ancients. Almost all the rest fell, as is the practice among such creatures, into one of two adverse camps. The partisans of Malaxation believed that our food was kneaded, minced, and ground from our teeth to our anus, and that these operations released elements of heat and moisture which the body required. The defenders of Dissolution contended that saliva and the juices contained in our stomachs and intestines corroded our food, as vinegar can dissolve a scrap of fresh meat. Some, the shrewd politicians, maintained that trituration and malaxation played equal roles in this commonplace process. Those who took the last-named position were probably the closest to the truth, but the least well-equipped to attain it. Nevertheless, the Dissolutionists, the Malaxationists, and the Malaxo-Dissolutionists gave proof of splendid eloquence; all admirably refuted their opponents' views, and all offered unimpeachable arguments. But in all the meanders of their prose, there were hardly any solidly established facts or precise observations. They spent a good part of their energy in polemics and passed their time citing themselves to one another, like little ambassadors of chimerical kingdoms barricaded in castles built on sand, strongholds no one cared to capture. Soon we were inundated by dissertations and refutations, always complemented by requests for subsidies. Our only fruitful readings were Van Helmont's treatise on digestion and all the works of the brilliant physiologist Boerhaave, which some free spirit, from the safety of Holland, had fortunately just translated into French, and which we had to order discreetly from a Swiss publisher whom the hard times had compelled to print, in addition to works of the true Reformed Faith, everything subversive of Catholicism which was produced in Europe. We could not assimilate the indigestible prose of a certain Stahl, and with him our abstract studies came to an end.

I like to think, Jean-Jacques, that contrary to all the simpletons who today call themselves your disciples, you would not be squeamish about the subject of my labors. The scoundrels who invoke your name and who pretend to know Man in all the truth of his nature have made him into a pale, bloodless ghost, without flesh and without a multiplicity of passions; and the said Man, one may suppose, never shits or fucks. I endeavored to observe in myself the diversity of the digestive operations. I swallowed a meal without chewing it, making note of the disturbances I thus created in my stomach and in the formation of my stools; on the following day, I consumed an exactly similar meal, but slowly and deliberately, and I made comparisons. I admired the tranquil, empirical prodigies of nature: how our teeth coarsely grind up our food; how it works its way to our stomach; how it remains there long enough to undergo subtle, almost alchemical transformations; how we draw vital elements from our food; how the residue of these mysterious operations is sent on its way out of our body. Everything in this process, including the turds which were its final result, appeared to me worthy of interest and admiration. I learned how the medical profession described stools—according to their consistency, the rapidity of their desiccation, their odor when fresh, their form, and their abundance. The reader may mock such application and such fervor; for my part, my fascination with this subject continues even today. I consulted surgeons and physicians, anatomists and naturalists. For weeks I went all over the city, visiting hospitals and private offices, making notes and sketches of all I saw and heard.

How to catch Nature in the act of digestion and discover its secrets? As I was beginning to fear for the health of my intestines, which protested with increasing frequency against the diets to which I subjected them, I was obliged to conduct researches *in anima vili*. My first series of experiments were at the expense of the stray cats of the neighborhood; there was nothing easier than luring them out of the vineyards and nearby quarries, where they lazed about all day long. Protected by long gloves, my workers flung the cats into large canvas sacks. I had devised a barbarous engine, a sort of pillory which held the animals' limbs fast in leather sleeves. I sacrificed the beasts on the altar of digestive science. The first was a big tomcat, mangy and wild, with a robe of frightful orange fur. I incised the animal's side and slit open its stomach pouch to observe its contents. But I had misjudged my undertaking. From the start, when I had placed the beast in my newly invented stocks, it had cried out so piteously that I was certain it could be heard as far as Paris. Then, when I made the incision, it set up an indescribable howling, and without thinking, I loosened the pillory. The poor animal escaped, breaking both its hind legs in the effort, and began crawling wretchedly around the floor of that hellish place, searching for a way out, and leaving behind a trail of mucus and blood. I overtook the creature without difficulty and cut short its suffering by crushing its head with a blow from my boot. The second cat was luckier: It scratched me from my elbow to my fingers, I let it go, it leaped through the window, and I never saw it again. The third nearly removed one of my eyes, and I wrung its neck without further ado. As living animals seemed to present too many difficulties, I resolved to divide my investigations into as many cats as, according to my calculations, there were steps in the digestive process. I made one cat go hungry; then I fed it and killed it at the end of half an hour. A second cat was allowed to live half an hour longer. And so on; I disemboweled each animal immediately after its death, and thus I was able to follow the entire progress of the food as it was decomposed. One day I inadvertently slew my neighbor's Grisette; its mistress complained bitterly, and the price of her silence was very high. In the end, the villagers grew agitated, not only because of the malodorous vapors caused by my experiments, but also because of the proliferation of rats and mice over the entire hill of Chaillot; they suspected me of some kind of horrible sorcery. As for me, it was no use my believing that animals have only a vegetative soul; the cries of the unfortunate beasts too terribly resembled those of human victims tortured by the justice of men. I gave up cats. It was then that an old taxidermist of the Jardin du Roi called my attention to a certain variety of falcon which could serve my purposes. In exchange for a louis, an intrepid Savoyard removed some of these birds of prey from their nests on the eastern façade of Notre-Dame, and with their providential aid, I made decisive progress. It was the habit of this species of hawk to swallow its sustenance and then to regurgitate it in order to feed its young. I took advantage of this singularity, making my falcons swallow small cylinders of various metals and then observing the degree of corrosion in the cast-out cylinders, noting the kind of metal used and the length of time between swallowing and regurgitation. Next I trained a particularly docile young male to consume small sponges infused with meat juices; when he cast these out, they were soaked with his gastric liquid. Thus I obtained vials of digestive juices; I sought first to determine their composition, and then to reproduce them by carefully measured combinations of alkalis, lime, and acids.

Simultaneously with all this, Monsieur B—— encouraged me to continue my endeavors in regard to Hercules. B—— dreamed, I believe, of proving to his friends that their dominant passion was less subtle than his own; that, all things considered, fucking was nothing in comparison with the process of eating, refining matter, and expelling its remnants. I spared no effort: I went to the general hospital and blithely dissected pricks in order to examine as I pleased those spongy organs which an erection gorges with blood. I had read a sufficient number of licentious books to know that a hanged man's *membrum virilis* underwent, *in articulo mortis*, a most unusual expansion, but I had no success in penetrating that particular mystery. On the other hand, I contrived to make acceptable sperm, which the most knowledgeable whores in Paris would have been unable to distinguish from the real substance. And so, little by little, our Hercules came to life. He was neither divine nor even human in the beginning, for he consisted of a simple trunk, without head or arms, screwed to a rocking chair to which the client could impart the movement she desired. I say she, but at first there were more gentlemen than ladies desirous of sitting in our Hercules' lap; it seemed that his uncouth character offended female sensibilities. It was upon B——'s advice that I had offered this model for sale; he expected that a clientele so particular about objects of pleasure would communicate to me all the imperfections of my invention; which was, in fact, what happened. However, it sold very well, in all the capitals of Europe.

Numerous clients urged us to civilize our Hercules, to give him that veneer of humanity without which, it seems, the majority of our kind cannot reach the heights of pleasure. Soon

Hercules was provided with articulated legs; he swived standing upright or on his knees with the same constancy, and, it goes without saying, he could be placed on one's bed and ridden. This second model supplanted the first and sold even better. Hercules received a head, a pleasant countenance—as pleasant as a porcelain face could be—powerful arms, delicate hands, and the most beautiful wig in Paris. I was particularly proud of his skin: It was that of a stillborn lamb, and I had labored over it for a long time, assisted by the best leather workers. I strove to compose a scent which would mingle the smell of male skin with the fragrance of the most refined fop, and the addition of this luxurious detail brought me many compliments. Of course, the most essential part of our work was the mechanism which was to set our heavy machine in motion; for the creature we were devising must needs have the suppleness of a living thing. By the end of a year, we had made such considerable progress that we were ready to present our Hercules, whom we dubbed a gay deceiver. We planned to display him with due solemnity to B———'s regular Monday visitors. Curiously, we had a great deal of difficulty finding a woman who would assist our demonstration by publicly submitting to such an experiment. The trollops were perfectly willing to participate in the most unrestrained debaucheries, provided that the congress were with their own kind and that their price were met; the notion of a machine repelled them; and all the more so in that it perfectly imitated the human form. We first presented our Hercules in private, in the fall of the year seventeen hundred and fifty, to Madame Paris. That generous soul congratulated us profusely. We had limited our fellow's capacities to one hour; if we wound up his mechanism to its maximum tension, he could fuck for just so long and no longer. Madame Paris laughed heartily at this limit, saying that it was thirty times as long as the vast majority of her clients required. In the end, she became so absorbed by our project, so carried away by the novelty of our artifact, and so sympathetic to our predicament that she made us a proposal which we should never have dared even to dream about on our own account: She offered to take a personal part in the public deflowering of our seducer. We quickly accepted.

The day fixed for our presentation arrived. An immense bed was set up in the middle of the great ceremonial salon on the second floor. As the reader may imagine, none of Monsieur B——'s regular guests absented themselves on that particular evening. B——, who had conceived the idea of covering our man with a black sheet, pulled it off as the final stroke of eight o'clock sounded, to the amused applause of the little company; and Hercules appeared, in the simple trappings of his nakedness. To begin, we granted the members of our audience a right of inspection, so that they might assure themselves that they were not the victims of some prank. I was charged with conducting the exhibition of our creature. I showed that Hercules' legs were independent of the floor, and that they gave a solid sound when struck. Then I undid the skin of our man's trunk, discovering his metal chest, with double panels that opened in the center like a jewelry case. Each of the guests was permitted to inspect the mechanism as he pleased; I invited the Maréchal de L—— to draw his sword and verify with its blade that no one was hidden inside. He did so, and then I was obliged to adjust poor Hercules. At that very moment, Madame Paris entered, greeted each of those present with exquisite grace, and quickly removed her clothes. The scene unfolded: After placing several pillows on the bed so that she might recline at her ease, Madame Paris lay down upon it and bravely spread her legs. B—— and I placed our gay deceiver in an appropriate position for his task, firmly braced upon his broad hands. Our benefactress slipped between his arms, took hold of the respectable instrument with which we had endowed our machine, and blithely inserted it into the opening which Nature had formed to receive it. At a sign from B——, I released the mechanism, and our Hercules began fucking heartily, with a persistency worthy of admiration. Madame Paris did not remain inactive, rendering blow for blow, flailing about, and loudly demonstrating that she was as fixed on her business as our man was on his. After swooning with pleasure, she turned over on the bed, offering Hercules her majestic posterior; and he, without a pause, performed a new feat of impassive regularity. At the end, Madame Paris writhed like a she-devil flung into a holy-water stoup, thrashed her pillows, cried out, and reached a climax so violent that it unsaddled her valiant cavalier. The suddenly dismounted lover collapsed on his side, and the assembly watched as he discharged a copious barrage of white spurts. At this denouement, the audience rose as one, cheering and clapping. The Duke de C——, whose inclinations were a secret to no one, approached the disordered bed, dipped a small batiste handkerchief into the freshly emitted sperm, tasted it, and complimented me on my recipe. I promised to provide him with it, should he wish me to do so; he replied that he preferred receiving such a tribute in its natural state, and upon this stroke of wit, the demonstration ended. Hercules was carried into an adjoining room, whereto the company retired as well, taking seats around a table in order to recover from all the excitement. The supper went on for a long time. In the end, we drank a final libation in honor of Madame Paris, and the last carriage left the courtyard in the Rue Saint-Honoré around midnight. Only then could B—— and I return to our gallant Hercules, who was all alone and waiting for us in the dining room on the first floor.

And now, Jean-Jacques, if you prefer illusion to reality, curse your brother and read no further. When we had sent all the servants away, when we were certain that we were alone in the dining room and had locked all the doors, we hastened to our automaton, opened the double doors of his trunk, and released three secret springs, thus causing two mirrors to appear. These were very precisely disposed so that their reflections of the interior works quite distorted their appearance. Removing the two mirrors, we exposed a sort of niche, where, drenched in sweat and nearly fainting, our accomplice awaited his deliverance. We bathed his forehead with iced water and rubbed his limbs. Finally, he completely recovered his senses; and the three of us supped together until dawn, unknown to anybody else, tirelessly recounting the events of that memorable evening and savoring them anew. We had just duped the most skeptical minds in Paris, at a time when Paris was well supplied with such minds.

What had led us to perpetrate our deception? Despite my incessant labors, and notwithstanding the considerable resources which B—— placed at my disposal, I had known too many failures and was prepared to lay down my arms, convinced that it was not so easy to imitate a living thing. I spoke of this to B——, but to my great surprise, he would not agree. He refused to give ground to the believers by acknowledging, even if only in an implicit fashion, that nothing but the intervention of a god could explain such a miracle as that of generation. Exasperated, he determined, not without malice, to take revenge on his own impotence by dragging his unbelieving friends down with him in his fall. He found it particularly satisfying to abuse their credulity precisely in the matter of debauchery, wherein many of them prided themselves on excelling and concerning which they delighted to tease their chaste friend. And so, despairing of giving our inert Hercules a veritable prime mover, B—— had conceived the idea of equipping him with an auxiliary.

As a man curious about everything, B—— loved to frequent not only the troupes of wandering minstrels and acrobats who traveled back and forth across Europe like desert nomads, earning a wretched living by dancing or exhibiting trained bears and exotic birds, but also the misshapen creatures whom public credulity wraps in a cloak of malevolence and calls monsters: snake-women, giants, dwarves, cripples of every kind. Throughout Europe, B—— was known to be fond of such anatomical curiosities and, indeed, of all the aberrations which Nature, in her great abundance, could supply. Inevitably, anybody who possessed one of these creatures came to the great house in the Rue Saint-Honoré and presented the prodigy to B——. It was on one such occasion that he had met a Spaniard named Chico, an acrobatic dwarf of formidable vitality and suppleness, despite the horribly deformed legs which further diminished his size. As a child, he was taken in by the local priest, but Gypsies carried him off from his village when he was thirteen. He was very fond of pleasure and entertainments, and he passionately loved women, to whom he spoke in an astonishing farrago, the product of his incessant peregrinations in Europe. Women liked him and were far from distrusting him, considering him rather as a kind of domestic animal. They laughed a great deal at his compliments and his pretensions, but Chico was not a man to lose heart. He cheerfully declared that yielding to a dwarf was an act of no consequence, barely amounting to half a sin; and that, moreover, Nature having made all things in proportion, those ladies ran no risk of being indisposed by such an instrument as his (on this point, he lied; having seen the said utensil in action, I can say that Nature, out of her infinite bounty, had accorded Chico a generous compensation for his stature). Many women yielded, laughing all the while. The miniature swain earned his living by exhibiting himself in learned circles or at fairs: Stained with walnut, he was an African pygmy remarkable for savageness; wrapped in an animal's skin, he marvelously portrayed a Patagonian, roaring whenever someone tossed him a sou. B—— had undertaken a search for this interesting personage, and had found him in Germany. The dwarf spent so much money on gaming and women that B—— had no difficulty getting him away from the troupe that exploited him; B—— paid Chico's debts and brought him back to Chaillot.

After Chico's arrival, my task remained quite arduous. I was obliged to learn how to build a secret drawer into an ordinary piece of furniture, and how to set mirrors in such a way as to deceive the eye of an observer. The members of the audience naturally had to be given the opportunity to examine the interior of the automaton at their leisure, but they must not find anything. I conceived the building of two hiding places, and I invented a very simple trick of which I was rather proud. To begin, I showed the spectators the first compartment, which was inside the automaton's chest; I encouraged them to put their hands into it; and then I closed it up again. Next, I created a diversion by opening Hercules' head. That part of the automaton was of no consequence to the rest of the machine, but it always captivated the uninitiated audience. While everyone's attention was thus distracted, Chico silently slipped out of the second compartment, where we had hidden him, and into the first compartment, which was located above the second. After the second compartment had been duly inspected, Chico once again took up his position inside it, for only from there could he activate Hercules' arms and legs by inserting his own into an arrangement of sleeves. He had spent hours practicing the operation of that strange external skeleton. As for Hercules' member, you will not be surprised to learn that Chico enthusiastically agreed to lend the automaton his own; it was simply a matter of inserting it into a sort of stocking made of lamb's skin. B——'s guests, of course, warmly congratulated me for the perfection of this imitation, and Madame Paris confirmed that that particular piece deserved all our praise.

We helped our hero extract himself from his hiding place, where he lay in a languor of inanition. We regaled him, we complimented him heartily, and we sent him back in a fiacre to the workshop in Chaillot. So unsure had we been of succeeding that—as I now began to see—we had not thought about what sequel we should give to our jest. Should we leave our skeptics in doubt? Should we undeceive them tomorrow? Dawn was breaking over the rooftops; we adjourned the discussion until another time. B——, whose replies had been most evasive, thanked me and implied that our collaboration was reaching its end. If I wished, I could retain the use of the workshop on the Chemin des Vignes. For my part, I was surprised by B——'s coldness toward me, but I was so grateful to him for his many favors that I forgot this incident. One year later I glimpsed the reason behind his sudden aloofness. A rumor spread through Paris to the effect that Monsieur B—— had discovered the secret of a vital fluid and that he was demonstrating it by means of an automaton of his own fabrication. When I heard this, I surmised that for B——, an unbeliever fascinated by others' credulity, the enjoyment of deceiving the members of his circle had carried all before it. He never revealed Chico's existence to anyone, and the composition of Hercules' fluid remained a mystery. As the years went by, B—— began to voice his opinions in matters of religion more and more loudly; so strident were his claims that his vital fluid made man the equal of the gods that some of his set, among them the Bishop of M——, were obliged for the sake of prudence to make their visits less frequent, and soon they no longer appeared at their friend's Mondays. Time passed, and B—— was growing old. The year seventeen hundred and fifty-seven would sound the death knell for such men as he.

In seventeen hundred fifty-seven the Carnival began in Paris, as it did every year, on January sixth, the Feast of the Epiphany. I have always been fond of this festive period. Everyone puts on a disguise, as one does throughout the rest of the year, but with this difference: At the Carnival, one dons the mask knowingly. January sixth, seventeen hundred and fifty-seven, was a Thursday, and on that day some incredible news spread through Paris with a rapidity which defied understanding. In Versailles, a half-mad fanatic named Robert François Damiens had stabbed King Louis XV. Immediately, there was general consternation in Paris, and because the King was believed to be dying, masses were said for that insipid monarch, that notorious idler, against whom his subjects were otherwise wont to rail. That very evening the Parisians learned that the royal wound constituted no danger to the King's life. The hue and cry caused by this incident reached my solitude in Chaillot and B——'s sumptuous town house as no more than murmurs. In March of the same year I saw B—— again by chance, at the moment when the authorities solemnly announced the public execution of the culprit. B—— and I had both forgotten Damiens, and I was astounded that an unfortunate madman was to receive the honors of the Place de Grève. Invoking my curiosity about the human machine, B—— declared his readiness, as a man of strong mind, to accompany me to the spectacle. He rallied me: Did a faithful disciple of Lucretius not have a duty to look horror in the face? I was on the point of refusing when I remembered my master Saint-Fonds and the cobbler burned at the stake in Avignon. I accepted.

When Robert François Damiens appeared in public on the day of his execution, everyone could see that he was in perfect health. The sovereign's first thought, upon receiving his wound, had been to order that no harm be done to his attacker; moreover, out of precaution, he had immediately been given all sorts of antidotes to poison. Thereafter, the man had slept bound to a bed, so that he might not take his own life, and his cell was surrounded by a multitude of guards. Despots dislike having their right to kill usurped, and they make sure to exercise it as slowly as they can. On March twenty-eighth, seventeen hundred and fifty-seven, the buildings around the Place de Grève, the balconies, the roofs, and even the chimneys, were all crowded with people. Polite society was there in the best seats. The gentlemen posed as philosophers; the ladies affected horror, but soon, as they peered between their slender fingers, pleasure would contort their wicked mouths at the unfortunate culprit's cries. Numerous well-to-do burghers had taken care to equip themselves with spyglasses. Near two o'clock, a laborer fell off a roof and killed another man, but this incident discouraged no one. At a great price, B—— had procured a choice spot for us. We were on the third floor above a grocer's shop, on a balcony outside his cramped living quarters; this lugubrious day made the grocer's fortune. Monsieur B—— had him serve us refreshments and dainty items of food, all in the Turkish fashion so popular at the time and so compatible with the cruelty of the occasion. Before us lay the ground where the execution was to take place, marked off by ranks of archers on horseback and on foot. Suddenly, waves of serpentine movement passed through the crowd, for everyone craned his neck in order to see Damiens, who was approaching from a distance. People shouted abuse at the wretch, but no one dared to spit on him, so intimidating was the deployment of the French and Swiss guards. The procession entering the Place de Grève came from Notre-Dame, because protocol stipulated that the condemned man should make amends in front of the cathedral's main portal. The Seine was deserted; in order to avoid incidents, the authorities had suspended all navigation.

Robert François Damiens remained seated before his funeral pyre for half an hour, waiting while his torments were prepared. They began around five o'clock in the evening. I looked at the man, I imagined the disorder of his mind, and it seemed to me that I must accompany him to the end. To begin, the executioner and his assistants applied themselves to burning Damiens' right hand, the one which had committed the unspeakable crime. Until then, I had not known that a man could cry out so vehemently. Next, the executioner took from an assistant a pair of red-hot tongs, which he plunged into a bucket of molten lead before using them to tear flesh from Damiens' breast, arms, and legs. Then came the quartering. Four horses were yoked to his four limbs, but Damiens was strong, and his limbs did not yield. The executioner gave orders, and two fresh horses were harnessed as reinforcements, but their number still did not suffice. The executioner sent to the Hôtel de Ville for instructions; when his assistant returned, it was revealed that the municipal authorities had refused to give Sanson, the public executioner, permission to cleave Damiens' joints in order to ease the horses' task. Those in high places had judged that the regicide deserved the additional suffering which Heaven had been pleased to send him. In the end, however, they were obliged to let the executioner slash his patient. Half chopped off, Damiens' limbs finally gave way—first the legs, both at once—and the crowd rushed forward as though to fall upon the remains. But the guards lay about them furiously with the flats of their swords and drove the throng back. Damiens was still alive when, at last, the horses attached to his arms completed their task, and at fifteen minutes after six, the wretch's limbless trunk fell into the dust of the arena. The executioner and one of his assistants placed the four limbs and the mutilated body on the woodpile, while another, wielding a sort of ash shovel, scooped up the earth soiled by the sacrilegious blood of the condemned man and threw it, too, onto the stacked firewood.

I felt it then, in the deepest fibers of my being: The crowd is the most terrible of Molochs. I suppose that some of the future deputies who would later vote for the adoption of the guillotine were, in their youth, among the witnesses to that day's infamy. By replacing the horrible litany of tortures with the keen edge of a single blade, they doubtless thought they were putting an end to such horror; and so they did. But today I believe that the Damiens affair also set in motion something enormous, barbarous, and savage. Beginning with Damiens' trial and execution, the French were seized by a frenzy of desire for a true culprit; for it was the sentiment of all that the madman Damiens did not suffice. Some accused the Jesuits; others inclined toward the Jansenists; still others blamed foreigners. Everyone, from the prince of the blood to the humblest day laborer, had an opinion in the matter. They all felt touched by it, as if they were entrusted with a mission. And since no hypothesis concerning those who had armed Robert François Damiens against the King could bear serious examination, they set about forming vaguer, obscurer, more extravagant and intoxicating hypotheses. They invented labyrinthine plots, fantastic conspiracies, intrigues so murky that the devil himself could not have found his way through them. Madame Pompadour and her royal lover were the objects of extremely violent placards, and the forces of justice believed it their duty to show themselves merciless. During the summer of seventeen hundred and fifty-eight, a certain Mauriceau de La Motte dared to inveigh publicly against the precipitous fashion in which the Damiens affair had been conducted; in the beginning of September, he was well and truly hanged. Eventually, people forgot about Damiens' attempt on the King, but the general craving for culprits did not diminish. The day of his execution, in my opinion, saw the birth of the unquenchable thirst which led us to the Terror and its seas of blood. And it was likewise from that day that the *Philosophes*, as they were then called, began to be dealt some serious blows.

As a notorious supporter of the philosophical party, B—— should have been alarmed at these developments, or at least should have shown greater discretion; but habit is an imperious mistress, and B—— had grown old. In former days, he had enjoyed the protection of the Lieutenant-General of the Police, but now another had been named in his place, and B—— failed to take notice of the change. The cannonballs whistled incessantly around his ears: In seventeen hundred and sixty-two the unfortunate Diderot's *Encyclopédie*, which the censors had previously treated with great leniency, was banned; B——, one of its first subscribers, did not hide his anger. Then there was talk of him in the King's Council, and the Lieutenant-General had him watched. Not long afterward, the scandal broke out: For one of his friends who was much given to revelry and debauch, B—— had ordered the abduction of some peasant girls, but his hirelings thoughtlessly ventured upon the lands of an illustrious Duke, an intimate friend of the Chancellor and Keeper of the Seals. Moreover, as bad luck would have it, one of the ravished girls was the special object of the Duke's paternal affection. It required but a few hours to find her, weeping and bloody, in a secluded little house in Clamart. Leaving B——'s friend to his own devices, the police investigators rushed to the mansion in the Rue Saint-Honoré, and there, in B——'s writing desk, they found some copies of the seditious placards of which I spoke not long ago. B—— lost his head and immediately claimed that he had torn them off the railings of a garden; alas, the sheets in question bore neither holes nor traces of glue. B—— was therefore, to his great surprise, thrown into La Force Prison. As soon as he was shut up in his cell, and believing that he could count on his friends to help him, he wrote some twenty letters and had them sent all over Paris. Only when five days had passed and not one of the former companions of his Mondays had replied to him did B—— understand that he was lost, and thereafter he ceased all efforts to turn aside the thunderbolt about to strike him.

Within fifteen days, there was nothing left of B——; his house and his possessions were seized and his papers confiscated. He was allowed to engage a lawyer, who was, except for me, the only person who visited him in La Force; but he had great difficulty in finding one willing to defend him. At last, a certain Chevalier de Floris presented himself; his youth and the money B—— managed, I know not how, to extract from the King's zealous henchmen accomplished what it was possible to accomplish. B—— was spared a public trial. Until the judgment was pronounced, he received considerate treatment, for Floris had quite adroitly hinted at the existence somewhere of certain scandalous correspondence, which could plunge the royal court into an unending series of awkward predicaments. This was a brazen lie, but so plausible that B—— spent the remainder of his time in La Force in a spacious cell. After the trial, however, there was a dramatic reversal in his situation. Condemned to thirty years of imprisonment for crimes against the security of the State, B—— was sent to the fortress of Belle-Île, where he was not authorized to receive visits. He languished there for five years, during which time the inveterate gourmand received his nourishment from vile concoctions whose monotony inspired him to compose letters which I read with tears in my eyes. At last, after five years of this regimen, he was deemed harmless, as his health was failing, and everyone had forgotten him. His lawyer having been spied upon, the authorities had reached the conclusion that the letters of which he had spoken did not exist. At that point, B—— could have been set free; but to do so would have been tantamount to acknowledging that he had duped the forces of justice. They preferred, therefore, to strangle him, and to fling his body into a creek for the crabs to eat. I report the tale as I heard it several years later, when I once again met the former Chevalier de Floris, who in the meanwhile had become one of the most ardent partisans of the Girondists. He wept as he told me of B——'s fate.

But let me return to the weeks just after B——'s arrest. At first, I was simply dumbstruck. I spent the days in Chaillot, in my workshop, which had long since lost all purpose. For the first time in my life, I felt a deep discouragement and acute weariness. Madame Paris sent Michel to urge me to leave the city for several months. I promised to do so, but delayed my departure long enough for the police to come and arrest me. That very night, I lay in the Bastille. My jailers had no clear idea of how to enroll me in the records of the fortress, given that I had committed no crime. The governor of the Bastille received orders for my confinement, but no one could say how long I was to be deprived of my freedom, so he entered me in his register as a forger; forgery being a criminal act sufficiently serious to justify incarceration *ad vitam aeternam*, because the French are readier to pardon a murderer than a man who attacks the dignity of money.

As for Hercules—I must say the final word on that lamentable subject—his success had continued. When B—— was imprisoned, Chico, who had taken up with a former tumbler from Saint-Germain, believed his fortune was made, as he now considered Hercules his property by right, without thinking that there might henceforth be some danger in possessing such a machine. And so Chico, in the guise of Hercules, performed in an orgy organized for the Vicomte de D——, whose father had the King's ear and wished to teach his fool of a son a lesson, as he was weary of covering the lad's gambling debts, of paying henchmen to thrash all those with whom the irascible coward tried to pick a quarrel when he had drunk too much wine, and of compensating all those whose fields he devastated while hunting deer with a small band of useless young men like himself. In order to chastise his son, the Comte de D—— had secured the complicity of a Châtelet police superintendent named René, whose cunning and cruelty were proverbial. Duly instructed, René, at the head of a troop of fierce-looking police officers, burst into the Vicomte's private salon, where the said orgy was taking place. He found the master of the premises on

all fours, being buggered by Hercules. It cost René little effort
to terrify his victim. He assured the young man that to the sin
of sodomy, albeit mechanical, he had joined that of heresy, because his automaton aped the work of the Creator of all things
and because his vital fluid was none other than a piece of sorcery. The Vicomte threatened, implored, offered fortunes, all in
vain. René remained inflexible and sent the blockhead to a dungeon for the night, although the Vicomte believed himself cast
into it for eternity. His little group of companions, driven out
by kicks and blows, scattered into the neighboring streets. René
detained the tumbler, Chico's partner, and asked him many
questions about the vital fluid; the frightened tumbler thought
it a crafty idea to prove his innocence by revealing the deception of the automaton. René immediately slit his throat and
threw his body into the rear courtyard. And then the pitiless
superintendent knew one of the evil joys for which he had embraced his profession: He had an order to destroy Hercules, and
he had just learned that he could kill him. He threw the
manikin into his carriage, ordered the driver to take him to an
isolated clearing in the forest of Meudon, and there supervised
the erection of a makeshift stake with a pile of wood around it.
During all these operations, René was careful to give his orders
in a loud voice, so that the man imprisoned inside Hercules
would know his fate. In the end, however, René was disappointed, because Chico died without making his presence
known, and the superintendent returned to Paris in an extremely foul humor. The police officer who related this story to
me twenty years after the facts thought that the dwarf had died
of suffocation before the flames reached him. The officer, with
two of his fellows, had remained near the stake; while waiting
for the fire to burn itself out, they dug a ditch, into which, at
dawn, they threw the half-melted carcass of Hercules. This

deed, when it was made known in Paris, flatteringly enhanced René's reputation for inflexibility. I saw René again many years later; he prospered during the Terror, until he himself was condemned to lie under the guillotine's blade. He was saved at the last moment by the events of 9 Thermidor and died in his bed six months ago, surrounded by his loved ones. It was for such as him, I suppose, that weak-minded men invented hell; for it is indeed a hard thing to console oneself for the flagrant injustices of this world!

And so I was now a prisoner of the Bastille. So much foolishness has been written about that place since its destruction that I feel obliged to state the truth clearly: In seventeen hundred and sixty-two the Bastille was not the vilest prison in the kingdom; far from it. When the governor of the fortress received me, he informed me that I had at my disposal a modest but comfortable pension. I dissembled my surprise. I have never discovered to whom I owed that charity, although I have often suspected that Michel and Madame Paris had something to do with it. I had enough money to live comfortably, I enjoyed excellent health as I entered my fifty-seventh year, and I gave no thought to the future. The Bastille, however, was a fearsome place in one particular, namely that you knew when you had entered it, but you could never say when you would leave. A conversation which touched upon this theme sent a shiver down my spine: At the end of my first week in the fortress, I tried to give back the provision of two candles which the guard, in conformity with the meticulous regulations of the Bastille, allotted me each day; it was summer, and I had no use for those candles, which encumbered my quarters. My jailer laughed heartily and enjoined me to keep the candles for winter evenings. I, who had never in my life thought about the passing days, the passing years, having always lived like a happy animal, fond of my work and fond of my pleasure—I found myself suddenly plunged into the icy waters of time. I, who gave but little thought to tomorrow, was going to spend twenty-seven years in the Bastille; but only later did I read, in the eyes of others, that this was a terrible thing.

I was lodged on the fourth floor of the tower known as the Tour de la Comté, with a view over Paris. The fifth and highest floor of each of the Bastille's eight towers was generally left unoccupied, because prisoners kept there either froze or roasted, according to the season. On each floor, there was but a single, fairly vast cell, octagonal in shape. By leaving an empty space between the floor of each cell and the ceiling of the one below it, a zealous architect had made sure that secret communications between prisoners were impossible. The result was that each prisoner lived an incarcerated life of remarkable calm. Often, at night, when the wind stopped carrying the noises of the city to our ears, I was able to fancy myself in a desert, in a hermit's cell or a traveler's tent. Moreover, we were, I believe, the most comfortable prisoners in Paris, far removed from the grisly crowding in La Force or Saint-Lazare. Human society was reduced to that of the transient prisoners, who came seldom and stayed no longer than a week, and that of the few permanent inmates of the majestic pile, who offered few affinities with my character: swindlers of paltry intelligence resigned to their fate and gallows-faced villains as dull as a long winter rain. The only one for whom I felt affection was an Englishman known as Caesar. He was a person of quality not wholly in his right mind, and his prestigious family counted it a fortunate chance that their scion's madness had declared itself in Paris rather than in London. Caesar's father had demanded that his son be admitted to the Bastille to spare the young man the horrors of the general hospital, where his less well-born fellow lunatics were thronged together in frightful conditions, and because then the old lord could tell his aristocratic friends in England that his son had been imprisoned for libertinism. A rake cuts a better figure in the world than a madman, who elicits either horror or pity. The unfortunate Englishman's Christian name was, in fact, John; his quirk of calling himself Caesar was innocuous; rather more worrying was his recurring belief that he was the Emperor of both Rome and Constantinople. Every evening I played chess with him, and he invariably beat me, as he had beaten all the occupants of the prison. He asked me a thousand suspicious questions; he feared that I allowed him to score his victories out of deference to his rank. When I reassured him by declaring that such worldly grandeur meant nothing to me, he was overjoyed. He introduced me to Shakespeare, whom he admired above all authors and whose works he translated into flawless French for me. I loved the English playwright's mad, misshapen creatures, his unnatural princes, his admirable women; I did not yet know that those phantoms, which seemed larger than life to me, would soon appear in flesh and blood upon the stage of the Revolution, suddenly overshadowing the characters conceived by Corneille and Molière and Racine. As to the staff of the Bastille, I always saw them treat the prisoners with humanity, except on a single occasion, about which I shall speak again. In their conduct on this head, our guards followed the example of the governor, Bernard de Launay. He was a handsome man, with an air of imperious intelligence admirably belied by his conversation, which, according to the general opinion, was as flat as a paved footway. In those days, the French aristocracy seemed to produce more such amiable nonentities each year. He was inoffensive to whoever flattered his pride, and this weakness made him easy to manage.

In thus describing the Bastille and its occupants, I should not wish to suggest that imprisonment is an enviable fate. For one who has never known it, incarceration is difficult to imagine. To be unable to move about as you please; to have your walks confined to a courtyard so hemmed in that you hardly seem to be outside; to forget the existence of something called the horizon—all that may seem of little moment to one who only thinks about it, but I have seen the spirit of the most indomitable captives undermined by such things. As for me, I should have dwindled away like the rest, I should have lost my gaiety and even my reason, had not de Launay quickly concluded that I deserved certain ameliorations in my daily routine. For not only was I the most stable and well-behaved inmate of the Bastille, I also enjoyed the favor of an anonymous patron powerful enough to pay me a monthly pension. This mystery tormented de Launay so keenly that he tried to extract from me the name of my protector. I demurred, explaining that he was too highly placed for me to name. De Launay, who was bored in the Bastille and coveted the command of the Paris Arsenal, supposed that I might one day prove useful to him, and little by little I obtained some invaluable special arrangements. At the end of two years, I was permitted to loosen two of the six horizontal bars over the window of my cell; as you are a man of imagination, Jean-Jacques, I feel certain that this detail will not seem ludicrous to you. The absence of those two bars allowed me to push out the wire screen over my window and gain access to its monumental embrasure. I sat voluptuously on the ledge, letting my legs dangle against the wall, and from there, I overlooked Paris. The city murmured at my feet, and the west winds sweeping the sky lashed my face. I recalled my joys; I thought about those whom I had loved, about those who had been generous enough to love me. Since my arrest, I had lived chastely; captivity sank my senses into a sort of interminable hibernation, from which I awoke only rarely, lending Nature a hand as a healthful exercise, but without the passion I formerly brought to such activity. My memories, revived up there between heaven and earth, stirred my blood and gave me the desire to renew my ties to the world. I was granted permissions to absent myself from the prison, giving my word of honor to return at the stipulated hour. Then, like Antaeus touching the earth, I walked again on the streets of the city and recovered all my strength. In the beginning, I limited my patrols to the Faubourg Saint-Antoine and Vincennes, for I recoiled before Paris and its rumbling immensity. Before long, however, I found my way to a house of pleasure, where I enthusiastically plunged back into the buxom company of women. Another ten years of my life flew past like a rack of clouds.

During all this time, the scrupulous de Launay kept locked in his strongbox whatever part of my monthly pension remained unspent. Eventually, I found myself in possession of a sum which would allow me to purchase a house. I inspected every quarter of Paris before settling my choice on a building of two stories in the Rue du Petit-Musc. Its thick walls dated from the reign of Henri III and seemed built to last until the end of time, and it offered the advantage of two independent entrances. For a while after buying it, I hardly occupied it; to do so would have meant coming into contact with servants and neighbors; and oddly enough, solitude was often what I sought in the city. I traversed Paris, my old Lucretius under my arm, and sat under the trees of the Champs-Élysées, which at that time was rarely traveled, except for a heavy cart now and then. I read, I meditated, I trampled the grass until the day was gone; when it was no longer possible to read or when the wind freshened, I walked down to the Cours la Reine, amused by the ballet of fashionable carriages and flirts and fops. I cast a glance at the hill of Chaillot, which I had haunted in another of my lives, and retired, exhausted and content, to my prison bed. At other times, when the weather was too bad for walking, I went to a tavern, which had grown up in the shadow of the fortress in the Faubourg Saint-Antoine. There I read the newspapers aloud for the workers from the manufactories, to most of whom reading was unknown. Sometimes I wrote letters for apprentices who wanted to send news to their families in the provinces. And the years passed like the days, in the peopled solitude that prison was for me.

Of all the prisoners in the Bastille, only one made a lasting impression on me. I came to know the Comte de Sade in the year seventeen hundred and eighty-four. He felt great contempt for de Launay and made no attempt to hide it. De Launay took his revenge by subjecting Sade to a regime of barbarous isolation. Sade dwelled in the Tour de la Liberté (the architects of the fortress were wits), occupying, as we said in our jargon, the second Liberté, a poorly ventilated and sunless second floor, without any question the worst accommodations in the entire Bastille.

I cannot tell, Jean-Jacques, whether you ever heard anything of this man Sade, but it seems unlikely. Before you died, he had made one name for himself in the chronicles of the dissolute and another in the world of letters; but you hardly ventured into the second, and you had a horror of the first. For my part, I was already a resident of the Bastille when Sade became a terrible legend repeated by gossips. He must have been forty-five years of age at the time of our meeting. Perhaps out of affectation, or perhaps for a personal reason whose depths I could not sound, he insisted on being called by his former, youthful title, which was that of marquis, and there was none of his jailers who would venture to address him as "Comte," with the unsurprising exception of de Launay, who adhered to the letter of his prisoners' register. Did de Launay think that I could soften his enemy's heart toward him? That he could gain the Marquis' good graces by serving him up a lover of literature (for such he believed me to be, having seen me always with a book)? However that may have been, the day when I entered the second Liberté I learned that there is friendship, just as there is love, at first sight. I know not how our conversation began, but I remember that I immediately felt great fondness for Sade, who evinced as much sympathy toward me as a great nobleman could show an individual with no name. Badly prepared by the governor's counsels, I had expected to encounter a mad beast, thrown into prison by his legitimately horrified family. Had he been, not long ago, such an untamable lion? That I shall never know. Physically, our Provençal noble was a little man, not more than five feet tall. He was so plump that he brought to mind one of those enormous castrated cats, which are so potent in appearance until one remembers the operation they have undergone. Sometimes Sade was a person of such great gentleness as might pass for weakness, but suddenly he would make a show of extreme violence. Was he a bird of prey whose wings were being slowly clipped, day after day? A loud, harmless capon? Time would bring me answers to these questions, or, more precisely, I learned to measure their inadequacies. Later, I shall speak of my feelings on this point.

———

Very soon our friendship took a form more substantial than the minor art of conversation. The Marquis was poor, and the idea of extracting from him the patrimony of the Sade family had counted for nothing in the decision to imprison him in the Bastille. I had a little money, and I was frugal; no one was less frugal than Sade. I opened my purse to him whenever I could; he deigned to help himself to its contents by way of doing me a favor. His gluttony was admirable, voluptuous, precise, and inevitably costly. Sade could converse for hours about an exquisite variety of peaches, which could be found, preserved in bottles, only at the shop of an artisan in Montpellier, or about a macaroon made in Périgueux, flavored with pistachio nuts, an unequaled delicacy. One day I entered the second Liberté and found him beaming like an angel in Paradise: Contrary to their usual practice, his family had yielded to what they considered one of his whims, and he had received a cask of his favorite olive oil. For a month, the fragrance of Provençal dishes filled the courtyards of the Bastille, and Sade, who wished me to taste all of them, never tired of demonstrating the superiority of his forefathers' cuisine to the insipid ragouts of Paris. Before long, I was amusing myself by covering the length and breadth of the capital on his account, furnished with meticulous instructions, searching for a certain variety of marsh-mallow, for a box of incomparably refined chocolate wafers, for a citron syrup which, three months a year, a merchant from Bordeaux offered for sale near the church of Saint-Eustache. When I was so careless that I failed to carry out his requirements exactly, or so bold as to furnish a substitute for what he wished, Sade overwhelmed me with sarcastic abuse, just as if I had spent his money and not my own; how could I not love such a man? All my savings went to feed the sugared stream into which Sade plunged with wild delight, finding there a distraction from the bitterness of his present state. Yet, although I was glad to improve his ordinary fare, I could not but be worried about the effects of such indulgence upon his health. The Marquis needed exercise and a regular diet. The short promenades permitted by de Launay did not suffice, and for the rest, Sade had no notion of self-regulation: A large bag of sweetened marsh-mallows, once opened, was not put aside until it was empty; bottles of wine suffered similar fates; gorging on almond paste never sickened him. He formed a strange relationship with his inclinations; sometimes he seemed their slave, and sometimes he appeared to reign over them like a despot. Moreover, as I soon discovered, he fostered a passion which inspired in him a temperance and a rigor worthy of admiration: The Marquis de Sade was an author. During the first period of our acquaintance, he limited himself to showing me a large portfolio containing the few inoffensive little works which the royal censors had allowed him to keep. I read some of them; although I admired them, I was neither overcome nor touched, and I told him so. My frankness served me well. Finally convinced, after observing me for a year, that I was not a spy for the governor or the Lieutenant-General of the Police, he confided to me that he had been thrown into the Bastille less, perhaps, for the few sexual scandals in which he had been involved than for the enraged impiety of certain licentious writings which had issued from his pen. His libertinism would have been forgiven had he been sufficiently inconsistent to separate it from his radical atheism; but Sade was nothing if not consistent. He suffered the death-in-life of prison while shunning the façade of stoicism to which even the most furious sometimes resort. I told him that the impious literature held more interest for me than the other, whereupon he could restrain himself no longer and revealed to me that he continued to write in that vein, right under the noses of the governor and his henchmen. Now, for a wonder, it was more or less at this same time—that is, near the end of the summer of seventeen hundred and eighty-five—that the excellent de Launay, having observed my friendly relations with the second Liberté, came to my cell one fine morning and with great complacency proposed that, for the benefit of the Kingdom of France and the governor of the Bastille, I should spy upon the Comte de Sade.

When he made me this offer, de Launay did not even give himself the trouble of threatening me; his malicious smile spoke for him. And so I accepted his proposal without hesitation. He left my cell highly pleased with me and with himself. I waited until evening before making my way to Sade's cell. I recounted the whole affair to him, and we laughed heartily before pondering the means of parrying de Launay's thrust; for we had somehow to satisfy our governor, without harming Sade's interests or my own. Here is what we did: I procured some extremely licentious works, including *Thérèse the Philosopher* and *The Carthusians' Porter*, a volume I knew well. Imitating the Marquis' handwriting, I began to compile long extracts from these works, cobbling them together into a vague sort of story, which I made as filthy as possible. I brought a few pages of my masterpiece to de Launay, who rejoiced to see them. He read with delight what his ignorance took for the revolting product of his most depraved resident's imagination. The following day he visited me and announced that he wished to seize the entire manuscript of the prisoner de Sade. I dissuaded him from this course; let Sade finish his work, I said, and then the blow that falls on him will be all the harder. De Launay followed my advice. The guards received the order not to disturb the second Liberté when the prisoner was writing. Naturally, Sade took advantage of this policy by composing, under the very noses of his jailers, pages whose impious obscenity had no equal. For my part, I continued my labors on the execrable, licentious bone we were going to toss to that dog of a de Launay. At the end of three months, I could see his patience nearing its end. I turned over my bundle of pages to the Marquis, who slipped it between two straps of his bedstead. I informed the governor where he should look, and when next his victim went for a promenade in the courtyard, de Launay took advantage of his absence and stole the manuscript. He was even so cruel as to visit Sade the next morning; the Marquis pretended to be suffering great distress, which brought joy to the heart of our myopic and foolish Machiavelli. Sade pushed refinement so far as to write a letter to his wife, telling her that he had shed tears of blood at the loss of his manuscript; de Launay, who opened all his correspondence, announced this triumph to me with jubilation. And, being certain that his broken adversary would not soon return to his vile scribbling, the governor gave me provisional leave from my duties. The Marquis de Sade's blue eyes shone when we celebrated, in secret, our splendid victory. He passionately loved the theater, its darknesses and deceptions, its machines and masks. And to my further surprise, he favored me with a new confidence: The obscene pages he had written under the soldiers' noses formed part of a monumental work which, thus far, he had always managed to conceal from his guards' inspections.

The cool ingenuity of which he gave proof in this matter filled me with admiration. De Launay kept a meticulous record of the amount of paper that Sade received. The Marquis, however, had conceived the stratagem of removing a long strip from each leaf allotted to him and hiding the strips in the pasteboard covers of his portfolio, considering, with reason, that once they were accustomed to him, his guards would never think of searching for forbidden papers in the place where he kept his authorized works. In the solitude of his nights, Sade set down upon those strips of paper the treasures of his flaming imagination. One day, without a word, he handed me a handful of the strange pages; I went back to my cell, sat in the embrasure of my window, and so entered, as if by housebreaking, the oddest tale that ever was. Words fail me at this point, and I know myself incapable of giving a proper idea of such a work. At first, I thought I had to do with one of those lascivious novels destined to be read with but one hand. I felt a heavy disappointment: Sade painted a small group of libertines whose originals I thought I recognized, but who seemed too crudely rendered for me to take delight in their portraits. The obscenity that sprang up in Sade was of a unique and strangely powerful kind. In his philosophical head, debauchery became something methodical and tormenting; he drew figures which represented nothing, and yet one had the sensation that they were the cipher of the world. Soon I forgot the characters of his story and advanced into the petrified forest of human desire. A new Daedalus, Sade had conceived in the depths of his prison the most dizzying of all labyrinths, because it consisted of an alignment of pieces always identical to one another; as it was impossible to lose yourself in this maze, in the end you no longer knew where you were. I admired all this, but with doubled trepidation: What readers did Sade expect to attract? And what would become of him should a work so monstrous fall into the hands of a fool like de Launay?

The Marquis was too courteous to ask me for my opinion, but of too passionate a temperament to enable me to avoid pronouncing some sort of judgment when I gave him back his pages. Not knowing what to say, I found myself murmuring that the portrait he painted of humanity was very dark. Ten years after having said those words, I still blush as I write them. To my great surprise, Sade took no offense at my stupid observation. He looked at me with benevolence, smiling imperceptibly. Then he pointed out that he had already spent more than half his life in the prisons of his country, and that, in his judgment, he was thus justified in writing as he pleased about human society and the motives which governed it. I replied that the despotism of the present regime surely proved him right, but that there must exist some more tolerant, more enlightened society than ours. This time, he frankly laughed, heartily embraced me, and invited me to take a seat at his table, where we talked about a thousand other things. I questioned him, seeking to know whether he had followed, in the past, some master or model. Would you believe it, Jean-Jacques? The Marquis de Sade was your most devoted reader, and he deemed himself your best disciple. He adjured me to read your *Confessions*, saying that he was the only one who had descended more deeply than you into the depths of the human mind. I followed his counsel, and I shall say later what I thought of your memoirs.

It was in the beginning of winter, seventeen hundred and eighty-five, when the Marquis confided to me one of the causes of his anguish. He still feared, and with reason, that his writings would be seized from him and destroyed, and he would have preferred to lose an arm. By this time, his extraordinary work—a handful of whose pages he had submitted to my perusal—had attained a considerable volume and now bore a title. Those *120 Days of Sodom* threatened to take on alarming proportions and formed a suspicious bulge in the covers of his portfolio. It was therefore necessary to find a more secure cache for the manuscript. This proved to be less easy than it appeared. Out of idleness more than cruelty, the guards conducted, every month, a minute search of all the cells. Moreover, we were never left alone; the door of the second Liberté had to remain open, so that the soldier on duty, who turned his back to us out of respect for the prisoner's privacy, could hear everything that was said. These sentinels only turned around if an unusually long silence occurred, an irrefutable sign, for those simple souls, of a conspiracy. Resolved to find a hiding place inside the cell, we conceived the following stratagem. Sade, indefatigable Provençal that he was, undertook to hold forth (as was, in any case, his habit with me—I listened more than I talked) in a loud voice, while I retreated to a blind spot in the wall of his cell and worked, with infinite caution, at loosening a stone. This operation occupied our evenings for a week. Then, hidden from sight, I hollowed out a narrow but deep slit in the heavy stone. Every evening, I was obliged to return it to its place in the wall and cover the chinks with counterfeit mortar, duly soiled to match the color of the wall. This labor required a month. Sade was incapable of relieving me; it often vexed him that his rank had not permitted him the opportunity of learning any trade whatsoever, and in labor of the hands he exhibited a remarkable clumsiness. And so it also fell to me to glue long strips of blank paper together, arriving in the end at a roll five inches wide by thirty feet long. Then the interminable toil of copying began. Sade himself, of course, undertook that terrible task. The difficulties he had to overcome in the endeavor cannot be imagined. It was my turn to hold forth. He drew all sorts of papers out of his portfolio and read their contents in a low voice. Then he copied them, making corrections as he proceeded. He suffered a thousand tortures, for, in order to keep the manuscript to a size that might be stored in its stone tabernacle, Sade was compelled to write in small characters—a wearisome job for a man who for years had suffered from acute ocular pain. Nevertheless, the sufferer accomplished the feat at prodigious speed, covering the recto of his peculiar parchment in ten days and the verso in the same length of time; and the *120 Days* found a secure refuge in the thickness of those very walls wherein the world's stupidity thought to contain the Marquis' singular genius.

Despite our triumphs, Sade continued to wear himself out. In the presence of that solitary man, why did my thoughts ineluctably return to the memory of Robert François Damiens' tortured body? What did the imperious feudal lord have in common with the obscure domestic servant? I believe that those two antipodean characters resembled each other in their suffering. Of course, Sade's fate appeared infinitely preferable to that of Damiens. The latter was immolated upon an altar medieval in its barbarity, and in a manner so fiendishly cruel that he was the last man to undergo such a public outrage. Sade was the victim of a new order of cruelty, less spectacular, less bloody, but still terrible. The regicide was publicly torn to pieces; Sade was buried alive. He was daily subjected to mortifications which, taken one by one, seemed comparatively mild: a promenade cut short, a letter censored, an intimate search of his person. But all this, combined with his interminable sentence, constituted a frightful torment, which he endured far from the eyes of decent folk, who in any case would have found nothing amiss in his plight. And although de Launay was an authentic imbecile, while Sade was the most refined aristocrat of the Ancien Régime in France, these facts were of no account; the former had power over the latter, and that difference prevailed over everything else. It caused the Marquis to spend many a day searching for a means of exasperating the governor, harassing him with his vocal gibes and his written requests, and drawing ferocious, terribly precise portraits of his nemesis in every one of his letters. I had not the heart to be amused by the spectacle of so eminent an intellect wasting his energy in an attempt to overwhelm that bottomless abyss, the soul of a fool. It seemed certain to me that de Launay would have the last word, and that Sade was exhausting himself in vain. In this assurance, however, I was mistaken.

Years passed. In seventeen hundred and eighty-eight we went through a period of great alarm, for Sade obtained permission to transfer his lodging to the sixth Liberté—a cell which in summer was far too hot, but which he preferred because it received better light—and we were obliged to repeat on the sixth floor the ruse we had employed on the second. The ever more voluminous manuscript of the *120 Days* was given a new home, and I carefully obliterated all trace of its former hiding place. The winter of seventeen hundred and eighty-eight was so harsh that the arrival of spring, with its periods of bright, warm sunshine and its fresh, moist breezes, seemed to us like a resurrection. Fine vegetables adorned my table, while that of the Marquis was laden with fruits transported at exorbitant expense from far-off Spain. Once again, I read my Lucretius. I looked no more than sixty years old, though, in fact, I had some time since passed eighty. Assuming that my death was near and having no appetite for suffering, I hoped to be seized and taken while I was yet in good health. In the last week of April, a noise arising from the Faubourg Saint-Antoine caused me to raise my eyes from my book. A bloody riot had broken out in a factory that produced paper hangings; its proprietor, to his workers' fury, had lowered their wages. Sade complained bitterly about this uproar; not, obviously, because he sympathized with the merchant, a respectable bourgeois named Réveillon, but because such circumstances gave de Launay a pretext for forbidding the Marquis' promenades around the battlements of the fortress, walks that provided Sade with the only occasions when he could feel the light of the sun on his skin. The governor quickly suppressed them. He confined Sade's outdoor activities to the second courtyard, a gloomy hole the sun never entered, and where the prisoner was obliged, every time a visitor crossed his path, to huddle in a niche especially constructed for this purpose, so that he could not enter upon any relation with the passerby. While I consoled Sade as best I could, he plundered one of his stores of dried fruits, devouring apricots by the handful. In the course of the following days, to calm his agitation, I undertook to describe the turmoil to him according to the accounts of it which I picked up in the neighboring taverns, and I succeeded so well that in the end the Marquis rejoiced, already envisioning himself liberated by the people and borne in triumph to the capital. Nonetheless, several months passed without event.

The period of calm came to an end in the second week of July, and roving bands of citizens, hotly pursued by royal troops, could be seen from the ramparts of the Bastille. On Monday the thirteenth, the noise of the crowd, which heretofore had diminished toward evening and fallen almost completely silent with the coming of night, seemed instead to grow louder as the air cooled and the shadows lengthened. I approached one of our guards, who were soldiers from the Invalides, and asked him the cause of all this disturbance. He replied with an ill grace, because he and his comrades had spent the previous night shifting the barrels of gunpowder which Monsieur de Launay had requisitioned from the nearby Arsenal, and which the soldiers had been obliged to haul from the interior courtyard to the cellars. The mob had seized the Invalides without meeting any resistance from the troops; apparently, the force in the Bastille was preparing to withstand a siege. As was his wont, poor de Launay had proceeded in a manner directly opposed to good sense: In the entire Bastille, there was no more than a day's store of water in reserve, and the other provisions would suffice for two days at most. The soldiery thus had enough ammunition to blaze away until summer, but they ran the risk of dying from hunger and thirst before the month was out. Moreover, de Launay believed that he could count on reinforcements, in which belief he gravely overestimated both his King and the kingdom; but who, at the time, did not do the same?

The popular tumult did not subside, and I hardly slept during the night between the thirteenth and fourteenth of July, a night filled with cries and indistinct noises, pierced from time to time by musket fire. Our governor, who knew his military manual by heart—though he had never put its precepts into practice—replied to each musket shot with a salvo of cannon. In all my life, I have never been able to do without a night's sleep; so at the first light of dawn, when calm finally returned, I fell at once into the arms of Morpheus. In the general commotion, the guards neglected to awaken me, and thus I spent the first half of July fourteenth, our great national day, in my slumbers. Are you perhaps wondering, Jean-Jacques, what became of Sade? Alas! It seems that the man was ever a victim of the most savage irony. The previous week, the poor Marquis had been transferred to another prison, a move that came about in the following way. As I have said, the beginnings of the uprising in the faubourgs had engendered a mad hope in Sade's heart. Seeing in those riotous events the means to make de Launay lose his reason as well as his dignity, Sade set up a great cry from his cell window, shouting that the prisoners of the Bastille were being murdered. Addressing the people passing by as his neighbors, his fellows, his brothers, he exhorted them to cast down that citadel of royal despotism and caprice. For the twentieth time since taking up his post in the Bastille, de Launay officially requested the transfer of Monsieur de Sade to the asylum for the insane in Charenton; the stated reason for de Launay's request was that the prisoner Sade was fitter for a hospital than for a jail. And this time, de Launay was granted the favor, which hitherto he had always been refused; during the night of July third, he received orders to turn over Monsieur de Sade to the authorities at Charenton. As may be imagined, de Launay, hardly able to believe that his eldest and dearest wish had come true, acted with the utmost promptness in carrying out those orders. He went at once to Sade's cell, rousted him from his bed, consigned him to a numerous escort, and flung him into a fiacre paid for at his—the governor's—personal expense. The transport of Sade's effects was postponed until later, and de Launay remained for a long time on the parvis of the Bastille, watching the fiacre disappear into the night and savoring for as long as possible the barrage of insults shouted at him by his dearest enemy. As for the fourteenth day of July in the year seventeen hundred and eighty-nine, Donatien Alphonse François, Comte de Sade, lived through it alone, far from men and History, far from his books and his sweetmeats, naked under his cotton dressing gown, and surrounded by lunatics and fools.

PART THREE

Revolutions

At two o'clock in the afternoon of July fourteenth, the crackle of musketry awakens me. A smell of burning hay and fresh dung drifts into my cell, mingled with an acrid odor I do not recognize, but which will soon become quite familiar: the smell of burnt gunpowder. I rise from my bed. My door is closed from the outside, a state of affairs which has not occurred thrice in twenty years. I call out. Nobody comes. Thirst troubles me more than hunger, and quite soon my voice gives out. I lie down again and several hours go by, but I am never able to go back to sleep. Finally, a violent rush of stamping feet resounds from the stairway very near me. I drum on my door. A voice commands me to identify myself; I do so, and am advised to stand aside. The lock is dismantled and the door broken in; a fat man, his face blackened by powder and streaked with sweat, embraces me, loudly declares me a free man, and thrusts me toward the landing. I step out into a hail of applause from a small, disparate troop of workers, craftsmen, and bourgeois. I dare not speak of my thirst. I thank the people politely, but in an inaudible voice. Finally, a woman gives me a drink of water, bathes my face, makes me sit. I am assailed with questions about the whereabouts of the other prisoners. Thus far, only five have been found; I assure the crowd that this is an accurate count, but my corroboration of the number does not satisfy my liberators. They press me to reveal the location of the dungeons into which the forces of despotism have flung the bulk of their victims; they demand to know if I have witnessed any ghastly mass executions. I patiently repeat that the Bastille has fallen almost into disuse. Disappointment, immediately succeeded by incredulity, is visible on their faces: Life in prison must have affected me; the mistreatment to which I have been subjected has addled my mind. They abandon me and rush up to the floor above, hoping to find someone better informed. I go downstairs. An insurgent is holding a bottle. Rumor enshrouds me; I am a hero of liberty; I am offered a drink. The wine is strong and turns my head. I am acclaimed. In the general enthusiasm, I am handed a musket, powder cartridges and balls are stuffed into my pockets, and I am pounded with friendly claps on my back and sides. I walk out onto the esplanade, the scene of indescribable disorder, and I sit down upon a milestone in the Rue Saint-Antoine, where the mighty tide of the crowd finally strands me. I make an effort to recover my wits, sitting on my milestone and leaning on my gun.

Torn from my brief repose by an exceptionally forceful movement of the crowd, I realize that if I do not wish to be trampled, I must return to the fortress. A man is led before the people gathered on the esplanade, and only with difficulty do I recognize de Launay, whose face bears a look of infinite distress. He carries neither cane nor sword, wears neither wig nor hat. Artisans and workers cry out around him, and vagrants imitate him for their amusement. Some in the crowd enthusiastically demand that his head be chopped off. Others would prefer to hang him. Those with most imagination propose that he be tied to a horse's tail and dragged through Paris, but their proposal is lost in the ambient din. De Launay is going to die—everyone knows or senses his imminent fate—and the simple and terrible truth of the moment doubtless strikes even the man himself. He should try to die well, but instead he turns into a whimpering puppet. I am stung with pity for this poltroon, crushed as he is by the burden of having suddenly to represent, in the eyes of a furious crowd, years and years of despotism. The mob is drunk with its power, and with the wine its members have consumed by way of giving themselves the heart for an outrageous deed. Impelled by spontaneous compassion, I try to draw close to their victim, but the press of the throng prevents me. Six paces away, de Launay emanates a terror so abject that some onlookers divert their eyes from him in embarrassment; if in this instant he could find the courage to harangue the crowd, he could save his life. I see that one of his eyelids is prodigiously swollen, and that he is bleeding from his right ear. He says nothing. I finally reach his side, but he fails to recognize me. I support de Launay while a long procession sets out to bring him to the Hôtel de Ville, where his fate will be decided. A man whom I know by sight soon lends me a hand, and now we are virtually carrying the dazed wretch. My reinforcement, a cook by trade, is named Desnot. At first we advance slowly and with great difficulty, all the while receiving—Desnot and I—a generous portion of the insults and spittle meant for de Launay. He is called a mangy dog, a traitor, and other niceties of the sort. I foresee the moment when he will be torn to pieces by the maddened crowd, and I tremble for myself. To my good fortune, a cabinetmaker from the Rue Saint-Antoine recognizes me; in a stentorian voice, he declares who I am; and like the waters of the Red Sea, the rabble parts, making a passage for us to the Hôtel de Ville, and cheering me as well as Desnot, who puffs up his chest with pride. I am the object of everyone's gaze, for the rumor that precedes us like waves running before the stern of a ship transforms me into the Victim of Royal Despotism, Generously Supporting His Oppressor. I am the first Noble Old Man of the new times, which will be mad for such venerable figures. I believe myself nearly clear of the entire affair, but then our convoy again comes to a halt, near the church of Saint-Louis. There de Launay loses his head and resolves to speak to the mob, now that the time for speaking is past and his right course of action would be to proceed as quickly as possible to the haven of the Hôtel de Ville, which is but a few steps away. Deranged by fear, the governor spreads out his arms, rolls his great eyes, and shouts that he is being murdered, that he is innocent. At first, the crowd is touched, but just as a young soldier thrown into the heat of battle grows irritated by the pity he feels for a wounded adversary, turns his anger against the object of his compassion, and suddenly dispatches the unfortunate fellow, so, too, in the end does the throng pounce on de Launay and snatch him in its jaws with a violence which flings me ten steps away. He continues to shout and struggle, and in the confusion he deals Desnot, who has not released his hold on him, an inadvertent blow to the lower belly. The cook shouts in agony, crying out that he is slain. Then it seems that bayonets spring up around the two men. All at once, the governor's shirt turns bright red, and then darkens. His body rolls toward the gutter which carries refuse down the middle of the street. A few brave hearts, not to be outdone, discharge their pistols into the corpse's chest. As for Desnot, he is lifted up unhurt from the ground where he lay. A sword is put into his hand; since the dog of a governor injured him, it is only right that Desnot should take his revenge. Without hesitation, the cook steps over to the gory, miry heap of rags that was once a man.

He pierces the dead throat with the point of his sword, but handles the weapon badly and casts it aside. Then he draws a butcher's knife from a pocket in his vest and finishes the job properly, like a man whose occupation has accustomed him to working with all kinds of meat. People around him lift up the severed head; joyous clamor greets the tragic conclusion; and the crowd moves away to parade its trophy all around the city.

Night fell at last, along with torrents of rain coming in from the west. Drenched to the bone in an instant, I ran to the shelter of the nearest porch, while muddy streams spread across the entirely deserted parvis of the church of Saint-Louis and flowed toward the Seine, carrying with them the governor's blood and canceling it from the memory of men. His body had been borne away to serve some barbaric rite of profanation I preferred not to imagine. I was free, as the saying goes. I was two steps from my house in the Rue de Petit-Musc. I supposed that the King would send in his troops and order the police to recapture the prisoners of the Bastille in order to show who was master. Where could I find a safe place to sleep that night, I wondered, if not in the Bastille? I therefore retraced my steps. Upon the parvis of the fortified stronghold, amid the bars ripped out and thrown down from the cell windows, amid the charred, broken-in doors, stood poor Caesar, bent with the weight of his years, receiving the acclamations of the crowd. When our eyes met, the unfortunate madman hurried to my side; some of his admirers had seen fit to make him drunk with wine, and he stank all the more because the imperial triumph for which he had waited all his life had so upset him that he had soiled his breeches. I wrenched Caesar away from his drunken subjects and escorted him to the drawbridge. What might be called the provisional government of Paris had posted a detachment there to avoid excesses; I introduced myself to the person I took for the commander of the group. Deeply imbued with the importance of his mission, this neighborhood notary listened attentively to my explanations and granted us a pass written in a beautiful hand. Still supporting Caesar, I entered the devastated, deserted Bastille, where perfect calm reigned. In the second interior courtyard, I found the means of washing my protégé a little. We reached the Tour de la Comté; I installed Caesar on the third floor, where he fell asleep at once, and then descended to the floor below and lay down in my turn.

On the morning of July fifteenth, I awoke at dawn, calm and refreshed. I decided to inspect the fortress. My steps drew me, almost mechanically, to the sixth Liberté. There a lamentable spectacle awaited me; the cell was wide open and littered with the remains of Sade's personal effects. Tears sprang to my eyes at the frightful disorder: scattered handwritten pages, overturned bookcases, some torn volumes lying in a puddle of wine. The Marquis' favorite armchair lay disemboweled, its straw entrails spilling out. In the very center of the room, some slashed wall hangings and a writing desk reduced to kindling wood formed the vestiges of a fire which the pillagers had built but not managed to set ablaze, and which they had then bepissed and beshat together. A pestilential odor filled the cell. The perpetrators of this crime had not been among the little band which seized the Bastille. I knew those men well; they would have scrupled to steal so much as a handkerchief from the place. But beginning with the very first evening, the magnificent vessel of the Revolution drew to its wake a host of carrion feeders, who nourished themselves on its refuse and never disappeared. I hastened over to the wall, pulled the heavy stone from its lodgment, and rejoiced when I felt under my fingers the swollen roll of *The*

120 Days of Sodom. Slipping the roll under my shirt, I left the sixth Liberté forever. I went to Caesar's room and awakened him; he seemed to have completely forgotten the tumults of the preceding day. I turned him over to the guards of the Bastille but kept my notarial pass; then, hoping to sell Sade's manuscript, I went to see a bookseller of my acquaintance in his shop near the Tuileries. This was my reasoning: To find Sade and give him back his property would be a dangerous business, both for me and for him; to keep the *120 Days* in my building in the Rue du Petit-Musc would be to run the risk of imprisonment. To sell the work would be to give it a chance, however small, of escaping oblivion, for there were in Europe a dozen rich, jaded eccentrics whom the extraordinary obscenity of Sade's book would inflame, who would fight one another to possess it, and who would be obliged to shield it from the vigilance of all censors. I sold the document at a good price and returned to the Bastille that same evening.

As I enter the first courtyard, I am greeted, in a familiar way, by a stranger: a cordial man, sweeping of gesture and mighty of belly, with full, pink cheeks, lively, darting eyes, and a gourmand's lips. He introduces himself to me: Pierre-François Palloy, patriot. And, in equal measure, Norman, he says, and then favors me with the history of his family, occasionally questioning me about mine but never waiting for an answer. Palloy has learned my story from the gallant notary, with whom he is slightly acquainted, having once assisted his wife's brother in a trial of some delicacy. He proceeds to give me a circumstantial account of the said trial, and my head begins to revolve. At last, I discover what he wants from me. Pierre-François Palloy desires to obtain the services of a man who knows the Bastille—the Bastille, which the City of Paris has charged him, Palloy, a man of law, a man of business, and a patriot, with demolishing. I am surprised to hear that a fortress which has fallen on the fourteenth of July should be in the hands of a demolisher on the fifteenth, and I say so. The fellow laughs heartily at my remark and tightens his crushing grip on my forearm, which he seized at the start of our conversation and which he will later return to me, but only with reluctance. He hauls me into the nearest tavern; finishes a pitcher of claret; orders a second; and finally, his rate of talk undiminished, explains the business he is engaged in, all the while looking like a disreputable horse dealer.

For several years, the government had desired to close the Bastille, which was too dilapidated and costly a prison. Palloy had regularly applied to the city authorities for the post of director of this operation, which was a matter of public safety, but the decisions were long in coming. However, what the King of France had been unable to begin in three years, his people had accomplished in a few hours. Palloy was one of the first to storm across the drawbridge of the Bastille, in the midst of the flames and the tumult of weapons; or so he affirms. He shows everyone in the tavern the collar of his coat, where there is a hole which could have been made by a musket ball. Before our eyes, the patriot Palloy represents his taking of the Bastille. So convincing is his performance that the tavern audience applauds him loudly at the end. Then, in a softer voice, he takes up again the thread of his explanations. He knows all the gentlemen who make up the city council; his particular friend is the Marquis de La Salle, who is, as of this morning, the man charged with supervising the demolition of our Bastille; and who, moreover, is a charming, refined person, celebrated for the beauty of his lace cuffs, and an expert at every game of cards. He is, however, insofar as the work of architecture and excavation is concerned, a thorough incompetent. And so the excellent Marquis has charged his good friend Palloy with those operations, whose destructive aspects rather shock his aristocratic sensibilities. Palloy in turn needs a supervisor who is neither dishonest nor lazy. He speaks in plain terms. He likes, he says, my frank appearance and holds out his hand to seal our agreement. I consider my orator. I tell myself that Pierre-François Palloy is a shamelessly long-winded rogue, perhaps a madman, and certainly an eccentric. In short, I feel that I cannot but love the man. We reach an accord on my salary. Palloy gives me precise, judicious instructions, arranges to meet me the day after tomorrow, and then disappears, as swiftly as he came. I set to work.

My first task consisted in the hiring of a thousand workers—an undertaking all too easy, alas, in those miserable times! I began with the craftsmen: about a hundred altogether, including masons, carpenters, and locksmiths. I found some of them myself, in various taverns, and charged them with raising the rest. Notices posted here and there in the neighborhood immediately furnished me with hundreds of unfortunates who had no trade and could expect to do no more than haul debris and carry crates. I formed my battalions of craftsmen and with the help of my recruiters chose two men of experience and authority to oversee each group of twenty workers. At dawn on July seventeenth they were assembled and ready to work, awaiting my signal to begin. With the aid of a lever, I amused myself by prying loose part of a battlement atop those forbidding walls and sending it crashing down. It landed with a big, slapping sound in a ditch, accompanied by the laughter and cheers of my men. I did not have to wait long for Monsieur Palloy. Around nine o'clock that morning, he made his entrance onto the esplanade of the Bastille, at the head of a long, slow convoy of quarry carts, pulled by heavy draft horses from the Perche and the Boulonnais, which looked as though they had stepped out of an old engraving. At noon my laborers presented themselves for hiring, as they had been required to do, and awaited our further orders.

I innocently asked Palloy where we were going to discharge the rubble, the furniture, and all the little objects which the plunderers had neglected, and whose volume threatened to be considerable. Palloy was waiting for the question. He chuckled with pleasure, patted his thighs, and confided to me his real project. What he had refrained from mentioning to the Marquis de La Salle or to anyone in the municipal administration was that there was to be no question of casting away the ruins of the fortress. Palloy intended to use the stone and wood to supply twenty building yards, charge them whatever he paid his workers, more or less, and thus realize immense profits. During the two days when he left me alone in the Bastille, Palloy had not remained idle; he had procured an audience in the Hôtel de Ville. The Grand Electors, fearful that excessively violent disturbances would lead the King to send his troops against the Parisians, proposed to appease the populace by promptly razing the useless and despised Bastille, and they looked approvingly upon the prospect of allowing a thousand beggars to earn a little money in the course of a few months. Neglecting to mention his plans for the debris, Palloy had even obtained compensation for his trouble in ridding the city of the old fortress. And this was how, in the evening of July sixteenth, seventeen hundred and eighty-nine, Pierre-François Palloy, contractor, became the proprietor of everything that lay within the premises of the Bastille, with the exception of the weapons, powder, and archives, all of which the Marquis de La Salle, mounted on a splendid chestnut horse, gaily beribboned and carefully groomed, accompanied to the nearby Arsenal. Palloy owned an unused quarry not far from the village of Pantin, northeast of Paris, and that quarry was the destination of our heavy carts. Our workers applied themselves with great ardor, because Palloy had promised the most zealous of them employment in one of his building sites, and also because most of them, much exercised against royal authority, wished to be among the first to discover the secret torture chambers and the filthy dungeons which, according to rumor, were to be found in great numbers in the Bastille. Need I say it? They found nothing. With a single exception: One winter morning, we all rushed en masse toward a cellar from whose entrance, with great clamor, two young workers were calling us. I parted the crowd and entered. Bones were scattered all over the cellar floor. I told the workers that they had made no mistake and that a great massacre had indeed been perpetrated in that place; then, laughing, I showed them the pork ribs and chicken bones and beef carcasses which generations of negligent cooks had thrown into the abandoned cellar, which was situated three paces away from the kitchens. The legends concerning the prison governors who were torturers, the cages left over from the days of the diabolical King Louis XI, and the cannibal jailers nonetheless continued to spread throughout Paris and all its faubourgs. So valiantly did we labor that within a few months nothing remained of the mighty fortress but its razed foundations. And on July fourteenth, seventeen hundred and ninety, under tents pitched all over that immense space of level ground, the citizens of Paris danced until the coming of the dawn.

When, like everyone else in the kingdom, Palloy began to understand that the skirmish of July fourteenth would not soon be forgotten, he hesitated for quite a while. He pondered whether it would be truly wise to use the materials heaped up in Pantin for the purposes he had originally intended. As early as the summer of seventeen hundred and eighty-nine, people had started singing songs about the Storming of the Bastille, as it was henceforward called, and though many months passed, the song makers returned to the theme again and again, and the revolutionary turbulence continued. By December seventeen hundred and eighty-nine, most of the fortress was in Pantin. We then attacked the foundations, and in May seventeen hundred and ninety, the work accomplished, we discharged our workers. Earlier that same year, the winds of History had swelled the sails of Palloy's fleet, and its glorious admiral had been equal to the occasion. We made a prudent beginning on February sixth, seventeen hundred and ninety, by sounding the depths, that is, by going, Palloy and I, before the National Assembly and solemnly depositing there the last stone of the Bastille; the representatives of the people received our offering with sincere emotion. Palloy himself wept tears of great conviction. We returned to Pantin, and this time we put on full sail and embarked on the most remarkable, most systematic, and most brazen commercial scheme of the new era. In the presence of his notary, Palloy appointed two clerks whose employment would be to draw up little certificates attesting that such and such a stone, of such and such nature and dimensions, had indeed come from the Bastille. Most of the large stones from the fortress measured four feet long by two feet wide; under my instructions, sculptors were charged with carving models of the prison into these stones. Early in the month of September, seventeen hundred and ninety, Palloy conscientiously presented to the National Constituent Assembly the first of our sculpted stones, accompanied by its certificate of authenticity, at the bottom of which he had affixed a seal of nearly Spartan sobriety: IN THE NAME

OF THE PATRIOT PALLOY, DIRECTOR OF THE DEMOLITION OF THE BASTILLE BY THE WILL OF THE PEOPLE. His initiative was applauded as it deserved. Just as we had hoped, several newspapers gave accounts of the ceremony, and soon there appeared, printed in the same newspapers, in Paris and throughout France, advertisements announcing the possibility of purchasing a set of patriotic souvenirs. Our customers received a box containing a carved and certified stone, a map of the Bastille, and an engraving which portrayed the patriot Palloy, rushing to assault the fortress. There was also a booklet describing the battle of July fourteenth and adorned with an image representing the skeletons which had been found lodged in the Bastille's foundations. (Palloy had cut short my protests on this point, saying that the image, however inexact in fact, was nonetheless truthful as an idea, for royal absolutism had fed on the very flesh of the poor.) Each subdivision—or, to use the new term, department—of the new France received three of these boxes, provided that the new administrators agreed to display the souvenirs in the public places best suited to serve for the edification of the citizenry. Naturally, Palloy did not require the departments to pay for their patriotic treasures; all he asked was to be reimbursed for the expenses of transport, which, by a strange chance, were always larger than the sums he himself had been obliged to pay. Then, by virtue of a healthy emulation, all the newly named civil officials wished to possess their own genuine piece of the Bastille; and Palloy charged them heavily for everything. In town halls, in police headquarters, people ordered their souvenir sets from the Patriot of Paris. We were obliged to open an office, for which I assumed responsibility. We played the game properly, Palloy and I; under our superintendence, nothing went to waste; everything was transformed in the sheds we had erected in Pantin to shelter our artisans as they worked.

If metal pieces taken from certain walls had nothing attractive about them, we had them melted down and made into the balls and chains of the Bastille. From the several boxes of official papers we had concealed from the vigilance of the Marquis de La Salle, we fashioned ladies' fans and cornets, which were then filled with sweets; upon those pages which were blank but certified authentic, we had playing cards printed, but cards of a particular kind: Ordinary citizens replaced the jacks, and bourgeois gentlemen the kings. In our hands, the Bastille became an inexhaustible horn of plenty, bringing forth snuffboxes and medals, portable inkwells and toothpicks, while the doors of the cells, polished and varnished, became revolutionary card tables.

By the end of the winter of seventeen hundred and ninety, I had grown weary of our trade, and one morning I asked my excellent master for my freedom. Palloy protested and cried out that I was a renegade. He embraced me a thousand times, calling me his brother and trying to move me to alter my design; then, having failed in this effort, he allowed me to go in peace, but not before he made me promise that, should I write an account of my years in the damp dungeons of despotism, I would grant him the right of publication. I so promised and went off, choosing to cover the distance between Pantin and the capital on foot. It was early; I was alone on the road; spring was announcing its imminent arrival; during the night, rain had softened the ground, and the perfumes of the earth mounted to my nostrils. I would soon reach the age of eighty-six. Madame Paris had died some time previously, carried off by the smallpox before I could see her again and express to her the entirety of my gratitude. She had long since retired from her profession and lived amid general esteem. Her establishment, moved to some address in the Rue du Roule, survived her there in a new neighborhood unknown to me. One day, by chance, I walked down Rue de Bagneux. The mansion at number 19 was occupied by a lumber merchant. As for Michel, no one was ever able to tell me where he had gone after his mistress's death.

I had a better reason than age or nostalgia for quitting Palloy: I still felt curious about the world, because the world was changing. I state the case without shame: I believed in the Revolution. During the first year, one could perceive in Paris the ambient shimmer which bears the maddest of names: liberty. The Parisians walked the streets with an air of calm goodwill, and they had never seemed to me so beautiful. Small, trivial tokens of change enchanted me, because from now on, trivial things were important. A new custom prevailed in our theaters, for example: Not only was the name of the playwright indicated, but also the names of the actors in the play. Collections taken up to help the indigent were never so numerous as they were in those days. When the first anniversary of the storming of the Bastille drew near, the authorities resolved to organize a public feast, the Fête de la Fédération, and something that took place in Paris in connection with that celebration won me over definitively to the cause of the French Revolution. Here are the facts: Two days before the feast, people began to say that the earthworks on the plain of the Champ-de-Mars (which had been chosen as the site of the festivities) would not be finished in time. I betook myself to the spot. The artificial hills and ramparts remained appallingly incomplete, almost formless, for lack of sufficient numbers of workers. Here, far from its final state, sprawled part of the immense circular rampart where the deputies were to have their places; over there, the altar of the Fatherland, which had been erected in front of the Invalides, needed to be shored up. The rumor, it turned out, was sadly accurate, and it spread like wildfire. Within a few hours, groups began to form and converge on that muddy plain. Armed with wheelbarrows and shovels, and often with naught but their own resolve, the citizens of France, old and young, men and women, representing all conditions, received in that place, at their own hands, their first national education. It lasted two full days. Thanks to Palloy, I knew how to direct teams and organize tasks in sequence. Like the others, I did my part. And, through the diligence of a disparate, stouthearted, and joyous people, everything was made ready in time.

The feast of July fourteenth, seventeen hundred and ninety, was generally considered a perfect success. It rained for six consecutive hours that day, but the people made jokes about the storm, saying that God must be on the side of the aristocrats. Be that as it might, the aristocratic side did not prevail. The day's celebrations, however, brought me less happiness than the industrious festivities of the twelfth and thirteenth of July had done. The occupants of the official tribunes looked too rigid, too solemn, too starched. I considered them without comprehending what it was about them that displeased me. Then I looked at their hands, and I understood: They were clean. And I was struck by an obvious truth: In the immense procession formed by the assembly of various social groups, no children had been invited to participate, nor women, nor beggars, nor any of the old men who, only the day before, had been pushing and pulling heavy wheelbarrows, putting the final touches to preparations for a feast they would never attend. The Fête de la Fédération was missing only one thing, but the omission was terrible: the federated people. Moved by a strange desire to imitate the pomp of the Ancien Régime, the young Republic went astray. Above the great field, on the terraced steps laid out in the antique style, the constituted authorities occupied their lofty places! Of course, the people of France were there, behind the barriers, all the beggars of Paris, all the bourgeois from the provinces, all the artisans and all the peasants, come from every corner of the kingdom. They contemplated their representatives, and they were happy. They leaned toward the mirror of the Fête de la Fédération; enchanted by what they saw, mistakenly convinced that they recognized themselves, they acclaimed, in fact, their new masters. Many of these men and women were in Paris for the first time in their lives; they had traveled far to see the nation, and along the way they had indeed met people like themselves, in ever increasing numbers. On the twelfth and thirteenth of July, when they reached the plain of the Champ-de-Mars, the nation was there, because they were the nation; and joy swelled their breasts. When the feast was over, they left, believing that the nation would continue to exist without them, for they had beheld its gleaming countenance. They were utterly mistaken.

In the middle of fall in that same year, seventeen hundred and ninety, a bankruptcy about which I understood nothing carried off all my savings at one blow. I had finished furnishing my house in the Rue du Petit-Musc. I loved the Revolution, but although it occupied itself mightily with daily bread, it required one to earn his own. I accepted philosophically the end of my idleness. I now needed to find some person willing to give employment to an old man, even to one as spry as myself. I read the gazettes, I examined the notices posted in the streets, I went to every address, but I had no success. This lasted so long that I could glimpse the bottom of my coffer, and with it the commencement of misery. In the month of September, seventeen hundred and ninety-one, I placed my own notice, subtracting thirty years from my age, and received a reply; a very simple and very courteous note invited me to present myself as soon as possible. The note had been written on the back of a small handbill, which bore the address of an establishment called the Chinese Baths. I set out at once. I had never heard of these Chinese Baths. They were located at the gates of Paris, on the Picardy road, in a countryside where I had often gone walking in former days, but where I had last set foot some twenty years previously. I recalled the landscape as decidedly pleasant, with its orchards and dairies. A surprise awaited me. When I had almost reached my destination, I traversed, lost in thought, the tree-planted avenue which had long marked the limits of Paris. But when I raised my eyes again, I discovered a new section of the city, so large that it hid the horizon. Paris had spilled over into the Faubourg Poissonnière. What had once been the country was no longer distinguishable from Paris, except by its newness, its clean façades and wide, straight streets. The very passersby had a youthful air, which reminded me of the liveliest hours in the Palais-Royal. A powerful odor of dung and horses rose from the royal stables, built on that plain, far from the noise and confusion of the capital, in the days of Louis the Great. A whole population of iron craftsmen, master saddlers, and blacksmiths worked there, as well as the actors and others employed in the nearby theaters. A water seller obligingly directed me to the location of the Chinese Baths; I reached their gate without difficulty; and then I stepped back across the avenue to gain some distance and admire the building, which well deserved admiration.

The most Chinese attribute of these baths was their colorful decoration, which stood out against the gray of the neighboring buildings. There were three floors in each of the two wings; these were buildings standing on two sides and joined in the middle by a third, yet more imposing façade, which presented itself to the visitor. A grand portico doing its best (which apparently sufficed for the Parisians) to imitate the pagodas of the Far East opened onto a vast courtyard. Under the portico, water from two fountains coursed down sheer, artificial rock, surmounted by a plaster statue representing a sort of round-paunched, shaven-headed hermit holding a parasol. Other rocks, adorned with fauns and naiads, decorated the courtyard, as well as tubs containing slightly faded orange trees, in whose shade one could sip drinks, hot or cold, or eat sherbets. The baths were approached by climbing a flight of wooden stairs at the rear of the courtyard. These opened into an enormous salon, illuminated by torches night and day, so that the whole place was fragrant of hot resin. From the salon, the visitor gained access to the floors with the baths proper, which occupied the entire north wing. It was especially in the decoration of these various rooms that the architect, who probably never left Paris, had given expression to his most unbridled Chinese impulses. He repeated ad nauseam the motif of the dragon: on the tops of the doors, on the jade shutters of every window. His raging Oriental fever had engendered an orgy of the brightest colors: The façades were painted vermilion, the window openings saffron yellow; in the corridors, there were bright blue panels and tapestries of a soft, almost languid green, while the roof was all aglitter with glazed tiles, which looked genuinely Pekinese to me, and which came from Dijon. Above the whole fluttered slender banners, snapping in the west wind. The extravagant building accomplished the feat of being charming in spite of itself, and the Parisians frequented it in great numbers, together with many foreigners, particularly Germans, recognizable by the guidebooks they solemnly consulted for fear of traveling improperly.

Thus, looking upward, I passed through the gates of the Chinese Baths and loved that strange place at once. I crossed the garden, presented myself at the desk, and was requested to wait in a small office. A woman who looked to be fifty-some years old entered the room. She greeted me cheerfully and naturally, and asked questions about my former occupations; I spoke frankly of Madame Paris and the Rue de Bagneux, dwelling rather less on the little jobs I had done while in B——'s employment. I was on the point of dissembling about the Bastille, describing my part in its demolition while suppressing the fact of my residence therein. She spoke a few words, giving me some sort of explanation, but of what I had no notion, for at that instant I stopped listening to her words and harkened to her voice, rich with strange, almost singing overtones; it was like the voice of a foreign woman who has learned our tongue by ear, and it charmed me like the memory of an old air whose words I was unable to recall. She became aware of my agitation and fell silent. It seemed to me that I must respond at once to the secret call of that voice. I began telling her about my years in Geneva, my meeting with the Comte, my love affair with Denise. I even spoke about you, Jean-Jacques. She did not interrupt me. In the end, renouncing all prudence, I related to her the adventure of our Hercules, all in one breath, and for the first time since those events occurred, I wept for the friends I had lost. I caught my breath again at the end of two hours, more or less, astonished at having opened my heart to a creature I scarcely knew. I must have interrupted my own words somewhat oddly, for my hostess asked me whether I felt unwell. I pulled myself together, and as I reassured her on the subject of my health, I looked at her for the first time. She had a rather ordinary face, regular features, a well-formed mouth, white skin. Once again, I was amazed. My clumsiness, my diverse abilities, and the frankness of my replies spoke more for my person than any clever lies would have done, and she hired me. The Chinese Baths needed a kind of steward. I asked her when I might meet the master of the house. She burst into laughter and then told me that the house had a mistress, that her name was Sophie, and that I was in her presence. Then she led me on a detailed visit of her establishment.

We climbed an exiguous spiral staircase until we were just under the building's nearly flat roof. There was a succession of simple rooms, clean and bright, on each side of the corridor, which was hung in yellow silk. Those rooms were reserved for the workers, all of them female, employed in the Baths. Sophie paid them wages much higher than were usual in Paris. She knew that most young girls with no trade and no experience often had recourse to prostitution in order to augment their miserable income; but she absolutely required that no one should engage in that debauchery on her premises, for in Paris, such places as hers, originally dedicated to hygiene, almost always degenerated into bordellos; and then they fell into the hands of pimps and of the police and their snitches. Sophie's system of payments guaranteed the independence of her girls as well as her own. A large number of young girls from the provinces, fleeing the wretched poverty of rural life, came to Sophie, worked for a few years as maidservants in her employ, and returned to their villages, where their Parisian savings allowed them at last to make good marriages. The Chinese Baths constantly changed their domestic servants and enjoyed a reputation for honesty, or rather for absence of venality (for a certain degree of license was taken at the Baths, as I shall soon have occasion to relate).

Next we visited the cellars. The light of day reached them by way of an ingenious system of mirrors and was reflected off the whitewashed walls. Under the vaults, amid a forest of equally white columns, a dozen young girls, practically children, were busily at work. They looked like shades in a white hell. I say "hell," because the heat down there was heavy, moist, penetrating, as was the din caused by certain machines, which very much excited my curiosity, and which were lined up along the walls. Sophie explained their use to me. On the right were basins filled with gravel of different sizes, dwindling, layer after layer, to the finest sand, which was destined for water filtering; beyond the basins was the heating apparatus, which must be fed a steady supply of wood, so that the customers might have as much steaming hot water as they pleased. On my left hand stood a collection of deep tubs, where linen soaked in a mixture of ashes and soda, and some drying ovens. Such were the wings of the theater of cleanliness in which I was to play the director.

At last we walked up to the second floor. We were in the east building, which was reserved for men, and Sophie informed me that the arrangements were similar in the other two wings. The Chinese Baths received their customers in a series of small chambers, two paces wide by ten paces long, with walls painted to resemble marble. A spacious corridor lined with tall windows looking onto the street gave access to those private rooms, and I stepped into one of them. The place was striking in its gaiety and freshness. In the center, like an altar to cleanliness, stood an imposing copper bath large enough to hold two persons. Two enormous faucets were ready to fill it with hot and cold water.

Under the high window which gave onto the courtyard, a mahogany sideboard held all the equipment necessary to the toilet of the most refined dandy. I asked my hostess what sort of customers I might expect. She replied that the "Knights of the Rearguard"—her term for pederasts—were at home in the Chinese Baths, as was well known in Paris, but that all sorts of persons frequented her establishment, persuaded by its reputation for decorum. For her part, Sophie believed that some of those gentlemen came to the Baths with the idea of trying certain delights which go under the name of "Greek," and, because in her house plain-speaking Nature prevailed over the hypocrisy of proper behavior, she further thought that many of them fucked a man there for the first time. Their first man, according to Sophie, proved in most cases to be their last, as the majority of them did not find the business to their taste and went home disappointed, not because of the act itself, but because of having so easily tricked their desire and reached the heights of pleasure with a person of their own sex. The most philosophical, she said, were the slowest to recognize that an arse is, after all, an arse. The proprietress of the Chinese Baths told me all this with an equanimity which owed nothing either to the idiotic prejudices of common morality or to the affectation of libertinism, which passed for bon ton in Paris at the time. That simplicity alone would have sufficed to make me love my Sophie. For although I have not yet said it, I am sure you have understood, my good Jean-Jacques, you who felt your heart more keenly than anyone, and who knew men: I loved Sophie. As I write those words, the pen drops from my hand, and I weep. Let us speak of something else, or I shall never finish.

Whosoever came to Sophie's establishment with the practically naive but thoroughly respectable idea of having a simple bath could shut himself up in his cabinet at his ease, his privacy assured by a solid oaken door. He would ring for the maidservant on his floor, who entered, dressed entirely in white, and served him as he would have been served in any other bathing establishment in Paris. As for the man who came to the Baths in search of pleasures more substantial than hot towels and lavender-scented bathwater, he needed only to leave his door ajar and receive the neighbors who came to visit him. Such were the practices in the east building, which we jestingly called the Greek wing. The north wing, known as the Fraternal, was the resort of persons attracted by the other sex. The Sapphic wing was reserved for the ladies. I myself tasted the delights of the Chinese Baths, and it is to them that I owe a discovery. In keeping with the spirit of tolerance that distinguished her in all things, Sophie made her Chinese Baths the only establishment in Paris that welcomed members of every race known to mankind. And so word spread among all the disparate foreigners, mulattoes, and Jews of Paris, and many of them were Sophie's customers. I had never in my life looked very closely at the few Negresses whom one saw in Paris, but one day I found myself kneeling between a pair of ebony thighs. I thought I should die of pleasure as I kissed that pink and black diamond.

Sophie's singular establishment had a singular history, which I must recount here in a few words. Paris owed the Chinese Baths to a certain Francœur, a seasoned man of business from Picardy. Devoid of any personal vanity, but the shrewdest merchant of his race, Francœur had been wise enough to anticipate the city's expansion toward its faubourgs; thus, when the capital started to push out past the old boundaries, it was discovered that old Francœur had some time since bought several contiguous tracts of land around the royal stables, north of

Boulevard Poissonnière. He had dreamed that the new neighborhood would become a rendezvous for elegant ladies and fashionable gentlemen, and his dream was realized with prodigious speed before his eyes. Upon the death of his wife, Francœur left his native Amiens and moved into a handsome new mansion on the Rue de Paradis, where he soon began to entertain a set of table companions as pleasing as butterflies and equally enduring. In seventeen hundred and eighty-five one of these parasites introduced Francœur to the acquaintance of a former actress named Sophie. From the age of thirteen to the age of fifty, old Francœur had labored to enrich himself, first by the milling of flour, then in the commerce of wheat. He had never thought of love until love thought of him, and found him as defenseless as an ignoramus of fifteen. Francœur desired this Sophie above all things, and his wooing of her was long and respectful; as for Sophie, such elegance suited her taste. But to love the man's qualities was not to love the man, and Sophie told him so. Her frankness excited his admiration even as it broke his heart; nevertheless, he was incapable of doing without Sophie's company. To console himself, he resolved that whatever favors he might obtain from her would bear the inimitable cachet of free consent. And so, through an extraordinary refinement of generous attention, this man, so ruthless in business, of whom it was said that he had refused both bed and bread to one of his brothers ruined by speculation in India, this wide-ranging bird of prey, feared throughout France, determined to make the mistress of his heart independent of him.

When Francœur consulted an architect, the latter assured him that the Chinese style was very much in fashion. Francœur, having never lost his head for business, contributed an astute observation: He believed that the Parisians had for the past several years evinced a growing desire to have clean feet and clean arses. And as if a genie had waved a wand, the Chinese Baths rapidly sprang up on Boulevard Poissonnière. In the spring of seventeen hundred and eighty-eight, Francœur was able to give a munificent fête in his new establishment; all the guests were invited to wear costumes appropriate to the place, and the festivities went on throughout the night. At dawn, he placed the keys to the Chinese Baths in Sophie's hands, together with a nankeen wallet stuffed with documents establishing her as sole proprietress of the strange palace, still redolent of pine resin and freshly sawed wood. This pitiless speculator and delicate lover lived in adoration of his fair companion for two months before falling under the wheel of a fiacre near the Porte Saint-Denis and dying happy in Sophie's arms. She mourned Francœur sincerely, but in the meantime a young and cosmopolitan set of clients had turned the Chinese Baths into a fashionable resort, and this, combined with a solid base of local custom, made the enterprise, frivolous as it may have appeared, uncommonly profitable. At the age of sixty-six, the widow of a man whom she had never wed and dependent on no male for the administration of her fortune, Sophie was free.

Should anyone ask me to express everything I admire in a single word, my reply, coming from a man who took part in the Revolution, would seem strange to fools: Throughout my whole existence, everything *noble* has touched my heart. Show me proof of elegance, of generosity, of courage, and I am conquered. Sophie possessed all those qualities in the highest degree. With the advance of age, I have learned to give tremulous thanks to the wonderful coincidences of chance encounters. Shall I confess? I cannot bear to think that once I am gone Sophie will sink into oblivion; and thus here I am, speaking to one ghost of another. What losses those were, the deaths of two creatures who were so great in life! And speaking of great and small, my excellent brother, I wish to say that there is one thing in your *Confessions* which has always aroused my suspicions. Others would call it a minor shortcoming, but it never fails to irritate me. I refer to your repeated use and abuse of the word *little*. It always happens, alas, when you speak of your pleasures: The woman you meet is a little woman, the farm you visit a little farm, the wine you drink a little wine, and so forth. This strange and nasty habit—Sade and I used to mock it, for it exasperated him as well—became hateful to me when, after the Revolution and in proportion as it was betrayed, I watched all sorts of affected tastes and sentimental foolishness taking the place of the noblest passions. And it was from the well of *your* works, Jean-Jacques, that people drew up such treacle! The throngs of imbeciles who play at shepherding sheep, at picking cherries and gathering herbs, at living on the insipid products of a dairy— they think to imitate you! Though it be contrary to common belief to say so, I declare to you that men of genius are responsible for their descendants. You should not have renounced greatness; perhaps the Revolution would have been different; and Sophie would have met a different end.

Sophie: I shall never call her otherwise, because that was the name she had chosen for herself. She always refused both to respond to her family's name, saying that it was not hers, and to use the forename she was given at birth. Until she was twenty, Sophie was beautiful, but happily unaware of the fact. She was raised by a father of Dutch origin, surely a man of the world— an honored physician from the city of Arras, called for consultations from as far away as Flanders—but also the most austere of widowers, so Jansenist in temperament and so besotted by his daughter that he gave her a thorough and pious education, hoping to arm her against the ignorance which was the usual lot of her sex and thus to assist her in escaping Eve's fate: a strange, almost mad project, coming from a man who was himself pious, and who thought that beauty, for a woman, was a terrible gift of Nature. By the age of fourteen, if you are but charming, you will hear no conversation whose subject is not your pretty little face. You pay no heed to those first compliments bestowed on your youth, but fools come in legions, and they are moreover inexhaustible. At fifteen, you lend an ear to their nonsense; at sixteen, if they grow less assiduous, you tremble. What woman could resist such treatment? Sophie could; she resisted miraculously, in the innocence of her genius. Had her father not already felt an excessive passion for her, he would have loved her even more. The grounds of his devotion were precise and terrible: At the age of six, Sophie had contracted smallpox, and her mother, whom she adored and who adored her in turn, refused, despite her husband's entreaties, to leave her daughter's bedside. Three weeks passed, and then one morning the child awoke cured, without even the marks usually left by such an affliction; no scar of any kind marred her face. The following day her mother died. Sophie's father insisted on performing the autopsy on his wife himself. He opened her, examined her, closed her up again, and never revealed his conclusions to anyone.

Sophie was still weak from her illness and therefore not authorized to follow her mother's funeral procession to the family tomb. Later, her father summoned her to his study. He told her of his intention to give up the practice of medicine. By taking his wife, God had wished to chastise the pride of a man who, not content with admiring the divine creation, had sought overweeningly to pierce its mysteries; but this same God, in his mercy, had also wished to raise up the father by leaving him his daughter. For some little time, Sophie's parent went on in the same vein. Then he made her kneel at his right side, before the only window in the study, so that together they could give thanks to God for having called their excellent wife and mother back to Himself. After this, man and child descended to the courtyard. There, the widower had caused a fire to be built, consisting of all his wife's possessions. He and Sophie watched her mother's things burn for a long time. Overwhelmed by horror, worn out by illness, the child understood nothing. She could but conclude from all this that her father had suddenly been overcome by an inexplicable hatred for her mother; and from that day she loathed him in secret and grew up indifferent to an existence she believed she owed to her mother's death. Such a start in life made it seem likely that Sophie would find consolation for the world in the incense of religion, but while there are souls born hungry for that drug, others remain absolutely immune to its poison. Sophie belonged to the latter group. Piety ran off her like water from a duck's feathers, a fact unnoticed by any of her tutors. She received, nonetheless, the education reserved for women in those days. She was forbidden the reading of novels and the study of the sciences, activities which in equal measure corrupted the human heart. Edifying letters and essays, and selected fables, were her prescribed fare. The deceiving spectacle of feigned passions had no place in such an education, and so Sophie had passed her fourteenth birthday before attending, by chance, her first theatrical performance. The year was seventeen hundred and thirty-six. Sophie's uncle, an excellent gentleman, but plainly in his dotage, had accompanied Sophie to mass at the cathedral of Arras. For the feast of Easter, a pious confraternity had commissioned a mystery play on the Passion of Our Lord. Sophie's uncle was unable to see how anything bad could come of this holy entertainment, and he remained with his niece on the parvis of Saint-Vaast until the end of the play. A company of fearfully bad actors moved about on some well-worn boards. A potbellied, drunken Christ, enamored of his own person, lowed like an ox and found the sounds sublime. One of his confederates stood under an arbor and pulled faces like a conspirator, but it was impossible to determine whether he was meant to represent the apostle Peter or Judas. Two female roles completed the dramatis personae: Mary, whom no one had dared to defile by involvement in this profane spectacle, was painted on the scenery, joining her hands and wearing a sort of tunic, blue in color, with angular folds, and sprinkled with stars; as for Mary Magdalene, she hovered near the foot of the cross. Sophie, in her ignorance, believed that this role was played by a woman, when the confraternity had naturally entrusted it to a painted and powdered man. It was so unthinkable that Sophie would ever be exposed to the seductions of the theatrical art that no one had troubled to arm her against them. She showed no particular interest in this production, and her old uncle gave no thought to reporting the matter to his brother. And yet! The pitiful scenery, the unschooled players, the inanity of their speeches—Sophie saw none of all that, but a sublime lie which spoke truth itself. She returned transfigured to her paternal home.

A year passed, during which Sophie outwardly remained the sad child whose docility secretly delighted her father. When she was fifteen, she manifested a desire to complete her education in a convent, and employed such subtle stratagems that her father believed he had chosen the place himself. It lay a scant two leagues from Arras and, as it happened, its Mother Superior was a great admirer of the Jesuits—so much so, in fact, that she imitated their ways in all things, which included making sure that her young charges studied something of the actor's art. Mothers of good families accepted her view in this matter, thinking it not a bad idea for young girls in search of a husband to know how to appear to their advantage upon the stage of the world. It was said that the Mother Superior herself had, in her youth, given ample proof of a fiery and theatrical temperament. The convent of —— had therefore been endowed, at Mother Angélique's direction, with a small but well-conceived theater. There, under her pitiless and enthusiastic eye, Sophie learned the art of dramatic performance; and in the refectories, on walks, and in the rooms of the convent, she learned the art of dissimulating, of seeming and charming, which is the alphabet of such establishments. She excelled equally in both arts. One day, she reached her seventeenth birthday. Her father expressed a desire to see her again and came to speak to her of marriage. Mother Angélique wished to assist at the interview, for she secretly hoped to have found her successor in Sophie. But the girl bowed unequivocally to the paternal will. Her father tried to tell her something of her future husband, having even brought with him a miniature, an excellent likeness, for her inspection; but Sophie replied that she would go to the altar with her eyes cast down and that such curiosity was improper for a girl of good breeding. The old man and the nun looked at each other, both silently admiring this response. Then, in desperation, Mother Angélique revealed her secret project: She would make Sophie her successor. The girl threw herself at the nun's feet and kissed them in gratitude; nevertheless, it was impossible for her to displease the author of her days. The Mother Superior pressed her point. To bring the scene to an end, Sophie asked to be given two days to pray that Heaven might inspire her with the right decision; she would pass those days in isolation and fasting. Her request was granted, and the interview came to an end marked by great emotion. The Mother Superior and the old man withdrew, filled with admiration for their Sophie. Their admiration remained undiminished two days later, around five o'clock in the afternoon, when they were informed of Sophie's recent absence at vespers. She was never found again.

The conversation I have just described took place in the afternoon. For the following vespers, Sophie had gone to attend mass at the cathedral. To twist her pretty foot as she was leaving the service, before the eyes of an amorous graybeard; to allow herself to be taken to his house for the application of an ointment; to give assurances, receive assurances in return, and inflame him with caresses—all that had been child's play for a young woman who had displayed an admirable talent for the theater during the course of the past two years. He whom she had thus lured into her web was a certain Plouchard, a shipowner from Boulogne worth millions. At first, Sophie was enchanted by her own shrewdness, but the evening brought the clever girl some disenchantment, for she was obliged to pay Plouchard in kind, and though his needs were not great, his breath was foul. Two days later the couple was in Paris; six months later Sophie had her house. Plouchard went to Boulogne four days a week for his business; his first flames of desire had also been his last. His member was no longer much inclined to stand, but he delighted to know that Paris believed the contrary; his entire pleasure, of an evening, was to walk arm in arm with his young wife, counting the envious looks of the passersby, which intoxicated him, and to display her at the Opéra when the season came. After a year, Sophie grew coquettish; she desired new dresses and, especially, the most beautiful jewels. She cajoled mightily, simpered, and sulked when she must. Plouchard loved such coaxing, and he paid. In the evening, Sophie placed her jewels, following Plouchard's recommendations, in a deep, solid strongbox. When the strongbox was full, Sophie sold all her gems at once, for a third of their value, and did not return to her house. The following month Plouchard consoled himself in the arms of a young woman who was less winsome than Sophie, but who did not cost him a single diamond.

Sophie believed herself free at last. And she would doubtless have been so had she not discovered that she was, alas, pregnant. She then tried all the terrible remedies recommended to ladies who desire relief from such a burden, with the result that she nearly succeeded in killing herself. Her unborn child survived, however, and was delivered in due time, only to die almost immediately afterward. Sophie wept a great deal; the midwife assured her that she could bear no more children. Among the tenderest daydreams of Sophie's youth had been the thought of showering upon her offspring the maternal care and attention which had been so abruptly snatched from her. Sophie thought she would perish, but one does not die of grief at nineteen. She lived in Paris. She would become an actress. In the beginning, she despaired of her chosen profession. Uneducated trollops, their pretty faces agape with conceit; hussies who took themselves for the goddess Venus but had none of her attributes except the diseases which bore her name; powerful matrons, stupid as cows; and a few women of character and talent who flew far above all the rest—such was the state of our Parisian theater. Fortunately, Sophie's reserved nature allowed her to find favor with those of her sisters in art who had talent and who believed she would not supplant them; her discreet beauty threatened no one; and thus it was that she joined the company of the Comédiens-Français. Sophie's career of playing small roles lasted a long time, but only at the end of her first year did she grasp what most novice actresses learned within two weeks: Without an aristocratic protector, without a lover from the fashionable world, no great theatrical success was possible for a woman, whether talented or not. Sophie had yielded to Plouchard so that she might be able to follow her vocation; she refused to take another Plouchard so that she might exercise a profession for which she knew she had a gift.

In the year seventeen hundred and sixty, when an author took notice of her abilities and yet made no attempt to have his way with her, Sophie believed that the greatest chance of her career had come. His name was Charles Palissot, and he had written a satirical comedy, *Les Philosophes*, directed against the philosophers who were beginning to cause a great stir in Paris. He offered the leading female part to Sophie. Did you know anything of Palissot, Jean-Jacques? He assailed you vigorously in his play, representing you as man in his natural state, eating grass on all fours. Your friends Voltaire and Diderot received less mistreatment, but only slightly less. Sophie, like all Parisians, knew the philosophers in question; that is to say, she knew their names from gazettes and salon conversations but had never read a single line written by any of them. She took it into her head to do so, in order to enhance her performance in the role Palissot wished her to play. He obligingly lent her several of your books, as well as volumes of Voltaire and Diderot. She had expected boring, turgid rhetoric; instead the books she read struck her as lively, limpid when necessary, complex when the subjects required complexity. For Diderot in particular she felt a kind of instinctive sympathy. And thus Sophie found herself in an awkward situation. Having been offered an important role for the first time, she had not the heart to refuse to perform in Palissot's comedy; but to deride those authors was to demean herself. She had the audacity to send a note to Denis Diderot; in it she expounded her high idea of the theater and explained the delicate position in which her reading and her profession had landed her. In his reply, Diderot thanked the actress for having taken the trouble to read his work, exhorted her to accept the role, and even added some suggestions about playing Palissot's antiphilosophical piece in such a way that his malicious art would not compromise her acting. When word of this correspondence spread, the Parisians did not know which to admire more, the delicacy of the actress or the elegance of the philosopher. Palissot, alas, was not only stupid, he was nasty. And he was not only nasty, he was powerful. At court and in town, he had no lack of supporters, and they favored indefinite incarceration for the insolent seditionists who claimed to serve philosophy and instead fomented unbelief and rebellion far and wide. Seeing that it was too late to deprive the actress of her role, Palissot put on a good face. Sophie found it admirable that so vehement an adversary of the philosophers' ideas could display such chivalry. But Palissot had resolved to ruin Sophie forever without harming his play; and undaunted by the difficulty of so delicate a maneuver, our scribbler set his traps by night. He prejudiced everyone he could against Sophie. During the first two weeks, at every performance of his play, he made sure that the audience included a group of hirelings, experts in their field, who managed the feat of applauding all the author's witty sallies and all the good scenes when Sophie was not on stage, but storming and covering her voice when she was. At the end of a week of this treatment, people began to murmur that the company had been ill advised to entrust so fine a role to a barely mediocre actress. From one of her fellow players, a woman with a very small part, Sophie learned what everyone else in the theater already knew. Believing, in her indignation, that she could appeal to persons of good will, she published the story of this misadventure in an "Epistle on the Small Misfortunes of a Great Hypocrite." In the world of Paris, where the first rule of the weak is to dissemble, Sophie's letter was a terrible mistake. She was a woman, she was a victim who would not accept her fate, and she was beautiful. A quarter of all that might have been forgiven, but the whole made a potion too strong for the Parisian dogs to swallow. The pack attacked her everywhere and tore her to pieces. It was said that she had tried to give herself to Palissot, who had refused her advances, and that thus the cause of her acrimony was not far to seek. Her provincial dialect was the subject of mockery. Although she was not yet forty years old, Sophie was cut off from the art which had been the center of her existence. She found ways of continuing to exercise her profession—giving private lessons, writing booklets on acting for booksellers of every sort—and succeeded in making an honorable living, despite her profound melancholy, from which Francœur eventually rescued her. There were, of course, some charitable souls who tried to explain to the shrewd old man of business that he was infatuated with a fallen actress; but Francœur was too cunning to buy such gossip at face value and too rich for the slanderers to dare to repeat it.

Such was the woman who welcomed me to the Chinese Baths one September evening in the year seventeen hundred and ninety-one. I knew nothing about her then. We agreed on everything and concluded our interview. Night had long since fallen. The Baths had admitted the last customer of the day. Sophie undertook to accompany me to the gate. It had been decided that I would begin my employment the following week; I desperately cudgeled my brains, seeking a pretext for seeing her sooner; but all eloquence had deserted me. We were approaching the accursed boulevard; soon I must resolve to bid her farewell and to be sensible no longer of her walking by my side. As we said our good-byes on the pavement outside the gate, Sophie asked if she would see me at the meeting of the Poissonnières; in as natural a tone as I could muster, I assured her that I would be there. And I watched her disappear among the orange trees.

After Sophie withdrew, I rushed into the first tavern I could find, which stood at the corner of the boulevard and the Rue Saint-Fiacre. I asked the publican what the Poissonnières were and what the deuce kind of meetings they could have. He laughed a great deal at my question. It was in his very establishment, said the tavern keeper—a former carriage driver who had tastefully named his place of business the Coach Tavern—that the meetings of the Poissonnières were held. The Poissonnières, or "Fishwives," was the nickname they used in jest, because theirs was a women's club. I understood but a fraction of his words, which their author drowned in pitchers of claret, but I was able to gather that Sophie would be in his tavern the following evening. To gain the good graces of the keeper, I ordered a bowl of soup, which he served me himself, together with thick slices of black bread, which made a horribly loud crunching sound as I chewed it. As I supped without drinking any wine, my host gazed upon me, his eyes perfectly round, dazzled to behold such a miracle of Nature and Temperance. I left the tavern and set out in the direction of the Île Saint-Louis, slowly returning home. Sophie, I saw, must have concluded from my recent confidences that I was familiar with the patriotic clubs which during the past year and a half had flourished throughout the capital. A pleasant coolness was settling over the city, the stars shone in the mute sky, and the moon cast abroad its bluish light. I hardly slept. The following day crawled past. When evening finally came, I hurried to the Rue Saint-Fiacre.

You died before the appearance of the political clubs, Jean-Jacques. In the early stages of the Revolution, immense hopes arose in the bosoms of those who represented the fair sex; the most enlightened among them recognized a unique opportunity to consider questions of marriage and divorce, of wages, of women's education. After the fall of the Bastille, citizens' clubs sprang up everywhere. Their members read the news; drew up motions, which were then brought before the Assembly; debated all sorts of ideas; and discussed conditions in their neighborhood. Certain women who wished to express their hopes, and those of their mothers and sisters, before such audiences attended the meetings of some of those clubs. There it was revealed to them that the word "citizen," which one might have considered to be of common gender, was in fact a masculine noun. The clubs accepted the presence of women at their meetings, but in a most touching display of republican unanimity, the clubs of Paris, of the kingdom's other great cities, and of the smallest villages were in complete agreement on one point: There was to be no question of allowing female participation in even the smallest decisions.

In the Faubourg Poissonnière, there were those of the fair sex who rebelled against this state of affairs. Sophie became one of them when a deputation of women of the people came to solicit her, as the most learned and richest woman in the neighborhood, to join their cause. The little band attended one of the first meetings of the citizens' club of the Faubourg Poissonnière, which convened its members in an unused stable in the Rue de

Paradis. At first, the citizens received the ladies with enthusiasm, making delicate allusions to the stallions which had been formerly sheltered in that place. The ladies asked to address the meeting; the citizens exchanged bewildered looks. In their surprise, they were almost gracious in granting the women the right of speaking. The ladies began to expose their demands; the citizens became indignant. The president of the club offered to admit the women as auditors only. They protested, they implored, they raged; in vain. At that very moment, the same scene was being played out, in one form or another, in all the clubs of the capital. In the end, the members of the citizens' club of the Faubourg Poissonnière had recourse to certain traditional arguments which had proved effective in their stalls, in their workshops, in their homes: They soundly beat Sophie and her companions and threw them into the street. In the days that followed, the women deliberated. Abandoning their undertaking was not to be thought of. Their part, they decided, would be to preach by example, to demonstrate that their half of humanity was worth as much as the other. They founded a club dedicated to human brotherhood and put up notices announcing the club's statutes and its meeting place. A jester, thinking to deride the women, hit upon the idea of calling their group the *club des Poissonnières*, the "Fishwives' Club," thus opening the way to a thousand obscene jokes; but the ladies, in defiance, adopted the name as their own.

I reached the Coach Tavern with an hour to spare and took a seat facing the door, determined not to miss Sophie's entrance. Women came in a few at a time, passed through the room, and entered a large hall on the right, which the tavern keeper had reserved for the Poissonnières that evening. Two servants engaged especially for the occasion carried in heavy stoneware jugs filled with fresh water. Sophie still had not appeared. Some changes in the sounds coming from the big hall drew my attention. I went in; the meeting was about to begin. The object of my thoughts was there, apparently having come through the kitchen. Standing on a platform in a simple, unadorned dress, Sophie presided over the meeting. The hall, long and rectangular in shape, with a packed-earth floor and windowless whitewashed walls, offered nothing remarkable to the eye. Three benches, each with about five places, reserved for women with child and elderly persons, faced the platform, but the rest of the hall was empty of furniture, and most of the audience stood throughout the meeting. On the platform, against the wall, were stacks of straw-bottomed chairs. To my surprise, half of the thirty or so persons in attendance were men. Their presence was explained by the fact that Sophie had carefully arranged to begin her gathering shortly before that of the citizens' club, which met but a few steps away; and members of that manly assembly came as neighbors, half bent on jibes and mockery, as they noisily demonstrated, and half—though they would have let themselves be killed sooner than admit it—out of interest.

I had chosen well for my first encounter with those ladies, for their meeting that evening was one of the most tempestuous in their history. The subject of discussion was women's right to vote—a subject very much in the air, for in Saint-Ouen and Pontoise, women and even children had been invited to take part in a local election, on the grounds that the Nation was everyone's affair, from the moment he or she reached the age of reason. When Sophie reported these facts, having first announced the business of the meeting, a violent shudder ran through the assembly. Sophie immediately yielded the floor to a jovial, chubby woman, who turned up her sleeves as she mounted the platform. Disdaining to lean upon the enormous lectern—borrowed from a nearby convent—where speakers usually placed the pages containing their discourse, the enormous matron planted herself solidly upon her legs and began to harangue her audience, which fell silent at once. She had the wondrous eloquence of those who, not knowing how to write, work over in their minds, for days on end, what they desire to say. Pauline was a flower vendor. She was not clever, nor cunning, but she was sure of this: Women had a part to play in the Revolution, and everyone knew what that part was. Their duty was to produce children for the Fatherland: boys to provide it with arms; girls to provide it with wombs. Those girls, once they became women, were to raise their own little ones in love and respect for the Fatherland; those boys, once they became men, were to be worthy of the Fatherland by showing their sons how to die in its service. This was all the voting that a woman should desire, and the rest was madness, contrary to nature and common sense. At this point, declaring that she had finished, Pauline triumphantly stepped down from the speaker's platform, resoundingly acclaimed by her kind, who recognized themselves in her, and equally applauded by the men, who felt truly relieved to find that at least one woman in the place had not lost her reason. During all this time, I never lost sight of Sophie, who leaned against the wall to the right of the platform and seemed to tremble. I later learned that she was quivering with rage. But already a second orator, short, stiff, and dressed in black like a schoolmaster, was approaching the lectern. He declared himself a Jacobin; a murmur of respectful approbation arose from his audience. I must, therefore, have been the only person in the room who did not know what a Jacobin was. The species struck me as disagreeable, as the words of the citizen who represented it stank of the defrocked priest and the narrow-minded moralist. Crouched behind the lectern, he seemed to speak to his cravat, and his thin, piping voice conveyed the impression that he delighted in his words as though in a guilty secret. He commenced by demanding a universal right of suffrage, that is, one open to all citizens. This audacity caused some consternation, and there was murmuring to right and left. The speaker declared that we still had to agree on the definition of a citizen. Nothing was nobler, or grander, or more demanding than the sacred duty of voting. Who would thenceforth be worthy of the call to perform that duty? Must we not preserve universal suffrage from the hands of incompetents? From all those who remained unillumined by the light of reason? From all those who lived benighted in religious superstition? And did not women, alas, correspond to such descriptions? They must, therefore, be excluded; but at the same time, the purity of the electoral body must be guaranteed. The Jacobin revealed his panacea: Service at the Fatherland's most sacred altars must be reserved to those who proved—by their industry and sense of duty—that they were worthy to perform it. The tax rolls, he said, should be consulted, and everyone who actively contributed to the national prosperity would be a citizen. All the men and a good half of the women in the hall loudly approved the Jacobin's proposal. At this point, the woman who reigned over my heart, unable to endure more and eager to respond to the orator, used her prerogative as president and broke in upon him.

First she assailed the Jacobins. Many of their number were in the Assembly as the people's representatives, she said, and yet they refused everywhere to represent half of the people. They were the Pharisees of the Revolution: Outwardly, they promised their wives and their mothers the imminent arrival of Par-

adise on earth, when women would have the right of suffrage;
and inwardly, they believed that suffrage to be as far from us as
the heavenly Jerusalem, and they laughed at the naïveté of their
supposed equals. Next, Sophie directly addressed the women
in her audience. She called them her sisters and reminded them
that the language of men used one and the same word to des-
ignate the harlot and the free woman; that this word, unless it
referred to a young person still subject to her father, was defam-
atory; but that the word—"girl"—was also beautiful, because
it said that all women were sisters. At this point in Sophie's
speech, a baker, a woman as dry as a stick, could contain herself
no longer: She declared that she was no sister to the whores of
the faubourgs, who caused men to spend the money they ought
to bring home for the household. There was a murmur of approval in the hall, but Sophie would not be discomfited by so
weak a stroke. She returned to the attack, observing that it was
easy to play the moralist when one was sitting on heavy sacks
of wheat. Here the hall hesitated and divided, for bakers had
the reputation of letting families starve while they speculated
on higher prices. Sophie went on to evoke, with what seemed
to me wonderful eloquence, the condition of a girl of no account,
the poorest of the poor; she spoke of cold pavements and sad
confinements, of ever-lurking death, in the gutter and in dis-
grace. She enlarged her discourse to include working women
and the three injustices which burden them: in youth, a foolish
and trifling education; in the prime of life, the calamities of pregnancy, the suffering and mortal risks of childbearing; and, for
the rest of their days, servitude, to children and fathers, to brothers and husbands. Women, Sophie said, paid for three minutes
of men's pleasure with a lifetime of slavery, dragging iniquitous,
abominable shackles after them from birth to death. For several
long moments, the women in the assembly seemed transported

by her powerful words, for the accents of truth will always move hearts. It was only that Sophie spoke at somewhat too great a length. The tragic actress in her overcame the public speaker, and the audience drooped. The Jacobin, who stood in the first rank, began to applaud as if he were in the stalls at the Comédie-Française, to the great amusement of many in the hall. The more Sophie insisted, the wearier her listeners became. Universal suffrage seemed indeed desirable, but doubt and discouragement triumphed, and it was simpler to pillory the denouncer of the outrage than to contend with the outrage itself. Almost the entire assembly began to hoot at Sophie, and jeers drowned her words. To counter this outburst, one of Sophie's most devoted partisans, and from the beginning one of the most furious of the Fishwives, a strong, bony beanpole of a woman, a trafficker in articles for the toilet, seized a laugher by her hair and flung her to the floor. One of Marat's admirers, brandishing copies of his newspaper *The Friend of the People*, cried out that citizenesses were being murdered and that the counterrevolution had arrived, there as everywhere else. The emboldened Jacobin leaped upon the platform in order to shout that Sophie was not, after all, really French, but an Artesian at best, probably a foreign agent, and that before the Revolution she had performed in plays depicting kings and queens, while she had never been seen in any play written by a respectable bourgeois author.

At the time, I had no taste for public affairs, nor have I acquired one since. Moreover, I am sure I understand nothing about the subject; but I feel, it seems to me, with sufficient intensity, and that has always enabled me to oppose injustice whenever I encountered it. I had never in my life given a thought to women's right of suffrage. Had I reflected upon the matter in those days, I should have said that I was opposed to it, for women have always been the victims of priests and their superstitions, and allowing women to vote would surely play into the hands of those odious chimera worshippers. I was like my contemporaries: Although I was charmed by the fair sex, it had never occurred to me that women could wish to tread the stage of the world and play a part like everyone else. But the heartlessness of the crowd disgusted me, and I was so enraged by the baseness of the Jacobin's behavior that I finally rushed at the imbecile as he stood on the platform, still gesticulating, and seemed about to seize my darling Sophie's arm. With a bound I was upon him, I struck him, and this poltroon, at least thirty years younger than I, with muscles twenty pounds heavier than mine, began to moan like a beaten child, fell on his knees, and covered his head. Now, however, the eloquent baker advanced upon me. She dealt me a prodigious blow and I fell backward, fortunately landing upon two old fellows sitting on the front bench; they cried for help, they cried murder, and cut me repeatedly with their canes. With some difficulty, I extracted myself from their clutches and mounted the platform, where Sophie, using the lectern as a ram, had felled the baker. Two parties quickly formed: On our side, several resolute women, with Sophie at their head; and on the other, a band too numerous for us even to imagine the possibility of defeating them and wrought up to the highest pitch of excitement, as is always the case when the weak apprehend their unhoped-for superiority. Most fortunately, we occupied the high ground, namely the speakers' platform, on that battlefield, and from there we threw down upon our assailants' heads a quantity of straw-bottomed chairs, which caused some cooling of their warlike fervor. Soon, alas, our store of ammunition was exhausted, and our eminence invaded by our adversaries, who cried out in triumph. A horde of sturdy shopkeepers and bareheaded workers, all women, surrounded us, backed by several iron-handed artisans, and they bore us with marvelous speed to the exit, complementing their efforts with much spitting and punching, pushing and kicking. We rolled in the foul ruts of the Rue Saint-Fiacre. Fearing for our lives in that dark, deserted place, we ran to Boulevard Poissonnière. Our adversaries did not deign to pursue us, and the remains of our army, perhaps some fifteen persons, reached the gate of the Chinese Baths, covered with scratches and spittle, soiled with gutter mud, and almost content to have fought so nobly. Sophie congratulated her troops and invited us to recover human form in her apartments. Some preferred to return home immediately, for their way was long. We passed through the gates, each of us supporting his neighbor. I was trembling from fatigue, but also because I felt on my forearm, placed there like a wounded bird, Sophie's plump hand.

We spent some time tending to our wounds, applying the admirable unguents which Sophie drew out of a large chest, where she kept remedies from all over the world. I made some lint to line the bandages intended for the more serious wounds. One of our Amazons had struck her forehead on the corner of a bench and was bleeding copiously from a cut above her eye. We did not know each other, but we exchanged smiles. Should anyone ask me to recall an occurrence which justified the Revolution, I would, I am sure, evoke that evening; and my reply would be greeted with derision. I am well aware that History will grant no honors to the Battle of the Coach Tavern, yet what is History to me, if the victors write it while their hands are still smeared with the blood of the innocent? But I see that I have failed to describe the composition of our valiant little company of militants. There were two midwives from the neighboring faubourgs; three workers who had been in the first rank of the women's march on Versailles to demand bread and who were possessed of a strange and wonderful rage which never subsided, so that they burned with indignation as others might with love; two dressmakers from the Rue Bergère, who had come as neighbors; and, finally, three vagrant girls without house or home, the oldest of them not yet sixteen, all unskilled in any occupation, thrown onto the streets of Paris by the famines in the provinces, surviving on plunder and prostitution, and—as I soon learned— spending the rest of their time as the personal guard of our brave and tactless Queen of the Amazons. We all sat talking until midnight, recalling our great battle and preparing the text of a public notice which Sophie was to deliver to the Assembly the following day, so that the people's representatives might know the truth; and then everyone left.

I remained alone with Sophie. With a simple gesture, she took my hand and bade me follow her up the narrow spiral staircase of which I spoke earlier to a door opening onto one of the Chinese Baths' terraces. Sophie went there, she said, when she wished to think, to write, to be alone. I took a few steps toward Paris. To the west, the moon still illuminated the city, but the sun was beginning to turn the eastern sky pink. Sophie had not released my hand; I stepped behind her and was so bold as to embrace her as clumsily as a provincial schoolboy abandoned in a disreputable place. We did not speak. We did not move. Then she shivered and wished to return downstairs. In the kind of intoxication one feels in the first hours of the day, we drew up the statutes of a Fraternal Society of Citizens of Both Sexes, of which we at once became the first two members. The dawn was not far from breaking; Sophie stepped away for an instant to give instructions to her morning workers. Upon her return, she invited me, in the most unaffected way, to share her bed, and

I accepted her offer with equal simplicity. You may believe it or not, Jean-Jacques, but I tell you we fell asleep chastely. Drunk with fatigue and happiness, I struggled to hold on to my dwindling senses and enjoy those moments as long as I could, and in the half delirium of my effort I dreamed I was transported to a palace in India. A bluish light bathed Sophie's room, which was simply and curiously furnished in an oriental style unknown to me. We lay on a hard but pleasant bed placed flat on the floor. I fell asleep.

I awoke to a bright day. From the sounds of the city, I guessed that the morning was well advanced. Sophie was no longer there, and the bed had grown cold. I closed my eyes again. I thought of nothing. After a good while, the handle of the door turned. There was a sound of shaken fabric in the antechamber; the window was opened, the shutters squealed, and the room went dark. I lay on my back and pretended to be still asleep. The floor creaked softly. I heard a rustling of sheets, which heated my blood more than I can express. I felt soft, warm flesh press against me, and a hand pulled my nightshirt up to my thighs. Then I turned to the woman, smiling, and without opening my eyes, I flung my arms around her.

Sophie was sixty-nine years old. Her body was fat, white, and virginal. It seemed made for love's caresses, but not its buffets; when I grasped her to me, her hips would bear the traces of my fingers for days. She brought a muffled fury to the joys of love; the apex of her pleasure came in a long, soundless shudder. When this happened, I had to remain quiet for many minutes until she returned, it seemed, from a country of phantoms; then she would give me a sad smile, like someone barely rescued from drowning. I had always engaged in fucking with either nonchalance or enthusiasm, nothing else, and I passionately loved Sophie's odd gravity. But if I wanted to share her life, I must needs participate in the Revolution, and so I became something like her private secretary. In this relation, we quickly formed all sorts of habits, the most trivial of which were not the least dear to me. Our breakfast was a thick chocolate, which we drank between five and six in the morning, while I read to Sophie the abundant mail she received as a result of her tireless political activity. On fine summer evenings, we climbed to the terrace of the Chinese Baths to watch the day come to an end. We sat side by side on a bergère as I read aloud from the gazettes. I took down, at her dictation, responses to newspaper articles, drafts of motions, outlines of laws. And, of course, we talked, of everything and nothing. It often happened that I did not listen to what she said. It was not just that the sordid, petty intrigues which were the chief occupation of those revolutionary times bored me still, even though I had learned to appreciate their importance; it was also the vast delight I felt in abandoning myself to the sound of Sophie's voice, with its grave sonorities, refined and perfected by the theater. At the end of such evenings, we often fell asleep on the terrace, each leaning exhausted on the other—for the Baths fully occupied our days—and only the early dew would awaken us.

How had Sophie, who in private was gentleness personified, transformed herself for politics' sake into an astonishing harpy to whom more than one citizen, exasperated by her untiring pugnacity, would gladly have given a sound spanking? I happened to ask her that question, and she replied that something she had observed at the Fête de la Fédération had shocked her, though it apparently offended no one else: There was not a single woman in the procession supposed to represent the assembled

Nation; indeed, the only females were a group of young girls dressed in virginal white. Like me, and like so many others, Sophie had done her share of the work. But she raged and shook her fist and struck out with her elbows and showed her wheelbarrow in vain; the soldiers of the National Guard who defended the access to the Champ-de-Mars refused to let her enter the precincts where the representatives of reconciled France gathered around their King. Doubtless, many others besides Sophie were indignant that day, but on the morrow the vast majority of them returned to their everyday lives; Sophie's anger, unlike theirs, had not diminished, nor would it ever. That same evening Sophie composed a protest, which she then submitted to the representatives of the people. Her essay made some noise; a shrewd bookseller printed it by night and sold two editions of three hundred copies. From that point on, Sophie had the ear of the Parisian street. She never stopped submitting motions, petitions, proposals for new laws, and proclamations to the various National Assemblies, and her eminence in the Fishwives' Club gave her a still greater reputation. Calumny hurled some of its filth at Sophie, but it slipped from her without leaving a trace. Nothing escaped her assiduous indignation. She demanded a law concerning the determination of paternity; petitioned for the facilitation of divorces; demonstrated, after a meticulous inquiry, that a young woman in Paris charged with the elementary instruction of children was paid two-thirds less than a man similarly employed; alerted the city to the fate awaiting the children of the prostitutes who worked in its streets. Sophie was received politely, but when it became clear that the woman would not be contented with empty compliments, she was found to be infinitely less charming; when she brought along in her train a growing number of citizens, male and female, she became decidedly importunate. Within two years after the Fête de la Fédération, she was informed that the cause of women must yield to other priorities, which would thenceforth require the punctilious attention of the entire country, including the lack of bread, present and future wars, and restraints on speculators. Sophie did not allow herself to be taken in snares so clumsily set, but her partisans were not always so alert. In the end, she grasped that the gentlemen who managed the world, whether they were Jacobins, priests, or aristocrats, would always have better things to do than to liberate their kind's other sex; and this discovery, far from reducing her to silence, made her more desperately active.

And thus, little by little, my poor Sophie performed the feat of uniting the whole country—against her. At the very time when the people of France passed for her new sovereign, the Republic kept its women in a state of odious debility; what was known as the "weaker" sex was the Republic's Third Estate, the commoners. After less than three years of revolution, partisans of all stripes colluded to destroy Sophie: Royalists and émigrés hated her, because from now on they would have to tremble before market women; the Girondins, the Mountain, and even the Plain grew irritated, some because their wives were the creatures of priests, and others because the advent of Woman Unbound would mean the end of all moral standards in families. Sophie became the subject of personal jokes; and from jokes to insults is but a step. There was much sneering at the fondness for women which Sophie so ardently professed; drawings were circulated, as well as all sorts of rumors. This mud rose from the street and climbed as high as the speakers' platforms in some political clubs: One day when Sophie presented to the Club des Cordeliers some proposed law more in conformity with humanity than the one then in force, exhorting the gentlemen to listen to the movements of their heart, some members of the audience cried out that they would be delighted to perform movements for her sake, and several other more explicit obscenities, which the clerks agreed among themselves not to record, so as not to besmirch the prestige of the august club.

I trust you will be much aggrieved to learn that all those heinous dogs invoked you, Jean-Jacques. They even gave you a street—they changed the name of the Rue Plâtrière for you. The street was not the gayest, since many of its residents were unfortunate women who worked at home. But you had lived there, and whenever I turned into the Rue Jean-Jacques Rousseau, I sent a fraternal thought in your direction. I never ceased to find it strange that you had worshippers; not only because it seemed to me that revolutionaries ought to eschew all forms of worship, but also because, in contrast to most of your idolaters, I had taken the time to read your writings, and I had never found anything to suggest that you would have been enchanted by this Revolution of ours. Nonetheless, women in market stalls sold plates embellished with your image; in the public gardens, on fine evenings, nurses called out the names of legions of Émiles and Sophies, thus baptized in honor of your treatise on education. How could parents wish to engender the moralizing halfgrown idlers and the little madams, all airs and ignorance, whom you depict in that work? It must be that they have not read it. All the same, ought we to hold great men responsible for their posterity? In those days, I often replied to that question in the affirmative.

In proportion to her increasing unpopularity, Sophie found herself, with her faithful servant, pushed out toward the edges, toward the most disenfranchised women of France. Most of the companions who had fought alongside us in the Homeric combat of autumn seventeen hundred and ninety-one disappeared. Some returned to their native provinces. Others were laid facedown, in the name of the French people, upon our new masters' guillotine. The Club des Poissonnières faded away and a song composed on the subject, which did not fail to mention that a fish rots from the head, was the occasion for Sophie to give her activity a new direction. She had come to think that society, dominated as it was by men, condemned woman to a kind of slavery, in which she must serve her man from the bed to the kitchen and from the kitchen to the bed. Therefore, prostitution seemed to her not the lowest form of work for a woman, but the most brutally frank and least hypocritical. It naturally followed that one day in the spring of seventeen hundred and ninety-three, we made our way to the Maison de Force, the prostitutes' prison in the Salpêtrière, where we were sure to find the dregs of society. As a former resident of the institution had recommended, we arrived very early in the morning. At the time, most of the women sent to the Salpêtrière were indigents; several thousand such wretches were crowded into its confines. But the authorities had decided to shut up the commonest prostitutes, the beasts of burden of whoredom, in the Salpêtrière as well, and all the girls whom indigence had thrown onto the pavement found themselves punished again for their existence, this time by being flung into the insalubrious wards of that infernal institution. Sophie and I gave ourselves out as two Swiss travelers come to Paris to visit the charitable institutions, and the Superior General received us, favorably impressed by our early arrival and the austerity of our demeanor. I was disguised as a sanctimonious devotee of the human race, a type that had replaced the former sanctimonious devotees of revealed religion, and I appeared to have little time for pleasantries. Sophie alone spoke, inventing an accent meant to be Genevan, and talking so rhapsodically of philanthropy and of the prosperity enjoyed by those who had sent us, that the corpulent villainess who directed the less than charitable hospital, reassured that we had not been dispatched there by the authorities to reprimand her for her negligence, left us free to go about as we pleased and was very careful not to accompany us. As we walked on, Sophie whispered that she feared the noxious exhalations in the common rooms above all things; she appeared never to have crossed the threshold of such a place. A nun vaguely responsible for welcoming visitors—or so it seemed—was assigned to escort us.

The inmates were still asleep when we entered a long, dark room where some twenty beds were aligned, each containing two girls lying head to foot. A mephitic vapor emanating from the moldy bedding filled our throats. By the light of our lanterns, we could see faces, all of them with pinched noses and hollow eyes; the odor of the chamber pots could turn your soul as well as your stomach. And this was not even the incurables' ward! The vaguely welcoming sister informed us of a few facts and named a few figures in a weary voice; I confess that I hardly listened to her. It seemed that most of those unfortunate girls were poor wretches who had been surprised by the watch while trying to escape during the first cold days of the previous autumn, for they preferred to die outside rather than to live in those damp rooms where they were so promiscuously crowded together. Sophie wept but spoke no word. The long wards succeeded one another like circles in Dante's hell. When our visit came to an end, the day was well advanced, and we had seen more than we wished to recall. After having fulsomely complimented the Superior General, who found none of our flattery misplaced, we obtained permission to return in the afternoon and follow a company of girls of ill repute (as our hostess designated them, venomously pressing her dry lips together). In this regard, the Salpêtrière served as a sorting station: Whores were sent on to Bicêtre Hospital; however, since none was willing to admit her occupation, only those visibly afflicted by the pox were transferred to Bicêtre, where it was alleged that they received proper treatment. By no means ignorant of such maladies, I trembled when I recalled that the pox could hardly be seen until the final stage of the disease. The unfortunates who might be treated at Bicêtre were therefore already past all possibility of cure. But, as I was to discover there later that very day, the hospital was much more desirous of treating those patients than of curing them; death, even to those who were supposed to combat it, seemed the just chastisement for such immoral and corrupt behavior as prostitution. When we learned what was the usual treatment for pox at Bicêtre Hospital, we were horrified.

A complete treatment lasted at least six weeks. To begin, the patient was subjected to an extremely strict diet and then purged, bled, and soaked for several hours. Those who died immediately from these procedures were not the least fortunate, for their demise spared them what followed. It was indeed true, as the director at Bicêtre boasted, that after a few days, the poor girls' condition was much changed: If they survived, they were no longer capable of thinking, or protesting, or demanding anything at all. They became the docile prey of the nurses committed to their care, ignorant incompetents whom the new masters of France had deemed deserving of such employment: soldiers' widows, prolific mothers, poor things pale from inadequate nourishment, from working in bad air, and from the dreary pleasures of republican virtue. They inculcated into their charges a bloodless morale no less mortiferous and mean than the one formerly inculcated, in that same place, by the nuns of the Ancien Régime. During the course of six long weeks, the nurses rubbed into their patients' skin a malodorous pomade with a base of mercury; this lotion was supposed to rid the sick women of the poxy essence in their blood through mercurial transpiration (such was the bombastic jargon which issued with marvelous fluency from the mouth of the director, who had insisted on doing us the honors of the place himself). The patients did indeed sweat abundantly. Unluckily for them, the so admirably efficacious mercury had other effects as well: It burned their stomachs, and when the pain in their guts became unbearable, they were told that they were being punished in the part where they had sinned; or that those were the last symptoms of an illness in despair at being compelled to abandon its prey. It was less easy to justify another consequence of the absorption of mercury: The young ladies lost all their teeth. As for that, the director was prepared to remark to us—and here it was apparent he meant no jest—that at least the diet was easier to follow for those without teeth; and he went on to declare that customers would turn away from toothless prostitutes, who, I had no doubt, would thus be put on the road to redemption. Many of those woman awakened one fine morning to find their jaws stuck together by their rotting gums, in which case a barber had to free them with a stroke of his razor.

The strumpets' misfortunes, having made such fine progress, did not stop there. All those who did not die were declared cured; they were returned to the Salpêtrière; and after three months, in the majority of cases, they were released. That many of them left prison devoutly religious seemed peculiarly horrible, but not surprising, as they were catechized and preached to and confessed every day. Besides, considering the world they were in, many of those girls loved to think of another one. As for the recalcitrant, there was a particular treatment designed to convince them that it was advisable to observe, at the very least, the outward forms of holy religion: They were brought into one of the neighboring wards, reserved for the ladies who had lost their reason, and chained for the night to a bed shared by two madwomen. In the last stage of the venereal disease, some sufferers went insane, and this was interpreted as a victory for the treatment. Learned declarations were made, according to which the whores' uterine fury, checked by the mercury lotion, must have taken refuge in their brains. Such women were put in that ward, where they made an end of dying, aided by the dampness and the rats.

After we returned to the Chinese Baths, we discussed what steps we should take to help those unhappy women. I recalled to Sophie that my house in the Rue du Petit-Musc remained empty. It stood not far from the Salpêtrière and therefore seemed to be an ideal location for an aid office. In our early naïveté, we thought it proper to give succor to those women who were worst stricken. We would speak to a patient and eventually arrange for her to leave the prison; a hired actor went to fetch her, and a small gift to the Superior smoothed over quite a few difficulties. I suspect that she was not taken in by our subterfuge, but it was in her interest to remain silent, and that sufficed to guarantee her cooperation. We would receive the poor girl, dirty, gaunt, and dazed as she was, and bring her to the Chinese Baths, where we scrubbed her carefully; then she was given new clothes and meals so light as not to kill her. In most cases, the pox in its final stage caused ulcerous sores that destroyed the patient's nose and the roof of her mouth. The palate would often collapse, and pus and blood in the victim's nasal cavity would render her incapable of speech. I was obliged to fabricate, at our expense, some silver palates. Alas, they did not serve for very long, because those women rarely survived, and our costly benefactions were plunged into a bottomless abyss. We could not bring ourselves to recover the silver palates from dead patients in order to use the things again. It made no sense to continue stubbornly down that road. One day, overcome by weariness, I remarked to Sophie that it would also be of no use to press the so-called representatives of the French people; they did not represent even half of that people, as they excluded women and servants!

And so we reformed our policy. Prostitutes, we reasoned, must join forces in order to avoid falling into the clutches of brothel keepers or pimps or the police. We walked the streets of Paris, inviting girls whose charms were for sale to pay us a visit. Our experience in hospitals did us sad service: We avoided all the mercenary strumpets whose afflicted noses and bewildered air announced that they had not six months to live; we approached only the youngest and healthiest girls. Very quickly, clients filled the Charity House in the Rue du Petit-Musc. I wrote letters to one's parents, to another's betrothed; I made inquiries at the Foundling Hospital regarding the infant left there by a third client, who now regretted what she had done. Most of the girls, being from the Limousin or Picardy or the Basque country or Savoy, barely spoke French and could not write it. Despite the declarations of physicians who claimed that too much seed made the womb slippery and inhospitable, the girls were got with child more often than not. Sophie showed them how to avoid pregnancy without tricks or devices, how to use the English bonnets (which their customers loathed), how to recognize the signs of the different maladies of love. She continued to rain proposed laws and appeals upon the heads of the secretaries of the Convention; she persisted, for example, in urging the representatives to vote subsidies for teaching the children of streetwalkers how to read and write. Her obstinacy seemed to me fruitless; we had some quite nasty quarrels on the subject. The Charity House consumed the little spare time we had left, and we began to grow away from each other.

Poverty, the Jacobins' idiocy, even charity itself, often made me tired. I worked less and less, and I returned to my nocturnal perambulations of the capital. Like so much else, the nights of Paris had changed. Debauchery had lost the bright gaiety it had taken on after the Revolution. The number of beggars was disheartening; destitution compelled some of them to bawl out songs, while others scraped bows across discordant fiddles and some hurdy-gurdy players devoid of talent caused me to clench my teeth. Even the Parisians' costume was undergoing a slow metamorphosis: The wearing of colors by women was still tolerated, but men now wore only black and walked about with a ferocious air they thought of as Roman. The streets were filled with the priests of the new patriotic religion. The Revolution had had heroes; it fabricated martyrs. Praise was showered upon two dead boys named Bara and Viala. In the meetings of the Parisian political clubs, much time was now spent citing feats of patriotism as spectacular as they were absurd: A little boy of five years had given his leaden toys to the army, so that it could fashion musket balls from them; a young girl had denounced her older brother for planning to celebrate masses and then taken her own life so that she would not see her beloved relative die on the scaffold. I walked at random through the Parisian nights, but all I saw in them anymore were citizens; and it cost me much difficulty to recognize that they were men.

I have come to the point at which I must recount the worst moment of my existence, because what follows is a relation of the circumstances of Sophie's death. To save her life, I would have given my own, but fate wanted none of it, and I experienced the horror of outliving what I loved. It has always been hard for me to conceive that one could wish another's death; alas, my century has furnished me with innumerable examples of the contrary attitude. Sophie and I had known from the beginning that she had no lack of enemies. What we did not know (later revealed to me by a snitch, a regular visitor to the Chinese Baths and a frequenter of all the disreputable places in Paris) was that those enemies had, with the passing of the years, eventually formed a kind of clique, whose project was to render Sophie incapable of damaging their interests; for by that time uprightness and fidelity to the principles of the Revolution had become great nuisances.

In seventeen hundred and ninety-three Sophie submitted to the Committee of Public Safety a proposal for a law forbidding what was called "moderate correction," that is, the right of a husband to beat his wife, under the vaguest pretexts and without the least risk of punishment. Robespierre saw the proposal and, unfortunately, liked it; but by that time he was a hated tyrant, and everyone was already conspiring against him. All factions tacitly resolved to bring about Sophie's definitive ruin. She had annoyed the Jacobins for many months with her interventions in their dismal meetings. The Girondins appreciated no more than their rivals Sophie's whim of extending the right of suffrage to women and the lower classes. The Jacobins were angered at seeing themselves outflanked on the left; the Girondins feared what they called her excesses. The simplest method of getting rid of Sophie would have been to accuse her of counterrevolutionary activities; but her enemies feared that she would use the trial to turn opinion in her favor. It moreover alarmed them to contemplate, should Robespierre fall, the interdiction of the guillotine. They resolved, therefore, to confront Sophie with a formidable adversary: the market women of Les Halles. From the very first days of the Revolution, those women had been inside its turmoil. They had entered the fight out of hatred for the powerful and love for humanity. The second sentiment had not the weight of the first, and now citizens trembled before the market women, who could with a single gesture cause a man to be flung into a dungeon from which he would not depart save in a tumbrel. The women had come to love the spectacle of the guillotine in action; all day long they sat at the foot of the scaffold—where, as notable personages of the new era, they held reserved places—and chatted like gossips in a coffeehouse while the frequency of executions mounted to the very apex of horror and assistants or servants minded their shops and stalls. When the guillotine was exiled to the gates of the city, the people of Paris grumbled, and the women of Les Halles gave voice to their protest. Such were the stout, ferocious females whom Sophie's enemies planned to unleash on her. The market women would be easy to incite, for Sophie had recently threatened their revenues by opposing with great vehemence a measure to fix a minimum price for vegetables. It was only a question of waiting for the proper moment.

During a portion of the year seventeen hundred and ninety-three, one could feel that anything was possible: a return to the old order, new overthrows, new convulsions. For her part, Sophie believed that the Revolution was going to receive a new impulse, precisely because it seemed to be in its death agony. As it happened, the opposite was the case: In the autumn, women's clubs were forbidden. Because we could show that our club's statutes refused to distinguish citizens by the criterion of sex, we continued to hold meetings, and this legal quibbling gained us a few months. But with the aim of undermining our charitable work, a faction of the Jacobins succeeded in making solicitation illegal by enacting a measure which was both hypocritical and ineffective, but which permitted every good citizen to send streetwalkers to prison. Finally, in the middle of winter in the year II, the decree of 21 Nivôse, the work of the ineffable Fabre d'Églantine, plunged us into terrible difficulties; it simply forbade all prostitution, and its single effect was to make the practice of the profession more dangerous. I have often wondered why our virtuous revolutionaries were so violent in their persecution of those unfortunate women and of Sophie herself. I believe that they were conscious of their failure—the regeneration of the nation and its citizens had not taken place—and of the fact that to attack the powerful was now to attack themselves; and so they were obliged to find scapegoats. Prostitutes offered to their diseased imaginations a simple image of corruption. Because they knew the poor wretches were not guilty, they struck them all the more violently.

With the interdiction of prostitution, the streetwalkers' plight became even more appalling; the police carried out mass arrests and flung the unhappy women into Saint-Lazare prison, notorious for its vermin. Many of the officers charged with making such arrests saw in them a convenient means of extortion, with which they could threaten the youngest strumpets and thus obtain the enjoyment of their charms. It was not long before those agents of the law became pimps. Before the month of April seventeen hundred and ninety-four was out, nothing remained of our charitable work. While I was entreating Sophie to leave, to go to Louisiana or somewhere else, far from Paris and its rivers of blood and mud, she announced her intention to publish a new lampoon. The pamphlet's title alone was an act of suicide: "Can Politics Offer More Gratification than Lust?" Carried away by a fit of anger of the kind from which one does not recover, Sophie taught those dried-up men who hated the human body, those women whose greatest joy was to send off their sons as soldiers, who strutted before their market stalls and in the assemblies—she taught them all what liberty was, what courage was. So reckless of danger was she that the Jacobins attributed more power to her than she had; in the throes of their lunacy, they imagined that Sophie was an agent of the emigrated nobility, come to Paris at the head of her whores to enervate revolutionaries. And everything ended with the simplicity of a nightmare.

One day near the end of April, seventeen hundred and ninety-four, we were returning from the Rue du Petit-Musc. Sophie's last remaining loyal follower had just informed us of the arrest, by Saint-Just's orders, of Claire Lacombe and Pauline Léon. Although they, unlike us, had wished to confine women exclusively to their roles as the mothers, daughters, or wives of sansculottes—the notion of woman as nothing but a source of nourishment is a milky conception for which I hold you responsible, Jean-Jacques—our differences had never stopped us from admiring their devotion to the female cause. The two had been abandoned by the extreme militants, the *Enragés*, who had long supported them, and Saint-Just had pounced. Sophie and

I spoke about their circumstances, and about Anne-Josèphe Théroigne de Méricourt, whose misfortunes had made her mad and who had been interned at Charenton. We were but a few paces from the Chinese Baths when there was an indistinct commotion on the Boulevard. At first, we thought nothing of it, but then we were jostled, and I found myself separated from Sophie. I lifted my cane and cried out to her to run away. A blow to the back toppled me, causing me to strike my head against the shaft of a cart and fall unconscious to the ground. When I regained my wits, I saw that we had been carried up to our terrace overlooking the Baths; ten paces away from me, Sophie lay on a low bed. I thought that she had been stripped of her white dress, but I was mistaken. It was drenched with her blood.

It would serve no purpose to linger on this part of my story. Sophie died without me, on that terrace where we had been happy. I rejected those who tried to give me an account of her last moments; I wished to know nothing. The sworn priest of the parish refused to bury her, under the pretext that she had been an actress in her youth; the truth was that he was afraid to be associated with a woman whom, according to local rumor, the powerful personages of the day had wished to destroy. I had her body carried far from Paris, to a wood which shall remain nameless. I dug her grave myself, in a clearing, and carefully covered her up. I sowed the little plot with acorns and covered it with leaves, that its location might be concealed from those fellow creatures alleged to be of our own kind. I did not weep. I did not console myself. Philosophy, as I conceive it, is not intended to provide any justification whatsoever for events so calamitous; let religion proffer the vile and comforting lies. Nothing either can or should diminish the beautiful scandal of existence, its grace and its absolute horror, and especially not death. Sophie had lived, and lived well. That was enough for her and must be so for me. Let the rest of mankind do as well as she with the time allotted them upon the earth, if they dare, and if they can.

Meanwhile, the great cold gripping my heart had left me almost indifferent to life. I lived in the narrow well of my grief. Spring flew past without my taking notice of it; summer followed, and I could not say how I spent it. One fine day in the beginning of May, I received a letter from a person unknown to me, who lived in Arras and said she was Sophie's relation. A week later a woman wrapped in a black shawl presented herself at the Chinese Baths; she was small and bony, with a thin, pinched line across the bottom of her face where her mouth should have been. Apparently, it had not escaped this harpy that Sophie owned property, for she was accompanied by a fat, unctuous lawyer. The man became quite amiable when he saw that I had no right to Sophie's establishment and that I knew it. At that point, the lawyer's talk turned to morals: He and his companion had heard that these premises had been the scene of the most revolting acts. Was this report true? I gave a moment's thought to pretending ignorance, but it was clear that I no longer had much heart for laughing; so I acknowledged everything. The lawyer feigned indignation, the harpy incomprehension. That very evening, I left the Chinese Baths, never to return. I settled into my house in the Rue du Petit-Musc. I lived on little. Out of idleness, I read the newspapers. Public affairs were in a state nothing short of disastrous. The strange evil which had spread through the entire country, and which was known as the Terror, had also penetrated bodies and souls and sullied their brightness. Bereavements followed upon bereavements.

Everyone feared his neighbor; you shunned conversation of any kind lest your words be deemed improper and you yourself sent to the scaffold. Sons denounced fathers. A despicable rumor asserted that when Robespierre and his virtuous acolytes on the Committee of Public Safety, their cruelty flagging, wished to harden themselves anew in order to send another batch of innocents to the guillotine, they would read a few of Sade's pages. In the Picpus quarter, citizens living near the prison had lodged a public complaint: The Committee of Public Safety had caused to be dug, in the courtyard of that former convent, an immense pit, so that they might fling into it the hundreds of corpses their industrious zeal produced; an improved model of the guillotine now made it possible to collect the victims' blood; and to avoid befouling the streets, the dark juice was poured upon the bodies in the pit. The result of these operations was a dreadful stench, which rose into the empty sky, and the petitioners, the good citizens of the quarter, found it unjust that the aristocrats who had persecuted them in life should suffocate them in death. To come to an end, quantities of quicklime were poured over the whole loathsome stew, but the job was done badly, and the lime made things worse beyond all possible description. Then that insane pit was simply covered up, and under the wagon-loads of earth, death continued its hellish fermentation until finally, with the arrival of the first cold weather, the local residents had grown accustomed to the pestilential smell. Sometimes, inadvertently, I murmured these words: five years! This was the length of time that had passed since the Storming of the Bastille. Tears sprang to my eyes.

I was waiting for a sign to make an end of things. Finally I believed that sign had come. Naturally, my poor Jean-Jacques, it was your most ardent and most terrifying disciple who was responsible for giving our Revolution the coup de grâce. Robespierre proclaimed a Festival of the Supreme Being in the first days of the month of June, seventeen hundred and ninety-four, and I decided to attend the celebration. It took place in the presence of an immense concourse of people; the head of the march appeared on the esplanade of the Louvre; and at first glance, I perceived that the festivities would be a worthy product of that despicable monotheist's weak and well-ordered imagination. All over the capital, from dawn to dusk, there was a stupefying abundance of white: At a salvo fired from the Pont National at eight o'clock in the morning, processions of wives and mothers, girls and children, all draped in spotless white costumes, set out from every precinct in Paris. On the Champ-de-Mars, naturally renamed the "Field of Reunion," where the wheelbarrows of the Fête de la Fédération had rolled not so long before, the leaders of the Terror had ordered the construction of a sort of mountain, probably in their minds a type of Mount Sinai or Golgotha, with a tree on its summit, the Tree of Liberty, cut off at the base of its uprooted trunk in some national forest near Paris; next to it rose an absurd column, adorned with laurels and so many other pedantic symbols that it was difficult to discern what it represented; scattered, vaguely Greco-Roman temples decorated the rest of the field. The good people of France, whitened as though by some spell, assembled first near the National Garden, formerly known as the gardens of the Tuileries. (Although the Parisian parks had lost none of their bright charm, many of them had lost their names, as had innumerable streets, bridges, and buildings.) A population of pallid ghosts advanced in good order through a strangely altered city. It was impossible to refrain from thinking about sheep being led to the slaughter, without any need on the shepherds' part to resort to force. The excellent Robespierre, of course, was determined to eradicate atheism from the State, for godlessness was a horror to him. To justify the establishment of the Cult of the Supreme Being, he had declared incredulity an aberration left over from the time of tyranny, an aristocratic vice like tobacco or pederasty. But the inanity of his new religion was such that some old republicans were heard to murmur, on the day after the festival, that it would have been easier to restore the former Church of France.

The virgin-white festival was above all a celebration of children, for a veritable pedomania had seized France's new masters. The precincts of Paris had convoked all the women who were with child and placed them in the front ranks, where they made a sorry sight; some of them gave birth in the first house they came to. A brochure written by one David had been distributed to the boys and girls; it specified the moments when the children must smile. And smile they did, like little lunatics; some of those younger than the age of ten, not daring to weep, could be seen biting their lips. It had been decided that adolescent boys would march in arms; the privilege made them swell with pride, as happens with those who have not known war. In addition, the Festival of the Supreme Being disappeared under wagonloads of flowers, which were everywhere, covering the ground, blooming in windows, decking the allegorical cars. This abundance produced a cloying, sweetish odor, which found a visual equivalent in the streams of pale-colored ribbons, dainty pinks and timid blues. As I gazed upon those pathetic children, I could not but consider the contrast they formed with the little five-year-old beggars who, a few paces away, behind the former Palais-Royal, could be bought for almost nothing from the pimp Duclos, violated, and killed, without leaving any trace; and then I recalled that in seventeen hundred and ninety-one an old sansculotte had sought to persuade me that such abominations would disappear from the new world. I wondered whether we should ever succeed in finding some less-than-abominable employment for the black evil which lies in the human heart, which Sade understood, and which is but the opposite of the jejune sentimentality whose incense bearer was the bloody Robespierre. It is true that Robespierre avoided the company of women—a practice for which he received great credit in the new era, when he would have been condemned for it in the old; and it is also true that his only known passion, apart from those connected with the public good, was the eating of prodigious quantities of oranges.

The ceremony—as bloated, stiff, and formidable as an elaborate construction of pastry—went on and on. After Robespierre gave a speech, the orchestra played a French symphony, neat and dull, like a pair of ballroom slippers. Then, after the symphony, came a new ceremony: A monumental allegorical composition, representing among other things the monster of Atheism, had been raised on a circular basin in the Tuileries. Apparently, the monster possessed large ears and large teeth, but it could not be identified with any particular animal, being part lion and part sea serpent. The president of this august assembly solemnly set fire to Atheism, which was consumed, I know not how, in a matter of seconds; then, once the smoke had cleared, Wisdom appeared, a tall woman with teats resembling the back of my hand, no arse at all, and the stern air of a church chair renter constipated from gorging herself on sacred hosts; the flames which had singed her had but increased her invincible coldness. Once again Robespierre stepped to the rostrum and regaled us with a final discourse, which no one heard, as the wind had shifted. After that, the white specters of the dead

Revolution again formed a procession, which crept from the National Garden to the Field of Reunion. I wondered how the Supreme Being, assuming he had existed to that point, could survive a cult of worship so pompously tedious; but I refrained from sharing my reflections with the crowd. Some weeks earlier a young man was guillotined for having refused to uncover his head during a discussion of Voltaire; and no songster had ventured to compose a satire on that incident. On the Field of Reunion, an enormous chorus sang, to the tune of the "Marseillaise," some exceedingly bad verses, which included this refrain:

> Ere we can sheathe our swords,
> And Victory embrace,
> We vow, we vow first to destroy
> The tyrants' bloody race.

Even the worst things come to an end; after the singing, the crowd dispersed.

I remained for a long time on the banks of the Seine, which calmly flowed, indifferent to these follies. How could we have come to this? To all appearances, no one found anything objectionable in that monstrous alliance between the stupidest elements of Christianity and the narrowest elements of rationalism; how was that possible? My thoughts returned ineluctably to my prison companion. I had tried to see in Sade nothing but pessimism and outrageousness, and now I resented History for having proved him right. The most unfeeling reasoners had built the guillotines; the cruelest of men had thrust those beribboned children into the streets of a dead city. Today I believe in Sade's infinite gentleness, in his sadness, and I say that had we only read him, deeply and entirely read him, we might have taken the road that leads to the end of all fear. I am thinking not only of the Terror which has just fallen, but also of the one which forms the basis of human misery. I myself, not long ago, defended the guillotine: At the time, we were seeking a manner of execution more humane than the barbarities of the Ancien Régime; moreover, or so I thought, we would thus abolish the differences between the execution of a nobleman—to whom the honors of the ax were due—and that of a beggar. I recalled that in the spring of seventeen hundred and ninety-two, thinking it my duty to observe with my own eyes the functioning of the newest judicial instrument, I had watched, from one of the windows of the Hôtel de Ville, the first decapitation by guillotine. When the blade fell, a sinister noise arose from the crowd. I thought this an expression of collective abhorrence, but I misunderstood it. An old municipal officer disabused me: The crowd growled, he explained, because the spectacle was too brief and too unadorned; the people missed the gallows, the tortures, the cries and contortions of the condemned. A mortal chill went through me. Besides, the inhumanity of the proceedings was now apparent to me in all its horror; and the future showed that mechanized executions made judges readier to pronounce a sentence of death. Once their disappointment was over, the crowds found means of amusing themselves; they followed the tumbrels that carried the prisoners, and they compared the rolling of the various heads. As for you, Jean-Jacques, you were well inspired to die before your fame spread. Now France is covered with little Rousseaus who have all of your defects and none of your genius. Woe to him who would break the fastidious uniformity of equality's cowardly despots! Each of them reigns as a tyrant over the little realm of his person, and he cannot cease counting his treasures. Jealousy has become the national passion. A fine lot of disciples! At the time of the September Massacres, these little Jean-Jacques filled the streets, weeping at the plight of the persecuted Nation, and all the while tearing off aristocrats' heads as children do butterflies' wings, and violating the women in the Salpêtrière by way of teaching them republican morality. Everything in your works which your humor refined and subtilized has been aped most crudely. They have killed you, because weak men love to kill what they love. I, for my part, have remained alone, lost and wandering in these new times. After the Festival of the Supreme Being, I considered that I had seen enough; and it was then that I resolved to die. But I was not yet done with my indignation at the turn the world was taking, and I procrastinated.

I first set about securing my retreat from Paris. I sold the house in the Rue du Petit-Musc and reserved enough of the proceeds from the sale to provide myself with a small pension. Having no heir, I gave the rest to the Foundling Hospital. That same day, returning to my hotel, I passed the Tuileries Palace, where the Convention met, and I heard that citizen Amar was about to speak. The name sounded familiar, so I entered. When I saw the fool—for such he was—I instantly recognized him: He had in days gone by advocated the suppression of women's political clubs, and in a vengeful pamphlet, Sophie had taken care to mention that this citizen Amar, a bloody pillar of the Committee of General Security, had been convicted on more than one occasion for failing to pay various alimonies. Since then, Amar, a tall, blond man with the hands of a woman, a fellow as pitiless toward the weak as he was satisfied with himself, had prospered like a cock on a dung heap. I listened to his address. He proposed to the Convention a decree assigning women to the role which was theirs both as a right and as a sacred duty: that of wife and mother. Of mother more than wife, naturally, because those creatures must not divert the citizen from accomplishing the sacred missions the Fatherland required of him. This virile proposal immediately received the approval of all our estimable deputies, the representatives of the French people. The date, it appears, was 9 Brumaire in the year II. Amar was mightily applauded; he turned red with the pleasure of it, and mopped his brow.

A few days later I visited citizen Palloy, who had passed unscathed through all the revolutionary turmoil, having always wisely kept to his place as a maker of profits. Palloy still directed innumerable enterprises. He greeted me warmly and offered to take me again into his service; I told him of my plan to withdraw from Paris. He had just acquired a small farm north of the capital, and I smiled when he revealed that the farm was on the outskirts of Ermenonville, where I knew you were buried. Ermenonville was now called Jean-Jacques Rousseau, and under its new name, Palloy informed me, it had become what one could call a place of pilgrimage for the idolaters of the new republican religion. He proposed to let me occupy the little farmhouse free of charge, in exchange for some odd pieces of work; I accepted. Jean-Jacques Rousseau gave me an excellent welcome, my dear brother. I settled into my new dwelling, which was in fact an old hunting lodge. Palloy hoped, after making some improvements, to rent it to the notables of the new regime, who would surely desire, on occasion, to breathe the same air as the divine Jean-Jacques. The villagers expressed surprise that a venerable veteran of the Bastille, such as I was, should refuse to visit the property of the former Marquis de Girardin and stand at your grave. I extracted myself from difficulty by saying that such a visit would excite too much emotion in me, and that every authentic patriot carried Jean-Jacques in his heart. This formulation was much admired, and for months I was pointed out in the streets as the noble old man with the long hair who had spoken so stirringly. It is true that the French were mad to put wreaths on the remaining old men's heads now that most of the others had dropped into the hampers of the guillotine. When I disclosed my age, there was a general outcry: I looked thirty years younger! And the inhabitants of Jean-Jacques Rousseau at once attributed my excellent health, the happy result of Saint-Fonds' instruction and counsel, to my republican virtue.

The noise of the world no longer reached me. I learned only by chance of Robespierre's execution; the Committee of Public Safety and the Committee of General Security, having eliminated the counterrevolutionaries and their own partisans, had been left with no choice but to attack each other, and Robespierre had lost. The guillotine was brought back to the Place de la Révolution for the occasion. When they placed him under the blade, the Incorruptible was already bound to a plank, because his jaw had been shattered by a pistol ball at the time of his arrest and he could no longer stand. The least movement caused him to howl in pain. Thus perished the man-midwife of the infant era, accomplishing in his own person the union of torture and the guillotine, of the old barbarism and the new. I wrote these pages during the following six months, without stopping to read over my words. I was finishing my story when I heard in the village that it had been decided to transport your remains to Paris, a city you never liked. This undertaking was due to the late Robespierre, who worshipped you, and who, when he learned that Voltaire's bones were going to be moved from Ferney to Paris, had led other overbearing patriots in a campaign of indignant protest. What? Preparations were going forward to pantheonize a petty nobleman who despised the populace, a friend of the King of Prussia, an occasional courtier, while the Citizen of Geneva was left to rot in the mud of an émigré aristocrat's park? That could not be: A decree was voted, and Robespierre's fall changed nothing in this regard. The citizen-mayor of Jean-Jacques Rousseau was charged with organizing the ceremonial transfer of Jean-Jacques' corpse from his tomb to the gates of Paris. The venerable citizen Laroche let it be known that he would accompany the remains to the capital. The citizen-mayor was delighted to be able to display me as the most ancient monster in his little republican fair. The ceremony was to take place in the beginning of October.

You died in Ermenonville in seventeen hundred and seventy-eight, returning from a walk in the park the Marquis de Girardin had conceived in your honor. Now an unjust decree perpetrated in the name of the French people had dispossessed him of what he honored most. In the matter of your tomb, Girardin had exhibited his habitual generosity: He had himself designed a resting-place worthy of you, at the far end of the largest lake in his park, on an island crowned with poplars. Nothing could have better suited you: You were alone, as you believed yourself to be all your life; you rested in peace, separated by the waters of a most tranquil lake from men and from the times. Girardin at first expressly forbade all disembarkation on the shores of your island tomb, but soon he was obliged to yield to the growing number of pilgrims who came to Ermenonville, rented a boat, and returned home to tell where they had been. The festivities of seventeen hundred and ninety-four lasted three entire days. They began worthily enough, with a vigil to which, most fortunately, only a few of the faithful had been invited. There were about thirty of us, more or less, counting the handful of servants who carried torches and the workers charged with the digging. The night was mild and the sky clear when we entered the park. At the other end of it, the Isle of Poplars awaited us. We approached it along the western shore of the lake, passing the dark mass of the hill whereon Girardin had erected several charming follies, which formed bright patches of reflected moonlight. We lingered for a few moments on the shore, looking out at your island, lulled by the rustling of the wind in the tall trees. Some long flatboats carried us in a few moments to the foot of your tomb, a sort of sarcophagus in a somewhat hesitant style. The workers set about their task. We stood in silent recollection for a long time before your remains, which had been placed on a sheet. Then we returned to the château, where our lot was makeshift beds. The following day a slow journey began: We went by way of Montmorency, traversing hamlets between two rows of peasants with their hats in their hands, and throngs of children and women and men in botanists' garb; many onlookers were in tears. We reached Saint-Denis, after which you were made to travel the road to Paris in the direction opposite to that taken by the funeral processions of the many kings who in former days were buried there. We passed before the basilica without casting a glance at its broken stained-glass windows or its decapitated saints.

In the evening of October the ninth, we were in Paris. The urn holding your assembled remains was placed under a temple built on one of the basins in the Tuileries; the temple was flanked with six torches; young poplars uprooted from their ground were supposed to represent the island at Ermenonville; and on the rim of the basin, small cups sparkling with little flames illuminated the scene. This was the Parisians' vigil, and they came in great numbers all through the night. Around one o'clock, the moon rose, and one could see the people of the lower classes, who recognized their own, weeping for you. The basin where your urn stood was the same one on which Atheism had been burned to please Robespierre and his Supreme Being. There was much murmuring when people pointed reverent fingers in my direction: I was the Past. The indefatigable Palloy had, of course, offered France a bust of you, carved out of rubble from the Bastille, which was like the True Cross inexhaustible and would therefore come to seem somewhat miraculous. The bust was carried to the place where the Bastille had stood, because people believed that you had brought it down. I should like it if that were true, that I owed my liberation to my brother. At last, on the tenth of October, there was a solemn passage from the Tuileries to the church of the Panthéon. As I recalled in the beginning of my story, I was seated in the tribune of honor. From there I contemplated your funeral cortege. Surely alone among all those present, I contemplated it without illusions.

I have returned to Ermenonville. My arrangements are made: My ashes will be scattered at the foot of the cenotaph on the Isle of Poplars, which is, as it were, the image of your posterity. I want my dust to fertilize the earth. Death to me is an absolute end and nothing else; I think little of those dull philosophers who aspire to appear before it wise and well behaved. I shall put into my end the last passions of my life: the joy of an existence accomplished, anger if I feel any, fear if it comes to me. I have pondered for a long time what fate to reserve to the singular account which I am concluding today. And this is my decision: In a few moments, I shall carefully wrap my manuscript in tarpaulin. I shall betake myself, alone and unbeknownst to any, to your Isle of Poplars. I shall deposit my pages in the depths of the tomb you should never have left. Will they be found someday? I shall never know. In the fullness of time, the smallest drops of water overcome the hardest rocks. I have done what I could, gently, to add to the disorder of this world. He laughs best who laughs last.